Genghis Cohn
Does His
THING!

"Romain Gary's Genghis Cohn is doing his
thing in Tahiti . . . magnificent in the sand
and sex sequences, equally superb as the
conscientious rebel, the nonconformist with
a cause"
> —*Saturday Review*

**"Genghis Cohn continues his dionysian
dance . . . an outrageous funny burlesque
. . . delightful"**
> —*St. Louis Globe Democrat*

*"Cohn is Everyman, Adam, the Wandering
Jew, the fountainhead of man's love and the
sinkhole of his guilt. Dancing furiously, Cohn
is a cosmic provocateur—puncturing bal-
loons of hot air, making love instead of war
. . . madman . . . libertine . . . genius. . . . He
becomes that most dangerously subversive of
men: a free man"*
> —Playboy

Other SIGNET Titles You Will Enjoy

The
Guilty Head

Romain Gary

A SIGNET BOOK from
NEW AMERICAN LIBRARY
TIMES MIRROR

Translated from the French by Romain Gary

COPYRIGHT © 1969 BY ROMAIN GARY

Library of Congress Catalog Card Number: 78-92535

This is an authorized reprint of a hardcover edition published by The New American Library, Inc., in association with the World Publishing Company.

 SIGNET TRADEMARK REG. U.S. PAT. OFF. AND FOREIGN COUNTRIES
REGISTERED TRADEMARK—MARCA REGISTRADA
HECHO EN CHICAGO, U.S.A.

SIGNET, SIGNET CLASSICS, MENTOR AND PLUME BOOKS
are published by The New American Library, Inc.,
1301 Avenue of the Americas, New York, New York 10019

FIRST PRINTING, AUGUST, 1970

PRINTED IN THE UNITED STATES OF AMERICA

CONTENTS

To the memory of Lenny Bruce

1

The Adventurer

Chong stared at the outcast in pained dismay. This was one of those moments of reluctant brotherhood when a man, witness to another man's downfall, somehow feels his own dignity assailed. The American hung his head low, in the classical attitude of shame and humiliation: Cohn was a great believer in classicism. He couldn't work up a tear or two—too much is too much—but he did manage to adorn his mug with the proper expression of dejection and guilt. After all, he had just lost the right to bear the proud name given him in the Larousse Encyclopedia: "MAN: a mammal of erect carriage."

The Chinese had caught him red-handed. Cohn had broken into the kitchen through a window, and when the worthy owner of the Restaurant Paul Gauguin—The Best Genuine Cantonese Cuisine in Tahiti came down the stairs, his suspenders hanging down to his heels and his belly button bulging over his open fly, he had found the American squatting on the floor, lapping up the pussycat's milk from the saucer.

Though he had probably never read Spengler's *Decline of the West* the Chinese was deeply grieved by the spectacle of an American citizen in such a shameful situation.

"You should be ashamed, Mr. Cohn. The United States is a great country. An American who falls so low in the Pacific while his nation is struggling heroically to stem the red peril—"

"Yellow," muttered Cohn.

"Red," snapped the Chinese.

Chong Fat was a French Chinese, a staunch Gaullist who spoke with the strong Corsican accent that several generations of gendarmes and customs men had implanted

9

in Tahiti like Western flowers, though the dominant accent of the island was somewhere halfway between that of Burgundy and that of Auvergne.

"We're all ashamed of you here, Mr. Cohn. The future of the free world depends on the prestige of the United States. You should know that."

Hanging his head humbly and tracing circles on the floor with his big toe, Cohn acted out the humiliation of the Star-Spangled Banner. You've got to show respect for the moral universe of other people, especially when you have just broken open their cashbox. The money was in the back pocket of his jeans, which was bulging outrageously. Cohn was careful to keep his ass turned toward the wall.

He had closed the cashbox as soon as he heard Chong Fat coming down the stairs, and had barely the time to run into the kitchen, squat on the floor, and grab the pussy's saucer.

"Mr. Cohn, you're a perfect disgrace."

Cohn was flattered. He had always suffered from an insatiable thirst for perfection.

He scratched his crotch, promising himself once more to drop in at the pharmacy and get some gray ointment for the little devils. You must never forget the little ones.

"Pardon me," he apologized coyly, as one should among well-bred people. "I caught crabs."

Cohn, whose name was not Cohn and who was not American, saw himself as the worthy heir to those Spanish adventurers of the Golden Age called *picaros,* who, according to Posada of the University of Salamanca, probably stemmed from Juan Valdés, fake conquistador, fake papal nuncio, among another hundred false identities, who was hanged in the year of grace 1602 and whom the people had lovingly dubbed *hijo de puta,* son of a whore. His legend still lives in Castile, in tales of endlessly reinvented and splendidly embroidered adventures, always ending in his triumphant escape from the hands of Authority. The *picaros* had prospered at the expense of the Spanish establishment for more than a century and a half. They were mockingbirds and parasites with a vengeance, the first anarchists and dissenters, rebels past all hope or belief, whose only aim was to cheat Authority and Power in all its forms, Church, kings, grandees, merchants, police. They were scoundrels, in a proud and challenging way: contemptuous of a viciously corrupt society, they took great pride in being frank rascals. Cohn was trying to recapture the free spirit of these long-vanished pioneers.

10

"I'll have you deported, Cohn," the Chinese yelled. "I—"

Cohn raised his eyes. "Cut it out, baby," he growled. "For some time now I've been making a good living by providing the people of Africa and Asia with a stimulating image of Western decadence. I remember spending a very pleasant month begging in front of the American Embassy in Ghana, the perfect symbol of defeated Colonialism. It was excellent for the African morale. I stood there, under the American Eagle, holding out my hand, the epitome of white nonpower. In the end, the American Ambassador paid me off: a hundred and fifty a month, on condition that I go and do my stuff in front of the French Embassy. Unfortunately, the *Herald Tribune* got wind of it and published the story, and the new government of Ghana kicked me out as a Chinese *provocateur*—"

It was true, too. At about the same time, papers were talking about two other *picaros* who had been making a living in San Francisco by claiming that they had bombed Hiroshima and could not overcome their sense of guilt. Guilt was real blue chips these days, you couldn't go wrong with that; invest in guilt and you're sure to make a killing. One of the two guys had been getting as much as seven hundred bucks for a public appearance and ended up having a whole chain of stores selling guilt souvenirs of Hiroshima to the guilty public. Everybody loves to feel guilty about Hiroshima or Vietnam, it shows that you are innocent. People love to feel responsible, that makes them a civilization. The moment a perfectly innocent son of a bitch feels he's got blood on his hands, he knows he's qualified as a human being. Guilt is moral status.

Out there in the night the surf was breaking against the reef in a fairly good imitation of Cohn's indignant heart. Only the mighty ocean had the vocal means needed to speak in the name of man.

One of the two guys had vanished in time, but the other went to jail because he was a fake and an impostor and had not bombed Hiroshima at all. Had no right to claim the credit for it. It's copyrighted, a thing like that. International law. The guy who had truly and honestly rubbed off Hiroshima and who was the only one who could claim the credit had sued him and collected damages.

". . . Then I came here to Tahiti to help the natives. Acting out the decadence, decline and fall of the West, in an agreeable climate and pleasant surroundings. Big white man *kaput*. He's finished. Reduced to lapping up pussycat's milk. I'm acting out here the end of the white bastard. It's the yellow bastard's turn now, and they're welcome. Well, no matter what color the skin, as long as them bastards are around. 'Man shall prevail,' as Faulkner said in his Nobel Prize acceptance speech, meaning exactly that. Jesus Christ, d'you realize what that means, 'Man shall prevail'? Hair-raising. See you."

He waved to the indignant Buddha and jumped out of the window, the thirty thousand francs snatched from the cashbox bulging pleasantly over his right buttock.

2

The Vahine

The Tahitian night—it was called "Mother of Delights" back in the old days, when things still went by their real names—enfolded Cohn in its voluptuous softness. He felt he was entering a kind of ethereal whorehouse where invisible servant-mistresses welcomed him with open arms: each whiff of air bore the suggestion of some essential femininity, full of secret throbbings, of tender sighs and promising murmurs.

The Milky Way dragged its tail of light-years among the waves. The lagoon, the masts of schooners, the palm trees, lay still in that ephemeral peace that moonlight can give to the eye and sometimes to the heart. Somewhere, deep below all this soothing tranquillity, the long-extinct volcano that had given birth to the island reminded Cohn of long-gone flames and burned-out hopes. It is from those passions that stones are born.

Mingled with the sound of the surf, music, shouts, and laughter were carried by the evening breeze from the direction of the shacks where Maori and Chinese were celebrating the capture of the Bastille by the people of Paris. It made Cohn's legs tingle: he loved dancing. Somehow, dancing made the world lighter upon his shoulders. He often thought Atlas was a dancer.

Under the violet and yellow flowers of the *maa* tree, of which Gauguin wrote: "I would be tempted to describe it as the most beautiful tree here, yet this would be too hasty a pronouncement, as each day brings a new discovery and an even greater wonder," he saw Meeva standing among

12

the silver shadows, her breasts and hips bulging under the light cotton dress, with all the round, full splendor of archaic forms.

"Here is the dough."

It seemed to him that Meeva resembled Tohatoa, Gauguin's favorite model. Her lips had exactly the same soft fullness, and her serious, slightly sad eyes, her catlike nose, her heavy hair, recalled those of the immortal *vahine* whose photograph Cohn had long studied in the local museum.

Meeva came from the Tuamotus; she had arrived in Papeete only nine months ago, and during the time that had preceded their fortunate meeting, she had managed to make herself quite a reputation. Cohn had met her at the funeral of Raffat, the famous author of *Human Inflation* and *Down with Hunger* who had spent the better part of his life fighting starvation throughout the world. At fifty-five, overcome by indifference and by the billions spent on armaments and on the race to the moon, by hatred and ideological madness, Raffat had given up his humanitarian crusade and had ended up in Tahiti, where he took to sex the way others take to drink. His despair and frustration seemed to have taken the form of a virility that knew neither age nor limit nor surrender. He was still receiving delayed telegrams of congratulation and encouragement from the intellectuals who rallied around Bertrand Russell, but Raffat expressed the opinion that these messages could not be referring to his failures in India, Africa, and in the so-called "third world" in general, but rather to his more recent efforts in Tahiti, which were crowned with considerable success. Cohn thought that perhaps the most hilarious aspect of screwing is that it gives you a feeling of accomplishment. But then, you do build a better world during orgasm and it even lasts a few moments after the act. Sex is a kind of harmless euthanasia, the instant coffee of the absolute. It is a pleasant little suicide that brings both liberation and survival, and Raffat pursued this illusory end of seeking with such ardor that he gave up the ghost in Meeva's arms, which conferred a great prestige upon the new *vahine* but recently arrived from her distant islet.

In this Polynesian world that had retained none of its past, Meeva seemed to have kept a strong personal bond with the vanished centuries. She could go on for hours telling Cohn legends about the atolls, of water genies destroyed by the god Taaroa, and of the five moons with human faces that brought either bad luck or happiness to

13

the chosen ones. She spoke of how the god Taaroa had subdued the five moons and hurled them into the sea: that was how the islands of Bora Bora, Enuo, Huahiné, Raiatéa, and Tubuaï were formed. She spoke of the god Taaroa, of his red pirogues, and of his warriors as if she had slept with them too.

Her voice was at once sweet and curiously, hoarsely deep, with that guttural accent of the Tuamotuans remarkably similar to the German accent. Her father, chief of the Island of Takule, had been sixty years old when he begot her, with the help—thus spoke Meeva—of the morning moon, which, before dying at dawn, blesses a waking man with the power he needs to do his best. Her mother had bestowed her as a gift upon some friends who came from a neighboring island, Raroira, in keeping with an old Polynesian custom of offering your child to those who want an offspring who is not of their own blood, so that they could love him more. Cohn, who claimed that he could not understand folklore, legends, ancestral rites, the "living presence of the past," gods, myths, the opium of the people, never tired of listening to Meeva's stories; but only, he claimed, because she had a voice that somehow reached him in his most sensitive spot through some sorcery of vibrations.

"Cohn, why don't you try to be nice to people, for a change? All the *popaas* here hate you." *Popaa* is the Tahitian equivalent of "white folks." "They say you're subversive."

"To hell with them."

They were walking under the stars along Paul Gauguin Avenue, just across from the Paul Gauguin *lycée de jeunes filles.*

Sixty-five years earlier, the greatest moral authority of French Oceania, Bishop Martin of the Marquesas, had publicly called the dying artist a *vérolé,* a syphilitic scum.

The crash and roar of the surf always seemed more violent and tormented at night, because at the hour of darkness men read into it their own inner turmoil.

"Besides, they need me. I'm great for tourism. The outcast of the islands. Local color, you know. The magic of the South Seas. The artist as a pig and a rebel. Somerset Maugham. Leprosy. Syphilis. You name it, we've got it. We're doing fine. Gauguin will never let us down."

Cohn had discovered the great Tahitian cult of Gauguin shortly after his arrival on the island some twenty months before. The French authorities and the local worthies had let the painter die in utter deprivation, persecuted by

14

officialdom, not to mention the hatred of the missionaries, so tenacious that, thirty years after his death, the last survivor, the Bishop of the Marquesas, wrote to the Benedictine monk Henri de Laborde: "I wish silence would settle forever over the abominable creature." But now their descendants cherished the memory of the "abominable creature," whose paintings were worth millions and who had done so much to put Tahiti on the touristic and cultural map.

In his lost grave at Atuana, the man who had once written to his friend Monfreid: "When they say 'an artist, you know,' they have a kind of superior, ironic, and patronizing smile that makes my hand itch for a bomb," was the best public-relations man the Tahitian establishment could possibly have had.

In short, here was a myth, and Cohn settled down to milk it. He had successfully imposed on Tahiti a kind of posthumous tax on Gauguin, payable to him. The true benefits were moral. He was settling the rebel's and his own accounts with Authority.

Cohn had adopted Gauguin as his patron saint. Everybody in Tahiti knew his "House of Joy," named after the great dissenter's cabin in the Marquesas. Cohn's wild appearance and behavior, his feud with the missionaries, his deplorable way of life, and his defiance and baiting of the local establishment were earning him a considerable amount of artistic recognition. It had also the advantage of ensuring a certain immunity from official harassment and a kind of knowing tolerance. Nobody in Tahiti wanted another Gauguin on his conscience. For it is wrong to say that people are always making the same mistakes and that they never learn from history.

As for his "pictures," they were painted for him by students in the atelier of Paava, a good cliché imitation of the master's work. He signed them "Genghis Cohn," a pseudonym he had adopted as a tribute to another famous rebel. He had read his story before escaping and had decided to put the name on his forged American passport.

"Cohn, you are *fiu* again."

The most famous word of the whole Tahitian vocabulary, *fiu* could mean anything: sad, blue, bored, depressed, nostalgic, tired, languid. It covered almost all the unhappiness of soul and mind.

"It's because you think all the time, Gene. You mustn't. It can drive you nuts."

"Don't call me Gene. Genghis is the name. Genghis was a famous vandal, a savage conqueror whom, it is said,

God has chosen in His infinite wisdom to burn and destroy the sinful and the corrupt."

They said there were still some wonderful atolls in the Tuamotus, virginal sanctuaries of beauty and peace where no man had ever left his footprints. But Cohn knew he could never live on a desert island. He needed outside enemies. To live alone with himself would be cannibalism.

He often wondered why it was that he was so haunted by the world's beginnings, by the first dawn, the first pirogue, the first gleam of hope, when life was new and all the roads were still open. There was no retracing his steps. The chance had been given and played out. And yet the confused yearning was in him, and the lines of a poem by Yeats were echoing in his mind whenever the weight he was carrying on his shoulders became too crushing:

> *I am looking for the face I had*
> *Before the world was made.*

The soothing tenderness of the Tahitian night flowed over them and from the *maa* trees petals fell gently over their heads. Nature was showing compassion and, with each breath of the night, squandered her gifts on them. Moths fluttered against their moonlit faces and fireflies scattered their humble earthly stars around them. The ocean's roar had subsided, so no one now spoke in the name of Cohn.

"Come on. Let's dance."

3

Cohn Dancing

The Bastille Day huts run along the beach all the way from the outskirts of Papeete toward Pouaavia, and you could smell the bodies for miles around. It was a good, honest odor that admitted frankly where it came from. In every grass shack, a *tamure* orchestra had but one artistic goal: to outlast the dancers. In the good old days of innocence, the *tamure* was performed around the male partner's phallus buried in its natural home, where it belonged. The proud owner was supposed to hold back his inspira-

16

tion as long as he could, before letting go in final yelling frenzy, then yielding his place to another supporting pillar.

With a blissful grin on his face, his sailor's cap pushed far back, his eyes laughing, his black beard bristling, his rump thrown back, his conqueror's nose thrust forward, the gold ring shaking in the lobe of his left ear, his testicles bouncing like Yo-Yos, scratching his crotch from time to time to quiet the little pests, the sweat of blissful exertion streaming down his face, Cohn wriggled his butt, revolving faster and faster. Meeva, facing him, moved her hips frantically, to the delight of the tourists whom the guide Puccioni was inviting in a confidential whisper to "take a snapshot of that unfortunate wretch and his *vahine* —a tragic case, a past veiled in mystery—a typical example of the white man destroyed by his memories—what they were exactly, no one knows." When dancing became too much or, rather, not enough, Cohn would grab Meeva, take her out to the beach, and get rid of the last faint traces of himself for a few blessed moments. Though what he meant by "himself" has been an enigma since the very first time the terrified Sphinx took a look at man, and that, in Cohn's opinion, was how the stunned Sphinx turned into stone. Then he would light a cigar, walk slowly into the ocean, and cool off, standing in the water, proudly challenging the sparkling light-years above with the noble red glow of his Havana.

Toward dawn, Cohn led Meeva once more out to the beach, but this was pure bragging, and he found himself unable to make a good impression on her. He was worn out. He gave up and lay on his back on the gentle sand, under the stars. Sometimes one would fall. But most of them were well attached. Which made him think of the little ones.

"Remind me to get some gray ointment. Can you imagine that—crabs, in nineteen-sixty-eight? Medievalism!"

The stars were fading. The ocean was beginning to find its morning voice, still a bit sleepily. A huge red pirogue full of fishermen glided from behind the screen of coconut palms and remained motionless in a translucid world of its own, which was neither night nor dawn, neither ocean nor heaven. Now that old professional, the sky, was beginning to turn pink, then gold, then pale orange, in all the proper places and with the most satisfying effect.

"You old whore," Cohn said tenderly, looking up at the universe.

Meeva got mad. "Don't you call me names, you bastard. My great-grandmother, she fucked with King Po-mare the Fifth. It's all in the history books!"

"I'm not talking to you," Cohn said grandly. "I was addressing myself to heaven."

Nervous exhaustion was reviving his physical powers. At first he toyed lazily with the idea, then with Meeva, whose fresh lips helped him along with that curious coolness of lips which revives the flames instead of calming them.

The pirogues were lying in the shallow waters and the ripples were murmuring against their weed-covered sides. Cohn fought the temptation to jump into one of them and leave this shore behind him. He would have to come back anyway. The limitless ocean was an illusion, and that was why Cohn had settled for a sailor's cap.

The surf was breaking against the reef in a fairly good imitation of his indignant heart. The world of coral was disappearing under the incoming tide, leaving at its edges a panic life of crabs in flight toward some providential hole. The brotherly ocean was quiet, impressed no doubt with Cohn's inner thunder and turmoil. Around the palm trunks, the metal bands cinched there to protect the coconuts from rats were taking on the silvery glow of dawn, like those halos the Renaissance hatmakers placed on the heads of their saints.

From an abandoned fishing boat in the palm grove a human form emerged, stretched, and walked away. Cohn recognized one of those familiar fake relics that Thor Heyerdahl's epic voyage had left behind on every Polynesian shore. He was "Captain" Skip Ellis, a bum who squeezed out a living from the tourists by posing as one of Heyerdahl's Viking companions of *Kon-Tiki* fame.

The *tamure* bands in the grass huts behind them were still throbbing with their savage beat, but now, with the night gone, in the pink light of dawn, the music was beginning to sound like the heavy panting of an exhausted lover, unable to conclude and unwilling to give up. He felt suddenly annoyed by the beauty of the lone pirogue hanging out there, between ocean and sky, in the pink-green universe streaked with pale yellow, ready for the usual tropical fiesta of sunrise. The local color was overdoing it. So was Meeva. At that pace, after the night's exertions, it was no longer give-and-take, it was self-service.

"O.K., go ahead, help yourself," he said, sinking deeper and deeper into the sand under her weight.

"Cohn. There's a guy out there taking our picture."

18

Cohn looked up. Behind a coconut palm he saw a *popaa,* his head bent over his camera.

"What the hell!" Cohn roared. "A guy can't perform anymore without someone taking his picture! These bastards will end up by giving me a goddamn fixation! I won't be able to do it without a camera clicking away." He drew away from Meeva, still in full regalia. "Hey, you!" he shouted.

The man stared at him. He looked like a typical tourist gnat—Bermuda shorts flapping on his knees; black city shoes and socks over pink, sunburned legs; a Hawaiian shirt with "Aloha" written over his belly; and a Tahitian straw hat with shells around it.

"Excuse me," he said without a trace of embarrassment. "I was taking a picture of the sun rising."

Cohn was flattered. "Thank you for the compliment. Here it is, take a good picture and show it to your wife. It will do her good to see with her own eyes that it does exist after all."

The guy shrugged and turned on his heel. As Cohn watched him disappear among the coconut palms, a vague suspicion arose in him, a slight unease. He smelled danger. Were they spying on him? No, it was impossible. He had no fingerprints left and the plastic surgeon in Caracas had taken care of his face. There was simply no way of identifying him.

"What's the matter again, Cohn?"

"Nothing. Just thinking."

"I know you're thinking. I can see that. You've gone small again."

"Don't you ever have anything else on your mind, you bloody Tahitian conformist?"

"Do we fuck or do we talk, Cohn? That's what I want to know."

Cohn sighed. He had still to meet a *vahine* who was not a hundred percent romantic. And a century of sailors had left an indelible mark in their speech. The most beautiful and delicate-looking of these tropical flowers had a way of coming up suddenly with the most matter-of-fact slang of the Foreign Legion, something that all the throbbing-with-emotion and poetical accounts of "love in the enchanted islands" tactfully forgot to mention.

"O.K., we fuck. But then don't just sit there," he said severely. "Do something about it."

As she did, he watched the palm grove suspiciously. He had developed a sixth sense for danger. Though his "outcast of the islands" disguise proved itself a highly successful protective camouflage, he knew that they had not given up the search and that sooner or later they would search him out and put a well-deserved bullet through his guilty head.

Nineteen months earlier, Cohn had been hiding in Trinidad, kept by a whore from the Blue Cat, a gorgeous black creature with magnificent, bulging mass media. Her name was Lamartine Jones. Cohn swam, basked in the sun, spent his days staring at his brother-in-anger, the ocean, thoroughly enjoying his anonymity. The sacred fire was still burning in him, but it was safely hidden, unknown, undetectable in the heart and mind of that human flotsam washed up on the Caribbean shore. No one could grab it and set the world afire. Prometheus had stolen the sacred fire too early. The son of a bitch was a premature antifascist.

One afternoon Cohn was sitting on the empty beach at Belle's Point, near the Morgan's Castle, watching the Caribbean turn to dark violet, while the horizon beyond Elizabeth Island was still in the midst of its purple and yellow dealings with the sun, when he saw three men step out of the palm grove. They were some fifty yards away and they just stood there, talking to each other, one of them smoking a cigar, another wearing a shiny blue suit and dark glasses, and the third half hidden by the other two, showing only the top of his panama.

There was no one else on the beach, except for that immaterial yet living, red, pulsating presence of something or someone that sunset always manages to suggest with all the skill of an old charlatan.

Then the man in the white hat stepped forward, a machine gun in his hands, and began walking quietly toward Cohn.

Cohn was saved from certain death by the 5 P.M. busload of tourists appearing on the road. It was the hour of the daily Pan-Am visit to the Morgan's Castle. The bus was still a hundred yards away; the man in the white hat glanced back, then half raised his machine gun and fired. Cohn felt a sharp burn in his thigh and saw something that looked like a dozen snakes wriggling in the sand around him. He had the presence of mind to raise his hand to his heart, stagger, then collapse behind a rock and play dead.

The killer seemed convinced. The bus was now stopping by the palm grove and Cohn heard the tourists' happy chatter and laughter.

20

His face in the sand, but squinting toward the palm grove with a sharp eye, Cohn lay still. The wound was superficial but that was unimportant.

They were after him again.

He played dead till monsoon clouds had engulfed the moon, then made his way to the Cat in the shadows. He went up to the girls' sleeping quarters, where they rested when they were off duty, and sent one of them to get Dee Dee.

Dee Dee had been the partner of the prestigious preacher, Boysie Sing, hanged after ruling the underworld of Trinidad for twenty years, with a hundred murders to his credit. Books had been written about Boysie, and his greatness was still inspiring some of the best calypso singers. Although he was one of the island's richest men, Dee Dee had remained active, running the best whorehouses in Trinidad and controlling at least seventy-five percent of the drug traffic and gambling. He was doing this out of sheer hypochondria: he had been told that businessmen almost always dropped dead from a heart attack when they retired.

He was a sixty-five-year-old giant with Negro features, but strongly marked with Indian blood. He still wore a five-carat diamond in a front tooth in the old manner—to show how rich he was—to the embarrassment of his daughters, who had married into the island's social elite. Cohn showed him his bleeding leg.

"Who done that?"

"They're after me, Dee Dee. They tried to kill me. I've got to get out of here or I'm a dead duck."

"Who's they?"

"Castro men."

Lightning flashed from Dee Dee's diamond, followed by a string of oaths worthy of the great Boysie himself. If there was one thing Dee Dee hated, it was godless communism.

"Why?"

Cohn hesitated. "You have to trust me, Dee Dee. I can't say more. C.I.A. orders. I gave them the facts. I had to tell, Dee Dee. I know I'm no good, but I love my country. You can be a shit and a patriot, honestly, you can. Happens all the time. This is the great communist conspiracy, Dee Dee. They're out to get me. You've got to help."

Dee Dee planted his teeth into a new cigar. "Leave it to Papa," he said.

The next day the Trinidad papers were full of details about the body of a tramp found on the Morgan beach.

There was no clue to identify the body, they said, and the police were having a rough time trying to find the murderer.

That very night Cohn left the island aboard one of Dee Dee's tankers for Venezuela, where one of Dee Dee's best friends, a narcotic addict, gave him what is known in South America as a "new look." The surgeon did a brilliant job, and Cohn arrived in Tahiti with a brand-new face. All he had to do now was to burn his fingertips, which he did without hesitation. It was either that or getting rid of his head altogether.

Meeva was curled peacefully by his side, asleep in her veils. In the grass huts the *tamure* was dying, with only a few guitars still twanging and a shrill piano giving up its last. The ocean was stirring over the coral reef and hissed gently over the sand; the island of Mooréa lay greenish and violet in the morning mist.

Cohn walked into the lagoon and stood quietly in the cool green water, his arrogant pirate's nose raised toward the sky.

This was going to be an important day. If there was one situation he was determined to bring to a triumphant conclusion, it was his great personal feud with Verdouillet. He had presented the Tourist Office with an ultimatum: they had to decide who was more authentic, himself or that ignoble fake, Verdouillet. The manager had summoned the two Gauguins to his office that morning to announce his verdict.

4

Gauguin and Co.

The head of France Oceane Travel Bureau was sitting at his desk beside a huge globe topped by a panama hat placed on the North Pole. His full name was Hervé Bizien de la Longerie and, at forty-five, he was known as "The Napoleon of Tourism." Right now he was concentrating his efforts on Tahiti, determined, as he had said in a recent speech at the local Chamber of Commerce, "to make this Garden of Eden a better and happier place." Tahiti was going through difficult times. The forthcoming French nuclear test in the atoll of Mururoa was scaring the tourists away. Worse, however, was the growing competition of Hawaii, and disquieting news was now reaching Bizien almost daily.

Apparently, the decision had been taken to turn Hawaii into a kind of Polynesian "living theater," a faithful reproduction of the radically wiped out cultural past of the South Seas. The *tiki* gods, the temples, the legends and the religious rites, all the mythology and poetry of the Maori people, were to be brought back to life by the Western world's greatest ethnologists. Five million dollars were to be poured into the project.*

Yet if there was one thing Hawaii could never take away from Tahiti, it was the incomparable luster of the Gauguin myth. The romantic legend of his life, loves, and death, the billions of postcards and reproductions of his paintings were a never-ending source of free publicity for the "earthly paradise" and for that epitome of willing femininity, the *vahine*.

Bizien was betting heavily on that. He was preparing a Passion play, with every step of the rebel's Stations of the Cross faithfully reenacted, up to his death in the total solitude of his wretched "House of Joy." The most shocking episodes would, of course, be cleaned up. There would be no mention of Gauguin's nights of debauchery, so gleefully described by the artist in his letters to Monfreid: "The delightfully devilish child-girls have again stormed my bed. . . . I had three of them helping me to perform last night." The pornographic-postcard business would have to be omitted as well. The reality of the man behind the legend had now turned to dust and was unimportant. What mattered was the myth.

What was needed was a good man to play the artist. Bizien looked up once more at the two candidates awaiting his verdict.

Verdouillet was a high-strung neurotic and had to be handled with a certain caution. A sickly introvert, he did not fit the image. He lacked that physical aura, that rascally, defiant, big-nosed aggressive impact so evident in Gauguin's self-portraits. There was no touch of rebellion about him. He lacked presence and, to make matters worse, he actually believed in his talent, and probably had some, too. Bizien winced with distaste.

Cohn was another matter altogether: aside from an

* Miami *Daily News,* April 22, 1967.

undeniable physical likeness, he also resembled Gauguin strongly in his morals, and he knew how to keep the Founder's reputation alive.

The Napoleon of Tourism was watching the two rivals, absentmindedly whirling the globe on its axis. Verdouillet, pale, argumentative, and surly, was nervously scratching the funguslike growth of red bristles on his hollow cheeks.

Catching Bizien's eye, he started to complain bitterly. "I was here before him, and I have Gauguin's palette, his manner, his vision, on my fingertips. The tourists recognize it right away. Mr. Cohn has his paintings done by the students at Paava's school. You call that authenticity? And yet, when I express the wish to call my studio 'The House of Joy,' the authorities forbid the name to appear on my house, under the pretext that it is located on General de Gaulle Avenue. Open persecution!"

Cohn belched insultingly in Verdouillet's direction, leaned over the desk, and opened the second drawer on the right, where Bizien jealously guarded his cigars.

"Don't bother to ask, help yourself," the promoter said. "My wife is home alone, in case you're interested."

"Don't count on me there," Cohn said. "Hire somebody." He bit the end off the cigar, lit it, then pointed it at the enemy. "You are a fraud, Verdouillet. You simply don't look the part. You, Gauguin? Ha! It's an insult to my memory!"

Verdouillet turned yellow—without question his finest achievement as a colorist.

"My works are sold all over the world. Every dime store in America—"

"As for calling your digs 'The House of Joy,' just ask any girl you've pursued with your talent. Every *vahine* here knows that it's hard work to get out of you even the smallest format, certainly the smallest since the Chinese miniatures."

Bizien raised a pacifying hand. "Now, now . . . Verdouillet has the right to use his brush the way he can. The format has nothing to do with it."

"Lies!" yelled Verdouillet, on the verge of tears.

"You simply haven't got what it takes to follow in Gauguin's footsteps."

Bizien was beginning to feel that Cohn was a bit too cocksure. "Our friend Verdouillet has one advantage over you, Mr. Cohn. He has a personal link, a blood link, with our great man."

Verdouillet flushed with delight and said nothing, modestly.

"He's the grandnephew of the gendarme Claverie, the painter's implacable foe who never stopped persecuting him."

"Shit! I didn't know that," said Cohn, truly impressed this time.

"Verdouillet is a relic," concluded Bizien. "Can you imagine how moving it would be if we could have a direct descendant of Judas among us? A living historical link with Christ. Imagine that! What tremendous spiritual and moral authority such a man would possess!"

Verdouillet beamed with pride. "I have the papers to prove it. It was Claverie, my great-uncle on Mother's side, who helped Gauguin become a martyr. Remember how he dragged him into court? And had him sentenced, too."

Cohn always felt moved when he came upon a direct link, still alive, still warm, with one of the great stiffs of history.

There was an aura of authenticity there.

It was said that Judas killed himself. Cohn did not believe it. Judas had probably lived to a ripe old age, maybe long enough to end his days in patriarchal greatness, surrounded by the love and esteem of the faithful. No doubt, in the end, he had become a crashing bore, like all veterans, with his endless, repetitious accounts of the whole business, always boasting of intimacy with the famous Jesus of Nazareth. He was, after all, Judas, the original betrayer, and as such he could quite rightly claim to be the founding father of all our civilization. Old, vain, dotty Judas must have become insufferable in the end, demanding constant new marks of respect and gratitude, and flying into a rage whenever he found himself seated too far down the table.

Cohn knew he was not exaggerating or giving in to flights of cynical fancy. Perruchot's book, *The Life of Paul Gauguin*, offered definitive and shattering evidence on the matter:

The bully Charpillet had retired into the Haute-Saône, where he lived to old age. Those who were interested in the long-dead artist often visited the former gendarme. In their presence, the patriarch would willingly recall, with tears in his eyes, ". . . *le maître* Paul Gauguin, that extraordinary man, that unfortunate great artist, whom I had the pleasure of knowing in the Marquesas. He was like no man I had ever known before. HE WAS A SEER."

The ruthless gendarme, Claverie, Verdouillet's great-uncle, was even more devoted to the cult of Gauguin. He had retired to Montgaillard, in the Hautes-Pyrénées, where he had a small tobacco shop. In that shop, says Bernard Villaret, ". . . he displayed religiously a little glass case containing a small wooden sculpture by the artist he had persecuted with such venom, and who had become his idol. 'A relic,' he would say to a visitor, looking lovingly at the sculpture."

If there was an expression Cohn could not abide, it was "it is only human."

At that moment, the Napoleon of Tourism had a sudden flash of inspiration.

It was Verdouillet's reddish beard and blue-eyed, pale, sickly face of the born underdog that did it.

"I think I have the answer, Verdouillet."

Verdouillet blinked suspiciously. "What now?"

"You'll play Van Gogh."

"Holy Moses!" said Cohn, admiringly.

Bizien looked pleased.

Withdrawing even deeper into his perfectly nonexistent protective shell, Verdouillet watched them with extreme wariness. Without even knowing it, he was already assuming the part of Van Gogh: he felt surrounded by a conspiracy.

"You've got what it takes," Bizien said with an air of finality.

"But everybody knows Van Gogh never set foot in Tahiti!" Verdouillet whined.

Bizien shrugged that off grandly. "So what? Everybody knows Gauguin is dead. This is a re-creation, Verdouillet, for authenticity's sake. The relationship between Van Gogh and Gauguin is an essential part of the myth. It's known everywhere. Can you imagine you two shouting at each other on the terrace of a café? They don't have *that* in Hawaii. The tourists will wet their pants with excitement; the slides they'll take home! You know, back there in Arles there's a café, À l'Oreille de Van Gogh, with a big neon ear."

Now Verdouillet was having artistic scruples. "But I paint like Gauguin. I don't paint like Van Gogh."

"You'll change your style. Every artist's got to develop, you know."

The victim opened his mouth, but Bizien, with a broad wave of his arm, pushed the protest back down his throat before it had a chance to come out.

"It's Van Gogh or nothing," he said sternly.

Verdouillet was crushed. Cohn was beginning to feel strangely protective toward the poor guy. Vincent had always been pathetically defenseless.

"I'll take good care of you," he told Verdouillet patronizingly, trying not to laugh.

"Screw you." The wretch tried once more to argue. "I still can't see what Van Gogh's doing in Tahiti."

"Listen," Bizien said patiently, "and what are all the Polynesian art treasures doing in American and European museums? Let's say it's a sort of cultural exchange. We've taken their culture away from the Polynesians, we're giving them Van Gogh in exchange."

"And why does Gauguin have to be an American?"

"First of all, Mr. Cohn is no more Cohn or American than my ass. I have not the slightest idea who or what he is, and I don't care. Besides, the majority of the tourists here are Americans. They'll all be pleased. France has carried the burden of culture and greatness long enough."

Bizien rose from his chair. His eyes were gleaming with pure hate. Cohn recognized instantly the spark as coming from the buried but burning flame of a true *picaro*.

"Now, this little matter being settled, I have some work to do. I am going to push the 'Garden of Eden' side of Tahiti for all it's worth. That's what people look for here, and I'm damn well going to see that they get it. Just watch me. Not an amusement park: I leave that to the Hawaiian Disneyland. No, this is something our Minister of Culture, André Malraux, calls Le Musée Imaginaire, but brought to life. The tourists will make the trip by bus, starting from Adam and Eve and original sin, all the way to Victor Hugo in exile on his rock in Guernsey. I may throw Napoleon in, I don't know yet. Depends on how much money Malraux will give me. Something truly French, in the Gaullist sense, from Leonardo da Vinci's *Gioconda* down to the Egyptian art treasures at the Louvre, the sacking of Byzantium by the Crusaders, Jesus, Mark Twain, Goethe, the 'greater France,' our *mission universelle,* Picasso, Chagall, Pasteur, the Bible, the chateâus of the Loire, Moses and his tablets, everything that goes into the making of French greatness. All in natural setting. I may even have Malraux's permission to bring some of the Polynesian art treasures back from the Musée de l'Homme, at least on a temporary basis. Maybe a reduced model of Chartres Cathedral and a miniaturized Versailles. The tourists won't even have to leave the bus. I've got three miles of land above Pouaavia, enough to give the bastards the whole shmear, from Genesis to Brigitte Bardot. Don't

27

forget France has one advantage over the American Disneyland; we've a thousand years more of goodies than they have."

Cohn was enthusiastic. "Saint Anthony tempted by the *vahines*, surrounded by reproductions of the most famous pictures he has posed for—"

The great promoter was also warming up. "A Hilton and a casino on Mooréa, with roulette, baccarat, and American craps. A golf course at Atuana, where Gauguin is buried."

"Joan of Arc!" bellowed Cohn. "In a bikini!"

"Joan of Arc, in a typical Polynesian setting, next to Salome where she danced! The world's best!"

"Bach! It's a must!" roared Cohn, with a total, self-devouring hate.

"Bach, of course, with Saint Louis, Picasso, and a miniaturized Auschwitz! We must have a little Auschwitz, there are at least forty-percent Jews among the American tourists!"

"Auschwitz, Victor Hugo's *La Légende des Siècles*, recited by pretty Tahitian girls by moonlight—"

"God! You have to stick God in somewhere!" yelled Cohn. "It's a must!"

"They'll find a way of sticking God in, just leave that to them!"

"Napoleon on Saint Helena, have to squeeze that bloody bastard in somewhere, we need a touch of glory!"

"Genocide! We can't do without genocide! It's a must!"

"Kennedy! We have to have Kennedy!"

"Kennedy walking on the water!"

"Kennedy healing the lepers!"

"Schweitzer! It's ab-so-lute-ly essential!"

"Gandhi! Buddha! Fuck it, we have to have Buddha! It mustn't be all Christian! No discrimination!"

"Damn it all, the suffering of the American Negro, we've got to have that, it's a must!"

"T.V. in every room!"

"The Slaughter of the Innocents, somewhere or other! Essential!"

"Bishop Martin washing Gauguin's sores on his deathbed!"

"The Three Wise Men stealing gifts from the stable!"

"The pagan Queen Pomare on her knees, welcoming gratefully the first Christian missionaries!"

"De Gaulle discovering penicillin!"

"Sex and the moon, we've got to have that somehow!"

"O.K., the first man on the moon, masturbating!"

28

"Gauguin's national funeral, his ashes at the Panthéon! Malraux's great speech on the occasion! Gauguin rising from the dead and pissing!"

"A touch of Americana! It's a must!"

"Yeah, yeah, that's it! A touch of Americana! The assassination of the third Kennedy!"

Before settling in Tahiti, the man who called himself Genghis Cohn had been looking for a desert island in the Tuamotu Archipelago. But he thought better of it—he had a well-developed instinct for self-preservation. On a desert island, humanity would be reduced to himself. A scorpion-esque situation, making all settlement of accounts impossible, even in a purely symbolic and perfunctory way.

The Napoleon of Tourism was recovering his breath. Verdouillet, his mouth gaping, had shrunk into a state of terrified stupor. An exotic fly buzzed desperately against the window, trapped like all the others.

Cohn knew he was witnessing the dawn of a new era, the birth of a new faith, that of Tourism. Its fundamental law was that the murderer always returns to the scene of his crimes, but this time bringing along his wife and kiddies.

He left the office in such a state of shame and indignation that he did not overcome it until some thirty-six hours later, emerging from a bout of drinking of exceptional magnitude, even for Tahiti. He tried to remember if he had perhaps given himself away during this binge, but all he could recall was they had kicked him out of the Pink Pussy after he had got involved in several brawls; then he remembered himself dimly, standing minus his pants on the counter of Chez Ricco, thundering from this pulpit to his audience of sailors and whores that the greatest source of energy of all time was the *tupapau*, the human spirit, all you had to do was control it, it would keep working for you forever, the atom could go and fuck itself. Of course, with the human soul as energy, there would be a truly stinking problem of air pollution. He also remembered that they were forcing him back into his pants, and then he had tried to walk back home to his House of Joy, singing "Onward, Christian Soldiers," but had collapsed and passed out, while the constellation of the Dog shed its brotherly light over his head.

The Bradfords found him there, asleep in the middle of the road.

5

Cohn Dancing

It was that hour of first stirrings and rustlings, as Tahiti-Noui, the *vahine* of Tinoo Taato, the "Master of all Births," rose from her couch and donned her morning finery, while her servants carried away her veils of night, when Cohn came out of his alcoholic stupor and found himself stretched out comfortably on a chaise longue, his head propped on a pillow, on the deck of the yacht *Antinea*. He had often admired its white beauty. It was anchored on the very spot where two centuries earlier the Spanish frigate *Águila* of Máximo Rodríguez, the first white man to live on the island, had been moored.

"Jesus!" said Cohn as a particularly painful hammer blow banged his head. "Jesus!"

"An American, I see," said Mr. Bradford with compassion.

"Wichita Falls," said Cohn between clenched teeth, simply because he felt he was falling, together with the chaise longue, down a bottomless pit. "Good God, this is the worst hangover I've had in a week!"

He opened his eyes again and saw a woman with a pleasant enough face looking down at him. She was around forty, but still on the right side. Thirty-six, thirty-seven maybe, that's the best age if you want to inspire productive maternal feelings. The man had that pleasant, gray-haired look you see in magazine ads under the heading "How to retire at fifty on four hundred dollars a month," with the slight difference that the yacht alone must have cost three hundred thousand dollars. He took the cup of coffee that Lee Bradford offered him.

"It's none of my business," she said, "but you really shouldn't drink like that."

"That's the kind of advice that never made whiskey manufacturers lose their sleep," her husband remarked, in the painful tradition of congenial jokes.

Cohn gulped down the scalding coffee. He liked these good people already. He knew he would have to thank them in some appropriate way.

30

"You passed out in the middle of the road. It's a wonder a truck didn't run you over."

"I wish one had," Cohn said gloomily.

He wasn't exactly in a creative mood. Usually themes for improvisation never failed to offer themselves, but with that incessant hammering inside his head, he wondered if he would be able to invent something half decent. He shut his eyes with a grimace of pain, at which Mrs. Bradford went to the galley to get some ice for his young brow and her husband observed a compassionate silence, as was proper before such a spectacle of ruin. Cohn's clothes were repulsively filthy, sweaty, and covered with dust. His wild black beard was staging an assault on his hollow-eyed face, his nose projecting like the still-proud figurehead of a sunken ship.

Incredible as it was, Cohn for once lacked inspiration. Not one lie worthy of him came to his mind.

He called to his help the shade of his great forerunner, the immortal *pícaro*, Pedro Gómez, who had prospered in the seventeenth century at the expense of the Spanish establishment for more than fifty years, merrily trampling underfoot all the bigotry, pious lies, fake beliefs, and hypocrisies of his time, robbing the rich and not giving to the poor, and who is still remembered in Sevilla as "The Dancer." Pedro Gómez died at the ripe age of seventy-eight from an attack of priapism, a hard-on that lasted seven weeks despite all efforts of the nuns who had rushed to his bedside.

Mrs. Bradford returned with some scrambled eggs. She was wearing shorts, like all women who should not. She had fine buttocks, but of the kind that demanded either nudity or a skirt. This American couple had a graciousness of manner that was deep and spontaneous, made of goodwill and faith in their fellowman. It was out of the question to let them get away with that. Cohn felt he had no right to let them leave the island without enriching them with some unforgettable experience. The hackneyed touristic image of the "outcast of the islands" was simply not good enough there.

He ate the scrambled eggs.

"This is the first honest-to-God American breakfast I've had in a long time," he said.

"How did you happen to come to Tahiti?" asked Mrs. Bradford.

Cohn was eager to go to work on them. His hangover had not succeeded in dulling his natural goodwill.

31

"I didn't know where to go. This thing follows me everywhere. I'm a hunted man."

"The police?" asked Mrs. Bradford sympathetically.

"No, my conscience," said Cohn, plunging in headfirst without the slightest idea in which direction he was going to swim.

He paused briefly with an air of mystery and accepted a cigar while the Bradfords observed that discreet silence which is the best encouragement to true confessions. Really fine people, thought Cohn. You couldn't just leave them like that.

It had to be something about "guilt," of course. "Guilt" had become moral status. It raised your standards of ethical and cultural living. It was the Cadillac of social awareness. "Guilt" was class.

The un-American tragedy, or the importance of feeling guilty. The man who couldn't work up a bad conscience, or how the famous hit-parade song, "Hiroshima, You Destroyed Me," was born.

Cohn was ready. The puritan in him had never yet missed a rendezvous with the fire. The secret idealist had never yet failed to provide him with savagery.

A sharp, irresistible surge of joy and confidence in the future of the breed suddenly filled his heart. Man should treat galaxies like mere pebbles on his road and brighten his way with light-years.

He was ready to dance again.

"I'm the unfortunate son of the man who bombed Hiroshima. My dad didn't dare to look me in the eye, because of his tragic personal problem: although he was the man who had committed one of the most monstrous crimes in history, he was unable to work up any guilty feelings at all. He felt un-American and a terrible son of a bitch.

"He shunned the company of his fellowmen, crushed by that terrible guilt complex he had developed about not feeling guilty at all. He kept changing his name all the time, but the papers always tracked him down because he was a great American guilt symbol and a martyr of science. Dad was a simple man and he couldn't keep lying all the time, and he had enough of all the sympathy and compassion they showered upon him because he had committed such an atrocity.

"My mother came from an old family with very strict principles, so it was much easier for her; she was a natural for guilt, and so she began to have one Japanese lover after another. It was, of course, an attempt to seek forgiveness and atonement, and also to punish my father for

32

his sin. Consequently, there was a steady stream of Japanese visitors at our home, and for a while we lived quite well and my father didn't have to work anymore. We soon had a nice fishing place in the mountains and two cars.

"But then I began to run into trouble because of the reputation I had with the other kids, who knew I was the son of a man who had wiped out a whole city, and they all looked up to me for leadership and expected great things from me. It went to my head and I became a thorough hoodlum by the time I was fifteen. I was often dragged into court for juvenile delinquents, but then my lawyer would call in psychiatrists who would explain that I had in me a built-in need for rejection and punishment because I hated my father and wanted to punish him. I soon realized I could get away with almost anything. Those were the best years of my life.

"Whenever I ran across my dad, he was drunk. You must understand that he was a very ordinary person to start with; he was not equal to the circumstances he was caught up in, and he had bombed Hiroshima as he would have done anything else. He was not made for greatness. When he realized that they wanted to turn him into a martyr, a kind of crucified Judas, he did try. He truly did what he could to suffer morally. But he couldn't make it. There was something basically healthy and normal in him. He felt no remorse at all, no dreams of charred bodies troubled his sleep, and no matter how hard he tried to feel bad, real bad, the terrible fact was that he didn't give a damn.

"That's what finally broke him. He felt like a terrible un-American bastard because he simply couldn't work up a decent guilt feeling about Hiroshima, the way a whole nation expected him to. He was letting the country down. He realized he was a monster without soul and conscience. He began to drink heavily. He had always been drinking heavily, but now he knew why.

"From time to time Dad would call me from some bar to come over. We had a lot to tell each other, but we were both so scared, we were afraid to say things that we just shouldn't be saying, in our situation. Neither of us was up to it. Some people can take greatness, others can't. Dad lacked stature. It was all the Army's fault, he told me once. Before entrusting a man with the mission of atomizing a whole city, men, women, and children, the candidates should be carefully screened, to choose one of high moral conscience who is well educated and a humanitarian, a man worthy of the job. So we just sat there, without saying anything. But we understood each other.

"My mother was still going with Japs, but it was easier for her. As the daughter of a Methodist minister, she had a natural bent for self-punishment. Dad would sit there with me and drink beer, and then he would work up some courage and shout that he had had enough of being crucified as Saint Judas and that he didn't care a damn about being a great American guilt symbol and screw Hiroshima, the way he felt, he often wished he could go back and bomb the place again. I was almost beginning to like him, sort of.

"Dad felt trapped and watched by the whole nation; he suspected everybody of considering him a callous son of a bitch and he became violent and antisocial. Finally, he developed such an aggressive grudge and hostility that he held up a bank with a toy pistol. He was acquitted. Everybody understood he was merely trying to have himself punished for the act that had made him a Judas to the human species. The papers wrote up the story for all it was worth.

"Dad was smartening up. He was beginning to conform. His moral fiber was cracking, he was giving in. He was now enjoying his moral authority as a great American guilt symbol. He no longer ran away, cursing, when invited to sit on the dais of some protest meeting condemning the U.S.A. for this or that. But he refused to have anything to do with Vietnam. Dad had a strong resentment against Vietnam and the publicity it was getting. He felt it was a maneuver to distract the attention of the American public from Hiroshima and himself. Dad simply couldn't stand anybody talking to him about Vietnam. He felt slighted.

"At about that time Dad had been approached by a liberal group to run for public office on the 'American guilt' platform. The Russians were talking of giving him the Lenin Peace Prize. All the pacifist, humanitarian, and moral-rearmament circles were constantly after him, and there were always a couple of priests hanging around. He drank more and more. That offered the double advantage of conforming to what the people expected of him and of being enjoyable.

"Everybody expected me to become a queer, because of my father-hatred, and I had many offers. My psychiatrist tried to help me adjust to that prospect, but I refused to conform. I saw no reason at all why I should get it in the ass, merely because my father had wiped out a city, as if
34

that wasn't enough. I was beginning to feel that society was putting too many demands on me.

"That was when Dad showed up again. The papers had written that he no longer dared to look his son in the eye, so he turned up with reporters and looked me in the eye, just to show them. Then he stuck his tongue out at me. That was more than I could take. I grabbed a beer bottle and smashed it over his head. Next day it was in all the papers and America was moved to tears. They had always known I had it in me. The father-hatred, I mean. You just can't lick conformity. It's stronger than all of us.

"I suddenly discovered I had quite a reputation of my own. I was receiving encouragement from everywhere. I suppose people felt reassured to see that everything was as it should be. I was becoming that great American institution, the father-fucker. I was invited to lecture by Berkeley first, then by other universities. But there again, I didn't have the necessary cultural background. I had never been given a formal education. It was not enough to be acclaimed by the students as the number-one father-fucker in America, you still had to give them something more—spiritual leadership. You couldn't go far on the father-fucking platform alone. You had to have dialectics, and I didn't even know what that was. I suppose with a bit of hard work and studying I could've become 'the symbol of young America's dissent.' But I muffed the chance, I simply couldn't work up an interest; I didn't feel like changing the world at all. The last thing I wanted was to make the world a better place. I rather like people. If you make the world a better place, what are you going to do with people? Destroy them or something? I skipped town and ended up in Memphis, where I was kept by a whore.

"Then there was uproar in the papers, because the press had brought out the fact that, out of more than seventeen guys who claimed they had bombed Nagasaki or Hiroshima, none had actually taken part in the raids. They were frauds. The American Air Force issued Dad a document vouching for his honesty.

"You can't imagine how fed up I was with all this guilt talk. I became obsessed with the idea of joining the Air Force and bombing Hiroshima or New York or any place. I tried to sign up, but of course they didn't want to have anything to do with me, because of my dad. As the Colonel said, 'Sorry, you've got to leave something for others.'

"It was the whore in Memphis who finally convinced me to make the best of my reputation as the son crushed by his father's sin. She found a guy who wrote articles for me to sign and got me an agent who organized a personal-appearance tour. I picked up some dough that way. But Dad didn't like that. He came to San Diego, where I was lecturing, and told me to lay off *his* line. I was taking the bread out of his mouth, he said. Hiroshima was his; it was his life's work. Finally, our two agents made an agreement: I'd take the West Coast, and Dad'd cover the rest of the country.

"Dad could play the guitar a little, and someone had written him a folk song, 'Hiroshima, You Destroyed Me.' He made a record and it immediately outsold all the similar ones by Joan Baez and stayed among the Golden Ten for a year, at the top of the hit parade, just after The Animals. In France, they even made a highly successful film of similar inspiration, *Hiroshima, Mon Amour*. My dad and his bomb had started a real culture boom.

"I was beginning to truly hate my father. The son of a bitch seemed to have the golden touch. So I bought an electric guitar and started a little folk group of my own, with some kids who had just returned from Vietnam. But by then everybody in the business was on the same protest kick, and we never made it.

"You know the rest. My dad had started a real renaissance in folk singing; the bomb, radiation, Vietnam, racial discrimination, it's all become part of American folklore and cultural heritage, great ballads and songs of social protest and dissent for wonderful singers like Bob Dylan, Joan Baez, and hundreds of others, so that truly no one can say that Hiroshima had been bombed for nothing. Today, Dad owns a record company and a music-publishing firm; he has become the symbol of the American resilient spirit and moral fiber, the living proof that you can't lick a good man. He's always cited as an example of the rugged American individualist who had started from nothing—you know, the bomb really cleaned up that place—and who made good against all odds. It's what we call a 'success story.' Dad is of the 'pioneer breed,' they say.

"He never sends me a cent. He says he disapproves of my ways and feels I should stop being a drifter and do something. Whenever I ask him for money, he lectures me severely in his letter, reminding me that, thanks to blood, sweat, and tears, he rose to the top and all I have to do is follow his example. Maybe he's right. I don't know. There's still a war in Vietnam. Maybe I should enlist under an assumed name and go over there to share the sufferings of the Vietnamese people, beat the shit out of them, and become guilty. With a little bit of luck, they'll send me to drop the bomb on Hanoi, and then I'd be in. I'd come back home with a shaken conscience and lots of subjects for beautiful songs of social protest. But the truth is, I don't have it in me. Something's wrong with me, deeply wrong, maybe, with all my generation. We no longer have that nitty-gritty American grain in us. We're rotten. We just piss our lives away, because it seems we enjoy pissing more than life. I don't mean to say we wouldn't throw the bomb—no, that's not what I'm saying. But it's not at all sure that we'd throw it on the right people, on the *wrong* people, I mean, as it is in Vietnam. You can't trust us with a bomb anymore. That's very bad. That's decadence. We could just as well go and throw it against our own people, that's the way we are.

"Now, you may still wonder what I'm doing here, in Tahiti, looking what I am, that is, a bum. Well, I'll tell you. I have a little understanding with the Director of Tourism here. He lets me have the exclusive rights to the role I'm playing now in front of you, and when I grab my guitar and sing my famous 'Ballad of the Cursed Son' right in the middle of the earthly paradise, the tourists get a big kick. They always ask for an encore. I usually oblige with 'The Great American Father-Fucker,' it's very popular back home right now.

"So, you see, I'm beginning to make a name for myself, and when I reach this point in my story, I usually turn to the tourists and say: 'Ladies and gentlemen, thank you for your attention, and let me tell you this, in the great Paul Gauguin's own words, and I quote: "Screw you and your guilt feelings, and I want you to know that I am completely happy, that's how low I have fallen." ' *

"I don't feel a damn bit guilty about anything, you can't sink any lower than that. However, out of respect for my public and to assume my moral degradation completely, I even pose for pornographic pictures, just to prove that I am the true spiritual heir to Hiroshima, one of the greatest obscenities of all time. Here, look—"

Cohn took some pictures from his pocket and threw them on the table. They were reproductions of the famous postcards Gauguin had bought in Port Said on his way to Tahiti, which are now in the archives in the Musée de l'Homme in Paris.

Mrs. Bradford wept with humiliation, while her husband glared indignantly at Cohn. But Cohn felt safe, for he knew that the puritan in him was concealed from the

---

* Letters to Monfreid.

naked eye. The emerald waters, the quiet, still palms, the white beaches, and the distant sky surrounded them with that wonderful indifference of nature toward everything that, being human, could not in the least concern it.

"Please get off my yacht at once," said Mr. Bradford, livid with anger. "This is outrageous. I realize that your generation has no respect for anything, but still, there are limits to cynicism and provocation."

Cohn got up. "May I have a cigar?"

"Take it and be damned!"

Monte Cristos. Cohn took the whole box. He felt the extreme satisfaction of a crusader who had paused to sack Constantinople on his way to free the tomb of Jesus in Jerusalem.

"You can take the dinghy. Leave it on the beach."

Cohn didn't bother with the dinghy. He slipped into the water and swam on his back, holding the cigar box over his head. He saw Mrs. Bradford seize the pictures and throw them into the sea. What a thing to do! There were several interesting ideological positions in them that would not have been scorned by Mao Tse-tung and his cultural dogs.

The puritan floated on his back, the cigar in his teeth, his eyes filled with sky.

Beyond the lagoon and the beach, on the slopes of Orohena, the giant ferns rose above the blue springs and in the depths of the luxurious growth slept forever the empty sites of temples and gods that were no longer there. And farther away, toward the hidden Faaone, wide estuaries made to the sea offerings of the sweet waters of Vaihiria and Aozai. The ocean was beating his wings against the reef and a thousand white surf eagles spread out, rose above the coral bar, and fell heavily, losing their plumes. And everywhere over the green earth wandered the pink and blue horses of Gauguin, bestrode by giant *vahines* that did not exist, but that the conditioned eye had brought with it from museums and postcards.

Toward the peninsula of Taiaropu, fifty red pirogues, twenty oarsmen in each, sprang from memory and raced toward Bougainville's ship of two centuries ago, *La Boudeuse*, with their cargo of naked *vahines* as welcoming gifts.

Cohn stepped out of the ocean, crossed the beach, and walked uphill through the banana grove, with the ocher heights of Orohena towering over him. Gauguin had painted the mountain so persistently that it was amazing to find it still standing.

He found Meeva sitting gloomily in front of the house, a bright red pareu around her hips, her huge bare breasts looking as if they had just been stolen from *Okahi,* Cohn's favorite painting.

"What's the matter?"

"Cohn, we need money. The shopkeepers say no more credit."

"What about the twenty thousand francs I gave you yesterday, you bitch?"

"I bought myself a new dress."

There was no arguing with that.

Cohn the provider scratched his beard, thinking it over. There was that new bunch of tourists at the Palace.

"O.K.," he said. "All I need is a pair of clean slacks, a clean shirt, and my black-leather glove."

6

Cohn Dancing

Mataoa Jenkins, the manager of the Paul Gauguin Palace, a true Tahitian who numbered several authentic Maori among his English, Irish, and Chinese ancestors, looked at Cohn with all the arrogance of a man who had built a hundred-foot swimming pool under the nose of the Pacific Ocean. The sight of it always enraged Cohn. That pool at the edge of the infinite was too much for him. Now and then he would mount a personal commando operation, and several times he had managed to piss in it in broad daylight. For that reason, and for several others, Mataoa Jenkins was more than suspicious of the most notorious bum on the island.

"Mr. Cohn, we've asked you not to come here. The boat docked yesterday and we have only *respectable* tourists here. They won't need your—your services."

"I'd like to have my breakfast served on the terrace," declared Cohn grandly. "You can't stop me: this is a public place. I'm having a fit of respectability, Mato. Home-sickness, I guess. I need to see good old American faces around me. Nostalgia. It gets me from time to time. If you let me in, I promise I'll never piss in your pool again. Scout's honor. You must have changed the water five times already. You'll be doing yourself a favor, see?"

The manager inspected Cohn from head to foot. The rascal looked less disreputable than usual. He was wearing fresh pants and a clean shirt. His sea captain's cap and his beard were less filthy. He was even wearing a glove—just one single black-leather glove—on his right hand. For once the bum looked quite acceptable, except perhaps for his nose, which retained a sort of arrogance that somehow made it look more like an organ of impertinence than of breathing.

"All right, Mr. Cohn, but don't start anything funny here."

"You can count on me."

Cohn went to the terrace and looked around with a sharp eye. Good old American faces. He ordered some coffee, and as Marua, the waitress, left the table, he had the strength of character not to put an appreciative hand under her skirt. There he sat, quiet and innocent, while Mataoa hovered around like a vulture, ready to swoop down on him at the first sign of an incident.

After enjoying the coffee, Cohn leaned toward the next table and asked shyly, "I beg your pardon, but could I see your *Time?* I've been away from home for many years—" He hung his head and sighed.

"Please join us," said the old gentleman, with a pleasant flash of freshly capped ivory. "Chaffee is the name. Jim Chaffee, from Des Moines. This is my wife, Betsy, and my sister-in-law, Marjorie."

"Bill Smith," said Cohn, who always took great pleasure in inventing new, simple names for himself, in the faint but futile hope of both escaping from his true self and of attaining simplicity.

He joined them at their table. The hotel manager materialized immediately, ready to protect his guests. But Cohn was relaxed and polite. He was chatting quietly with his countrymen, that was all. Mataoa left.

"And you haven't been back to the States for two years," asked Jim Chaffee, with compassion in his voice.

Cohn shrugged helplessly. "What can I do?" he asked. "You know how they treat lepers at home. They lock them up. It's the law."

"Lepers? I don't quite—"

"I mean, as soon as the doctors told me I had caught leprosy, a few years ago—it's quite prevalent here, you know—it was out of the question for me to go home. Back there they lock us up in hospitals. Here they let us

40

move about freely—as you can see. They don't consider it contagious, except through direct contact."

He brandished his black-gloved hand right under Marjorie Something's nose.

"Feel it; it's steel. I lost all the fingers of my right hand. Eaten away. It's threatening to spread up my arm to the elbow. Of course, with Enelpha drugs, you can control it in its first stages, but I discovered I had it a little late."

The tourists were transformed into statues, of which one, that of Marjorie Something-or-other, appeared to be on the point of crumbling to pieces. She stared in helpless horror at the black-gloved hand that Cohn was poking amiably under her nose.

"Naturally, life's become a bit difficult. I can't work, and I can't ask my folks for money. They don't know anything about it. I don't want to break their hearts. Poor Mom, can you imagine, if she knew— But as a rule, people are good to me. Especially fellow Americans. They never let me down. They're the last good-hearted people left in this sad world."

He withdrew his hand slightly. He was afraid good old Marjorie would keel over prematurely. It was an extremely interesting human experiment. A fundamental feeling of decency kept these three old prunes glued to their chairs, instead of bolting and running away, as they were dying to do. Jim Chaffee, of Des Moines, his face ashen, was digging feverishly into his inside coat pocket.

"Of course, I'd be very happy—allow me—I don't have any cash. Would you take traveler's checks?"

"I had no intention of asking you for money," said Cohn in a rather hurt tone of voice.

"Oh, but *you must*—"

"No, really, please—"

"But I insist—as a fellow American—"

Cohn let himself be swayed. The poor old thing knew there was no way for them to flee unless they covered their retreat with a humanitarian gesture. The hotel manager, feeling something fishy was going on, began to prowl around the table again nervously. Discreetly, Cohn made in his direction an obscene Italian gesture with one finger. He finally accepted three hundred dollars in traveler's checks. It was better than the last time.

"Please excuse us, but we have to be going," said Jim Chaffee in a choked voice, jumping up from his chair as if projected by a spring.

"If I may, I would like to show you the island," offered Cohn.

41

"Oh no, no—good Lord, no, thank you! They're taking care of all that here."

They were all on their feet now. It was a most amusing and gratifying moment, when the thought that "Bill Smith" might want to shake hands was sending cold shivers down their spines.

"If I can do anything for you in the United States—" said Chaffee.

Three hundred dollars, thought Cohn. They certainly deserved something for their money. After all, it was the absolute touristic climax of their trip. They would be able to bore their friends to the end of their days with the story of the fine American boy who had caught leprosy in Tahiti. It was the perfect tropical cliché, pure Somerset Maugham, with just the right touch of the golden legend of the South Seas. He was really giving them their money's worth.

"You may take a snapshot of me and my hand, if you wish," Cohn volunteered. They were past listening.

"If I can do anything for you in the United States," Mr. Chaffee was repeating, like an automaton, drops of sweat beading his forehead.

"Nothing," said Cohn. "Well, come to think of it—" He lowered his eyes and sighed. "I hope it won't seem too sentimental, but— Please send me a handful of American earth, care of the hotel here. I'll carry it with me always. I know that sounds corny, but it's so far from home here—and—well, my poor mom— Oh well!"

The older of the two broads burst into sobs. The manager appeared at once, observing Cohn as if he had a bomb in his hand.

"Mr. Cohn, I've asked you not to bother my guests."

Jim Chaffee, of Des Moines, glared at him. "Leave him alone," he growled.

He turned to Cohn and searched desperately for something encouraging to say to him, something optimistic, something truly American.

"Keep in touch with our consul here," he said at last. "See him regularly. With him, you'll be in good hands, I'm sure."

Bewilderment gave Mataoa's face the blank look of stupidity. The two old ladies were crying, Cohn was wiping his eyes, and Jim Chaffee was snorting into his handkerchief. Overcome by so much emotion, Cohn opened his arms to clasp him to his breast, but Chaffee turned white and stepped back hastily. Cohn grabbed the copy of *Time* and held it out to his countryman.

"You forgot your magazine—"

They took three steps back in charming unison, horror-struck at the very thought of touching that contaminated paper.

"That's all right. Keep it, keep it—"

Jim Chaffee waved at him vaguely; then urging the women on before him, he retreated toward the hotel. Cohn pictured the three of them naked, drenching each other in alcohol, not missing the least cranny. He went to the desk and presented the traveler's checks.

"Cash those for me."

The lady put on her glasses. "Three hundred dollars? Whatever did you tell them this time, Mr. Cohn?"

"Old family friends, that's all," Cohn told her curtly. "Hurry up."

But it was too late. He heard the roar of a wounded rhinoceros and Mataoa Jenkins came charging down the stairs, his fine mask of a Polynesian totem twitching with hate.

"Don't you ever dare to set foot here again, you bastard! I'll teach you to scare the wits out of my guests with your damn lies!"

"You mean they complained?"

"Of course, what did you think?" roared Mataoa. "They've threatened to have me fired for letting lepers wander around here and bother the guests!"

Cohn felt truly shocked. "What heartless, callous people! I can't tell you, Mataoa, how this saddens me. I am *so* disappointed!"

"Out!"

He grabbed Cohn by the collar with one hand and with the other by the seat of his pants, escorted him to the door, and concluded the ceremony with a well-aimed kick that sent the outcast flying facedown into the dust. Cohn experienced a pleasant feeling of achievement. Once more he had done something positive for the white man's prestige in the South Pacific.

There were quite a few Europeans in the parking lot, among them the three brothers Vervieux, who had come to Tahiti from the Congo, where they had lost their two-generations-old family estate. Cohn was picking himself up from the dust and was beginning to walk away when the youngest of the three Belgians caught up with him.

"Hey, you."

A brutish, deadly earnest square, without a trace of humor in his somber face. Cohn was not entirely against colonialism. He thought that a few centuries of African

43

occupation of Europe would be a good thing. Western sex life was getting terribly automatic and joyless.

"You lousy bum, if you let the natives kick you around, it will soon be rape and murder here, just like it was in the Congo!"

Cohn's curiosity was aroused. "And whom, exactly, have you raped and murdered in the Congo?" he inquired.

The Belgian took a step forward, Cohn two steps back.

"You Judas-shit, the next time you let a native kick you in the ass, we'll see to it that you sink to the bottom and stay there with a stone around your neck!"

Cohn was always at his best when he felt torn between arrogance and funk. This time he came up with something truly creative.

"How dare you!" he said haughtily, with the strongest possible American accent. "I am the Consul General of the United States here, and I accept no lessons of white dignity from anyone."

The Belgian swallowed hard. "The Con—"

"Here is my card, m'sieur."

Among other useful tools of a true *pícaro*, Cohn always carried the card of the honorary consul of the United States in Papeete, a man he detested cordially, because the son of a bitch was constantly trying to have him deported.

Cohn walked away, whistling gaily. Gossip was the fastest communication medium in Papeete. Within hours the news of the affront suffered by the Star-Spangled Banner would be known everywhere, and the Honorable Thomas Jefferson, Jr., would wonder why it was that both the French and the Tahitians were looking at him with ironic grins. The whole thing had just the right touch of perfection. Cohn was an artist at heart.

Meeva was waiting for him at the side of the road in front of the Chinese store. To Cohn's disgust she was wearing blue jeans. There should be a law against Tahitian girls in blue jeans, he thought. He handed her the traveler's checks.

"Here it is. Three hundred. Cash it."

She took a *tiare* from her hair, a gorgeous white orchid, and put it lovingly behind her *popaa*'s ear. He took her hand. He liked to feel her hand in his, and he loved to walk along the ocean with her, holding hands and with a flower behind his ear. Somehow, it made him feel almost innocent, as if he were recapturing something, at least, of "the man he was before the world began."

The red yolk of the sun, so swollen that it seemed about to burst open and give birth to some new bloody epic, sank heavily into the ocean in a damp light of the world's beginning, assuming there could have been a light at the beginning of such a venture. Indigo and deep blue reigned over Moaréa, while the lagoon was already giving in to darkness. The palms were becoming silhouettes, still streaked with silver where the sand began, and the dead worlds of fossilized madrepores called "coral" raised above the lagoon their gray dungeons of life become matter, with miniscule yellow crabs scurrying among the seaweed.

Three hundred dollars was a good take, but some of it had to be squandered on painting supplies. A sad waste, considering that Cohn seldom touched the brush and was totally devoid of talent in that field. However, the tourists whom the guide Puccioni took to his House of Joy expected to find an artistic atmosphere there, and there simply had to be a lot of paint, "work in progress," and brushes around. Cohn was, like all crooks, a stickler for realism. The first prerequisite of a *pícaro* was credibility. You can't cheat without some authenticity. So he had run into debt at Smirnoff's painting supplies shop. He needed more money.

There was that newly arrived German whom he hadn't used yet. A German almost surely meant "guilt" and guilt was always a good chance of grabbing a ransom.

He mounted his Honda.

"Get on."

As he started the bike, Meeva began to sing. It was an old Maori song and it told how the sky had wooed the earth and how, sadly, their copulation had been crossed with misfortune. It was interrupted by a gigantic tide of the ocean, who was jealous of the sky and felt mad, because the earth belonged to him and he alone had the right to caress it. And so it was that, their inspiration having been cut short, the earth gave birth to a man-man, and not at all to the man-god the couple was expecting. Without a doubt, thought Cohn gloomily, the most disastrous *coitus interruptus* of all time.

"Shut up," he told her. "You make me *fiu*."

7

Cohn Dancing

They rolled along until they got to the coral beach, where
Cohn got off the motorbike and walked into the palm
grove on the soft sand that felt pleasant to his feet. Big-
low's villa, which the German *popaa* had rented, appeared
between the palms in all its white splendor. It was the
most beautiful villa in Pouaavia.

"Wait for me here."

He took off all his clothes. Completely naked, he rolled
around in the white sand until he had all the appearance
of some half-human animal that had crawled out of its
hole in search of a lizard or a turtle egg.

"Cohn, what are you going to do to that guy? You look
scary."

"Never mind."

He left her under the *mapes* and walked toward the
house.

On the other side of the lagoon thousands of coconut
palms were hanging their heads down, leaning over the
green and yellow water in an attitude of petrified grief, a
kind of floral imitation of all the Italian pietàs, of mourn-
ers and Greek choruses. They crowned the island with
a melancholy that grew deeper still as the shadows length-
ened.

The house, built by a Swiss architect and reputed to be
the most modern on the island, was surrounded by beautifully tended lawns, which was most unusual in Tahiti. The
grass began almost at the very edge of the lagoon, a real
achievement in gardening. In the midst of that superb
greenery, a distinguished-looking man sat in a chaise
longue, his mind quite obviously at peace, feeding his eyes
on infinity.

Cohn licked his chops. Obviously, an escapist. The son
of a bitch thought he had fled far enough, and he was
feeling safe here, away from it all. Well, he was going to
teach him that there was no getting away from getting
anything.

A gardener was watering the flowers. His name was

Muhuu, but he was better known as Popaul. He saw Cohn, and he gave way to a kind of self-defense reflex that came spontaneously to anyone in Tahiti who had ever had anything to do with the rascal. He dropped the hose and rushed up to meet him.

"What the hell are you doing here ass-naked, Cohn?"

"I had a swim. That guy out there wishes to buy one of my paintings."

"Don't start any trouble or I'll beat the shit out of you."

Cohn tiptoed toward his prey, experimenting with a series of interesting nervous tics. Not overdoing it, just enough to look authentic and inspire confidence. He decided on a jerk of his right shoulder, with simultaneous tics in his right eye and twitches in the corner of his lips, with a trace of epileptic foam, plus a little guttural cry not unlike that of a mongoose. It was this pathetic little animal cry that attracted the German's attention to the human presence at his side.

He saw before him a kind of naked guru from Banaras, or Calcutta, his face and body white with sand. This ghastly enough apparition was in the grip of a really frightful succession of nervous tics. With a shade of respect in his attitude, the man rose. On seeing that nudity, those spasms, those wild eyes and beard, he must have felt instinctively that he was in the presence of holiness.

"Please forgive me f-f-f—"

Three little mongoose cries, a sharp tic shooting from one side of his face to the other like lightning, and in a sudden moment of inspiration Cohn also decided on a slight stammer.

"—for bothering y-y-you."

With some relief, Cohn saw the man was old enough to have known History. White hair, a sensitive, slightly sad face, and thoughtful eyes. Cohn always liked to deal with men of quality, of sensitivity: the yield was better. It also gave him the slightly satisfying impression that he was settling accounts with himself as well.

"W-w-we're n-neighbors. I live in a c-c-cave near here. H-h-hiding, you understand. Wh-when I heard you h-had arrived at last—as I kn-kn-knew you would, s-sooner or later—" He held back his nervous tics a bit. No use wasting all your ammunition at a single shot. "P-p-perhaps you remember me?"

"I'm not sure, but—"

"P-permit me to refresh y-your m-memory. Cohn, Moshel C-cohn, son of Leiba Cohn."

"Martin Grutt, from Munich. Pleased to meet you."

47

"Y-you d-don't remember me," mumbled Cohn. "You've f-forgotten already."

The German looked slightly embarrassed. As well he might, thought Cohn. Eight thousand miles by plane, the end of the world, Tahiti, the earthly paradise—he thought he had left History far behind. The man gestured a bit helplessly with both hands.

"I'm sorry, but— Although the name does seem familiar."

The ocean laughed so loud against the coral reef Cohn was afraid his old brother-in-arms would give away the game.

"I sort of expected my name would mean something to you, even now, after twenty-five years. But still—*Cohn*—don't you remember? *The Diary of Anne Frank* and all that—the Warsaw ghetto— No? That doesn't ring a bell?"

A string of nervous tics, three little mongoose cries, a convulsive head and shoulder spasm, a brief, jerky little dance. The German *popaa* just stood there, *The Enchanted Isles* of Gonçalves under his arm. The red blossoms of the flame trees joined above them, while beyond the pointed pandanus trees the ocean was grinning, showing his wide teeth over the reef.

"When I heard you had arrived, I said to myself, 'Cohn, the time has come. You should report immediately. You can't keep running away all the time.'"

His eyes were wide open and glassy, struck with a nameless terror. To achieve true artistic perfection as he performed another brief epileptic dance among the orchids, Cohn thought of Professor Teller, the father of the hydrogen bomb, in order to get goose pimples all over his body. But it was too hot, and he had to settle for a slight drooling at the lips. When it came to art, Cohn was for realism.

"I've lived on bananas for twenty-five years. I've hidden underground like a mole. But for twenty-five years Cohn has managed to survive, and to escape the Nazis, while the rest of his family, his sister, his father, his mother, his brothers, all of them—"

A sort of Saint Vitus's dance seized him once more.

"Auschwitz! Auschwitz! Auschwitz!"

His eyes were filled with an expression of terror, where the other had no difficulty seeing six million Jewish corpses. Cohn heard a sensuous cooing among the flowers. Turtle doves. Tahiti lacked birds, so Bizien had imported these voluptuous little creatures whose tender outpourings squared so well with the legend of eternal love.

48

The German had turned deathly pale.

"I may assure you I had nothing to do with those hor-rors," he said in a strangely low, broken voice.

The gardener Muhuu was watching them, hose in hand. He was sure there was something fishy going on, and was waiting for the least sign to intervene. But Cohn felt se-cure. That distinguished-looking man had probably never been a Nazi. So he was going to pay the ransom. He had to. Only the innocent feel truly guilty.

Cohn improvised a very nice knee spasm, a true medi-cal first.

"You're probably wondering, where's the required yel-low star? But you see, here, we're in the Garden of Eden and I live naked. The law concerning Jews required that the star be worn on the clothing, not on the skin. Maybe you'll say that the law has been changed, and that now Jews have to wear the yellow star on their skin as well, because of progress, and because Fermi, Einstein, Oppen-heimer, and Teller were all Jews, but I didn't know it, I swear I didn't know it, I swear!"

If that son of a bitch with his kind, sensitive face thought it was enough to pay his plane ticket and rent a beautiful villa in Tahiti to escape History, he was fooling himself.

"That is all finished," said the German in an unsteady voice, as white as a white man. "Finished long ago. It will never happen again."

The idea crossed Cohn's mind that the tourist was going to refuse to pay the ransom, but he reproached himself at once for his base thoughts.

"I'm happy you came," he mumbled. "I've had enough of waiting and of fear. I've been waiting for twenty-five years—waiting for them to come and ship me off—back home—"

From the back of his throat came the sound of whin-nying, as from a terrorized beast—a human beast, of course. He stood still awhile, his eyes opened wide, his mouth twisted. Then he shook his head and looked around him, as if he had just come out of a trance.

"I live near here," he muttered. "We're neighbors. If you need anything—Cohn—Moses Cohn—I wished to welcome you to this earthly paradise."

He turned around and walked away like a robot. Then he joined Meeva under the coconut palms and got dressed.

"How much did you get for your picture, Gene?"

"Well, I'll be damned," said Cohn in amazement.

He had completely forgotten the ransom. That often

49

happened when he was in the grip of real inspiration. Nothing mattered then except dancing. Or trampling. Same thing. So what? He thought. Nothing wrong with a bit of art for art's sake, from time to time.

8

The Artist

Down below, toward Mooréa, the broken belt of the coral reef let the ocean in, and its white seed flowed steadily toward the welcoming shore with all the self-assured, majestic virility of Teona, the fecund father of all the seas. The foam still had the purity of the first act of creation and it was sinking into the sand with a soft murmur of pleasure. Thousands of palms bowed their heads at the foot of Orohena, who was the God of Anger before being bitten by the "flea of immortality," thus becoming a dead volcano. Its stark and rusty nakedness was covered with patches of green fleece that deepened into dark valleys, where the brightness of ocean and sky ended in mystery.

On their way back they drove up to Le Goff's place, bearers of good tidings. The adventurer had fallen upon hard times. A few days earlier, his *vahine* had come to see Meeva and told her tearfully that her beloved *popaa* was broke and didn't Meeva know another lord and master whom she could love devotedly for the rest of her life. She was tired of eating fish and she hadn't had a new dress in months. She was losing face, it was *e mea haama*. If there was one thing Meeva knew everything about, it was heartbreak, and she had kept pestering Cohn. As a matter of fact, Cohn knew of an opening and had already talked to Bizien about it. The promoter agreed that Le Goff had exactly the kind of blond, sad, and meek appearance needed for the job.

They soon heard the waterfall and saw the grass hut perched on a hill among the papayas, with their massive fruit hanging obscenely, like a kind of vegetable elephantiasis. The light, like everything else in Tahiti, was imbued with a translucent marine quality. It always seemed to carry within it the emerald greens, the sulfur yellows, and the transparent blues of the lagoon. They left the bike and

50

plunged into the tunnel of red and violet flowers leading to the shack.

René Le Goff was squatting, naked, before the hut, holding a fish over a wood fire. Sitting on the ground next to him, in a blue and white cotton dress, the *vahine* Taimaha was nursing her latest child, which had already been requested for adoption by the best families on the island. Cohn often wondered at the Polynesian custom of giving away their own offspring to strangers and adopting the children of others. The custom had probably originated when the rites of the religious sect of the Arii required believers to kill their own children. By giving their children to strangers and adopting theirs, they were getting around the oath without offending the gods.

Le Goff had a sad face, a blond beard, and hair falling down to his shoulders, and he was smeared with daubs of red, blue, and yellow paint.

"Hi, René. What's new?"

"Hi, Cohn. I think I got the clap again."

"It's the climate," suggested Cohn tactfully.

René sighed. With his splendid golden hair and beard, he looked like an astrologer Cohn had known in the Latin Quarter.

"Of course, I could get a shot of penicillin. But that poses a moral problem. In principle, I should heal myself by the laying-on of hands. If they learn I'm being treated by a doctor—"

"Ask Father Tamil, the Dominican, to give you the shot. He's O.K. He won't talk."

"It's embarrassing to go to another religion for help."

Le Goff had come to Tahiti three years earlier. In those days the British youth was marching through England by the tens of thousands in protest against nuclear madness and the "balance of terror." Le Goff claimed that he had tried to organize a similar protest movement in France, but he had had to bow to the fact that the French were much too individualistic to bother with the question of collective death. In fact, every Frenchman seemed to think that no greater consolation could come to him for his personal demise.

"First we tried a march to the Musée de l'Homme in Paris, naked and smeared with shit from head to foot, to symbolize our abject state of degradation and barbarity. We succeeded only in arousing a little curiosity, that's all. We kept at it for a few more months, but we were up against the most complete indifference. The French are cynics, you know. They don't believe in the end of the world. They just don't give a damn, and we were feeling like entertainers. So I said to myself, 'Screw you all!' I came here. When they saw me sitting here naked, my face all painted red, blue, and yellow, they took me for at least one *tiki* France gave them back. These people need to believe in something. They fed me. I became a kind of witch doctor."

Gradually, without quite knowing how, Le Goff began to heal by the laying-on of hands, except for lepers, whom he would not touch. Then, when there was a pretty one, instead of laying hands, he laid the *vahine*.

Then he had gone to pot completely, screwing and drinking; and though he still took himself seriously, flying into a rage when the fishermen from Buuva went to sea without first making offerings to him, the fact was that he had never managed to get on the list of "cultural points of interest" published by the Tourist Office, with the "must" attractions marked with three stars, a kind of Tahitian Guide Michelin. The village people were nice enough, bringing their *tiki* fish and fruit, enough to survive, but no one could get anywhere on the island without the tourist trade. Yet Le Goff still had dreams of glory.

"I'd like to get established on a firmer base," he said, puffing the Havana Cohn had given him. "I'd like them to build me a church."

Cohn laughed. He didn't believe a word about Le Goff's crusade against the bomb in France. All these blue, yellow, and red daubs of paint probably served to disguise a mug too well known to the Interpol police.

"What's so funny? Everybody needs material security. That way, when they stop believing in me, I'll still have the church. I believe in real estate."

The baby began to cry and Taimaha smiled at him proudly.

"Isn't he beautiful, Cohn? He's beginning to look like you. My sister has a boy by an English sailor, but he's not half as pretty."

"Are you sure I've slept with you?" asked Cohn.

He tickled the baby's nose, and the baby kicked and gurgled.

"See, he recognizes you," said Taimaha.

Meeva beamed approvingly.

Above the *matave* trees with their pink leaves, Gauguin's mountain was covered with a lush beauty that was less an act of nature than that of the human eye capable of discerning it. The naked blond adventurer with the daubed face, who might well be hiding behind all those

52

coats of paint the features of a Nazi criminal or an international crook, the man whose name was not Cohn, the two *vahines* who were only *vahines,* and the child who by some miracle could well become a man, were quiet among the flowers.

"Can you give me some money, Cohn?" asked Taimaha. "René hasn't received anything but lousy fish for the last three days. The doctor says I have to eat meat and starch. It's your child, after all."

It wasn't true, but Cohn often felt that all children were his. He gave them two hundred francs and told Le Goff to take the bus to Papeete and to report to Bizien that evening. It was urgent.

The evening sadness of the tropics fell over them as they left.

A rusty moon drifted along the lightning-streaked edge of an indigo storm, and the ocean still glowed with the remnants of the swallowed sun. The smoke from a pig roasting over a wood fire hung heavily over an invisible village hidden behind the palms. The mountain towered above him; it had come closer and seemed to lean over him in that startling sudden nearness of shortened perspectives.

The black Citroën followed them all the way to Pouaavia, then the driver switched off the lights and drove the car along the path into the clutter of palms and mangrove on the ocean's shore. The clouds lay dark and still around the moon and their shadows over the bluish sand were creeping slowly along the beach.

The man behind the wheel was wearing a white *judoka* vest, a huge Coptic Abyssinian cross over his chest, and heavy earrings of fake diamonds. There was the red Brahman's mark between his eyebrows. The Chinese sitting next to him had a round, flat face that looked more moonlike than the real thing up there in the sky. The cigarette he was smoking nervously stuck out like a last candle on a birthday cake. They sat in the dark among the dancing fireflies without exchanging a word, watching the orange light of the oil lamp inside the house. Then the light went out.

"Nothing again," Callum said. "Are you sure?"

"Sure," replied the Chinese. "My nephew's been watching him for more than three weeks now, and it happened twice. But I don't understand. I don't understand it at all, Mr. Callum. Why should such an important man as you be interested in that bum? Why should the great C.I.A. be so concerned by a lousy painter? Why? That's what I want to know."

"Maybe he is planning to kill the President."

"Him? He's a good-for-nothing."

"O.K., I'll tell you. The C.I.A. have discovered the only man in the world they know nothing about. It shook them. So they're taking care of that."

The Chinese shook his head disapprovingly. "Jokes," he said. "That's the trouble with your country. Jokes. That's how America has lost the war in Vietnam: joking. He is probably paid by the Communists to discredit the free West. I have written that in my report. Do you know that this *merde* has been walking for weeks around Papeete with a huge I AM AN AMERICAN button, pinned to his filthy shirt?"

The man with the silver cross laughed.

"Well, maybe that's why we'll probably get orders to kill him. He is subversive. He is damaging American prestige in the South Pacific. A saboteur."

The Chinese shrugged. "Jokes," he said.

The clouds were all over the moon now. The white man swore.

"We won't be able to see a damn thing," he said. "But we can still take pictures."

He patted the infrared Bordas camera he was holding on his fat thighs.

"Please, Mr. Callum, who is this Mr. Cohn?"

"Jesus Christ!"

The Chinese thought it over. "I don't believe it."

"I didn't say he is Jesus Christ. I said: Jesus Christ! It's an American expression."

The Chinese took another cigarette and stuck it in the middle of the cake. Why should the honorable C.I.A. be so interested in a lousy artist simply because he would get up now and then in the middle of the night and spend hours drawing in the sand? It made so little sense that it was becoming quite frightening.

The man who was watching the other two crouched behind the pirogue and made his second contact over the walkie-talkie at one A.M.

"They're still there, *mon capitaine.*"

"What about Monsieur Cohn?"

"Nothing so far. The house is dark. But you can never tell."

"I don't want Callum to take any pictures, Mozon. That's an order. No pictures."

54

"What the hell am I to do? Kill them?"

"*Amigo,* those two guys put together must weigh four hundred pounds. It's simply too much meat to dispose of, without attracting Monsieur Cohn's attention. Besides, there's an ethical problem. The C.I.A. is no 'enemy,' technically speaking."

"So?"

"Scare them off."

"*Bien, mon capitaine.*"

It was getting hold of him again and yet he had fought it back as bravely as he could. Sex was a good way of getting rid of your creative urge, and he had done his best, but now Meeva was asleep, and the compulsion was returning, growing irresistibly within his head.

He got up and lit the oil lamp. Moths flung themselves eagerly into the bright flame, which they probably mistook for a civilization. Cohn stood still, struggling against his true self, then put the oil lamp out, went outside, and looked into the night. No one. Nothing but silver there.

The island of Mooréa was arching its back among the stars. The ocean sparkled with billions of microorganisms, the dark violet clouds were shuddering with silent lightning, but the storm kept prudently away from the shore, as if to keep its fires at a safe distance from the Promethean hand of the man standing on the ocean's shore.

Cohn picked up a piece of driftwood and got down on his knees.

Then . . .

The night was silent and trusting. Nature seemed to be holding its breath. Only a low murmur on the coral reef, a furtive dash of a crab.

The man with the silver cross stood quietly in darkness, holding the infrared Bordas with telescopic sight. The Chinese was beside him. Down there below at the foot of the dune, Cohn, stark naked, was dragging himself on his knees, scribbling in the sand. The two men were straining their eyes. Then the clouds suddenly undressed the moon and the whole beach took on its pale-blue phosphorescent glow.

The man with the cross swore in a low, hissing voice. "Makes no sense at all."

"I told you," the Chinese said. "He is doing this all the time. Getting up in the middle of the night and drawing in the sand. Then usually he gets drunk. What is it all about?"

It looked more like a musical score.

Callum swore again. Well, let Washington worry.

He raised the camera.

The first bullet hit it almost instantly.

There was almost no sound, just the flat burp of a silencer. Then there were two more hollow belches and ten thousand dollars' worth of spying equipment lay smashed in the sand.

Callum heard a brief, stricken gasp and saw the Chinese go down by the car. Funk, sheer funk. They were both dressed in white and too fat a target to be missed by a professional. This was merely a friendly warning from the French. Americans, go home. Mind your own fucking business, Monsieur Cohn is *ours*.

"Get up."

"They'll kill us."

"The French don't kill their allies, they just scare the shit out of them. Let's go. We'll come for the car tomorrow."

They walked down the dune toward the road. Callum took a handkerchief out of his pocket and wiped the cold sweat from his forehead. He wasn't frightened. He was merely living some kind of a nightmare. The whole thing was now bordering on sheer madness. The French S.D.E.C. and the C.I.A. were showing a demented interest in a crazy musician who was getting up in the middle of the night to write music on the sand on a lonely beach in Tahiti.

"What was he drawing?" the Chinese began again. "Why on earth—"

"Shut up. He is a composer. Music. The C.I.A. is passionately interested in music. It's not generally understood, but the C.I.A. is a great cultural institution. There's nothing they wouldn't do for a pretty tune."

The coral laid bare by the receding waters swarmed with a panic life of crabs whose sudden dashes or petrified immobility recalled some nameless perils at the hour of Creation, a terror that had never left them. And in the sky, the pallor of the Milky Way itself was there like a trace of some primeval agony. Then, as the ocean began to swell again with the returning tide and the stars paled, Cohn threw his stick away. The ocean was creeping closer and closer to the writing on the sand, then over it, with an uneasy shudder, as if in fear that some of it would elude destruction. But Cohn helped the ocean, running over the lines, shuffling his feet, so that when the daylight would come, no trace of his music would remain on the shore.

Then he lay down on the beach and closed his eyes, smiling.

The passing storm still shuddered in the distance, then the celestial rumble subsided to a murmur in which the dreamer recognized the young voice of the world's beginning, as if nothing had yet been lost and the chance was still open.

I am looking for the face I had
Before the world was made.

9

The Enemy

He was awakened by a kick in the ribs and barely had the time to look around and make sure there was no trace of his creation left on the sand before the two gendarmes pushed him into the jeep. This was fine: as long as they were treating him like a bum, he was safe. The day when they began to show him the respect due to a Beethoven, he would be finished.

He was driven to the police station, charged with robbery, then taken to the Chief Inspector's office.

Apart from his greasy hair, parted asslike in the middle, heavy lips, and a flabby, shapeless sort of a nose that presided over the general dullness of his features, Chief Inspector Ryckmans had the smart, knowing look of a superior idiot. His eyes sparkled with imbecility. Cohn considered the man a worthy heir of the immortal gendarme Charpillet, who had drawn up the historical report against Gauguin because the artist had gone about the island "aboard an unlighted carriage." It was the only horse-drawn cart in the whole of the Marquesas and Tuamotu islands. But Cohn didn't really hold it against Ryckmans. Gauguin was at the time the only artist in the Marquesas and Charpillet the only cop. They couldn't miss each other.

In his ten years in the now defunct colonial police, Ryckmans had witnessed such fantastic reversals of fortune during the process of African accession to independence that he had come to regard all criminals as potential

57

political leaders. The Congolese post-office thief whom he had kept in jail for a year without a trial was now personally received by General de Gaulle as Head of State, and Paris was decked out in flags in his honor. His number-one boy in Brazzaville was now Minister of Health, and one of the "bandits," as they were then called, whom he personally had deprived of three front teeth after a riot, had become Minister of the Interior three weeks later. These tragic blows of fate had made Ryckmans one of the most confused, frightened, and mediocre cops in the world. His failure to smell out a future great spiritual and political figure among the African riffraff had dealt a fatal blow to his career. He was now serving in Papeete in a subaltern position. He considered his failure as a price good police paid to bad history and was giving in to melancholia and to persecution mania. The sly expression fixed permanently over his features was there merely to conceal his complete confusion, and he had a tendency to shake hands discreetly with every pimp or chicken thief in Papeete, after locking him up, convinced that he was dealing with a future president of the independent Republic of Oceania.

For some time now, a terrible fear had been haunting Ryckmans' sick mind: he is sitting in his office, everything is nice and pleasant, and then suddenly the phone rings and he is given the order to have a certain Jesus crucified. This ghastly thought kept him awake at night, and his wife begged him to think of something else, they had enough problems as it was. But in the light of his colonial experience Ryckmans was determined not to get caught unawares.

"You get the picture? I'm sitting here in Papeete, and the phone rings, and the Governor of Polynesia tells me: you will arrest such-and-such and you will have him crucified immediately. Paris orders. What am I to do? Can you tell me? Because, you see, I still have no assurance that this criminal element will turn out to be Jesus Christ, just as they had no idea in the Congo that Lumumba was going to be Lumumba. Well, they tell me, get the so-and-so and have him hanged, or whatever. What am I to do, for God's sake? Do you see my situation?"

"Bernard, honestly, nothing like that's likely to happen in Tahiti. Whoever saw Jesus in the Garden of Eden? All right, let's imagine the worst, let's imagine Jesus suddenly shows up here. You can always request a transfer. You're worrying yourself sick over nothing."

"It happens all the time in my job. Remember Guganda, in Nyome? Give that nigger the works, they tell me, let's make an example. Right. I carry out my orders, and what happens? Six months later, he's the new Prime Minister. Do you see it now? They tell a police officer: a so-and-so called Jesus, a troublemaker, teach him a good lesson, we don't want to hear from him again— What am I to do? Do I obey? Do I disobey?"

"Bernard, listen to me, before you see Jesus in Tahiti—"

"You can never be sure of anything anymore. He can come anyplace, under any name, where you least expect him—the surprise element, you know. They've learned a few things."

"Bernard, you have more important things to worry about than Jesus showing up in Tahiti. The children have got to go to France for their studies—"

"In the Congo I grab Kamato and keep him in jail: he becomes the new police chief. In Algeria I manage to keep Godard, the head of the O.A.S., out of the can: he becomes nothing at all. How's one to know? I am only a cop. Suppose they tell me, 'Ryckmans, we have a subversive element here, a certain Jesus.'"

"Bernard!"

"But look at Gauguin. He was an anarchist, a sworn enemy of Law and Order, eaten alive with syphilis— And now, where do our innocent little children go? To the Lycée Paul Gauguin! I'm telling you, there's no justice!"

"Are you going to get some sleep? It's three o'clock!"

"I went to see Bishop Tatin to discuss my problem with him. I said to him, 'Let's imagine we have a Communist government tomorrow and they give me the order to crucify a certain Jesus. What am I to do? Do you see my situation?' He said, 'It can't happen.' A bishop!"

"Bernard, for the last time, if Jesus comes back, it won't be in Tahiti. They don't come to Tahiti for that sort of thing."

"You remember Jamila, in Algeria? She died during interrogation. Because of a manufacturing flaw, the Perrier bottle broke and she hemorrhaged to death. Today Jamila is a saint in Algeria. Inspector Bigreux was kicked out of the police force—"

"I swear to you on the heads of our children that you'll never have anything to do with Jesus Christ as long as you live. Don't lose any sleep over it. It isn't worth it."

"You know, Father Safran kicked me out of church last Sunday?"

"Bernard, really, going to church to pray for Jesus not to come back! Put yourself in Father Safran's place!"

When he saw the number-one pain in his neck in Tahiti scratching his crotch in front of him, Ryckmans' cunning air became more pronounced, so that the smile swept away his whole face, leaving only his nose, by the sole virtue of its size, presiding over that feast of understanding and benevolence. If there was one man he hated, it was Cohn. But Ryckmans had taken all the punishment a cop could take in his dealings with history, and he had no desire to go down to posterity as the "dull brute who had never missed the chance to hurt the unfortunate genius who was to crown Tahiti with a beauty more eternal than that of its lagoons." He had read that only the night before, in an article about Gauguin, and these insults were aimed at his alter ego of the Marquesas sixty-five years before, that unhappy servant of Law and Order, the good gendarme Charpillet. Ryckmans had six children, and the thought that some day his offspring might read such horrors about their father gave him goose pimples. The new Gauguin was now standing in front of the police officer, scowling at him. Ryckmans smiled broadly at Cohn and felt a cramp in his stomach, an instant reaction to that act against nature.

"Ah, Monsieur Cohn. Please sit down. How about a cigar?"

Ryckmans was looking at Cohn with a benevolent and paternal eye. This gave him such a false appearance that Cohn felt like leaning over and rearranging his features. What made his mug more intolerable was the fact that on the wall behind, there were three large reproductions of Gauguin's paintings, including the fine *Rereioa*.

"Let's speak frankly," said Ryckmans.

"Drop dead."

On May 27, sixty-five years earlier, Ryckmans' predecessor, Sergeant Jean-Pierre Claverie, had given the final blow to the sick and fallen man who lived in the House of Joy. He had personally sentenced him to three months in jail and fined him fifty francs for writing letters insulting him in his official capacity as the representative of public order. And the most unforgivable aspect of the whole shameful business was that the Administration had asked Claverie, the plaintiff, to act himself as public prosecutor in the case.

"It's time we made peace, Mr. Cohn."

"You bloody well know that the judge in your crooked trial against me had no right to choose the prosecutor. As for naming your henchman Claverie to do the job, that was Nazism pure and simple. You won't get away with it,

60

Ryckmans, I'm telling you. I have influential friends in Paris. My art dealer, Vollard, and de Monfreid are right now approaching Malraux on this matter. If necessary, we'll go all the way up to de Gaulle. We're demanding complete rehabilitation and apologies."

Ryckmans' Adam's apple moved up and down spasmodically. Doctor Toulane, whom he saw regularly, told him that he had developed paranoid tendencies as a result of the moral anguish and psychological shocks to which he had been subjected in Africa.

"I am trying to save you from deportation. Chong Fat's lodged a complaint against you for robbery."

"Yellow lies. Anything to discredit a white man. They feel we're going under, so they bite."

"I've also received a report saying that you were up to your tricks again, with the passengers from the *Columbus*. I've warned you that the next time you pose for pornographic pictures—"

"I didn't pose. The bastards took the snapshots without my knowledge. I was swimming in bliss, when that traitor Puccioni tiptoed in with the tourists. My eyes were closed and my back was turned. Both our backs were turned, as a matter of fact. You know that position?"

"Then you made them pay."

"It was a matter of principle. They had no right to take my picture at such an important moment of my life without my consent. You just don't do that sort of thing. They should've asked my permission."

There was not a word of truth about this business of posing for dirty pictures. Another slander of his envious rival, Verdouillet. But Cohn had no intention of denying it. It was good for his reputation. It had just the right Gauguin touch and it added credibility to his disguise. The only thing that worried him was his voice. You could change your face and remove your finger prints, but you couldn't do much about your vocal cords.

He brought down his fist on Ryckmans' desk.

"Besides, may I remind you that Gauguin's bed, with its pornographic designs, which so shocked the Apostolic Vicar, is now in the Louvre. They paid millions for it in nineteen-fifty-two. One of the last letters Gauguin wrote before his death said simply: 'I'm beaten down to the ground, today, defeated. . . .' In June of nineteen-fifty-seven, that letter was sold in Paris for six hundred thousand francs. You can clap me in jail if you wish, but posterity will hold you in universal contempt."

Ryckmans said nothing. But he had learned a few things

in his dealings with history. Picasso, who painted such horrors, was considered the greatest artistic genius of our times. De Gaulle had been condemned to death for desertion, and today he was a monument. Nehru had spent fifteen years of his life in jail and he had become a myth. Lumumba, who stole money orders, had become a prophet and a saint. Jesus, who was an enemy of the establishment, had become a pillar of the establishment. Gauguin, who had given syphilis to hundreds of Tahitian girls, now had his Lycée Papeete, as well as his museum and his street. The gendarmes Charpillet and Claverie had become monsters in the eyes of posterity. The world turned so fast that everything ended up ass-backwards, and the sharpest cop, when confronted with history, could no longer tell if he was beating the shit out of a "bandit" or of a "man of destiny." Ryckmans felt drops of cold sweat on his forehead: he was suddenly having the awful premonition that sooner or later they would be celebrating Saint Gauguin's Day in Tahiti.

He rose from his chair, walked around the desk, and put a friendly hand on Cohn's shoulder.

"That's all right," he said. "I'll see that Chong Fat withdraws the charge. As long as I am here, every artist in Tahiti—and particularly you, Monsieur Cohn—can count on my support. I can't say I understand your work very well. When it comes to art, my tastes are rather conservative: Gauguin, Van Gogh—something classical, something I can truly enjoy—"

He saw Cohn to the door and shook his hand warmly.

"And keep at it, keep at it, young man. Work, hard work, that's the thing. Remember that our great Gauguin simply killed himself screw—I mean, working."

The first thing Cohn saw outside was Meeva, sitting under a flame tree in her new white dress with red flowers.

"What are you doing here?"

"The gendarmes told me you were in jail. I was waiting."

"It could have been a damn long wait, you know."

"Cohn, I'd wait for you forever, anywhere, all my life, even if it took several weeks."

They were squatting on the dirt road, holding hands. Above Papeete, on the flanks of Orohena, the giant ferns exploded in green petrified fireworks, and higher up, the mountain looked naked, its reddish hide streaked with the black and the gray of volcanic times. White *tiare* were twisting around the trees, and they looked like snakes transformed into flowers by the true gods, as a reward for

having so successfully encouraged the first cou[p]
the fruit of joy. That's why there were no snakes in
only flowers.

"Cohn, don't play with my ass in public. *E mea haamu*
It makes me feel ashamed."

He withdrew his hand, with the feeling of a sad personal loss.

"Come on. I'm taking you to Chong's for lunch."

The Governor of French Oceania pushed the cable away, then turned his gray, tired face toward Caillebasse.

"They're out of their minds," he said, his voice quivering with irritation. "It's some ghastly mix-up. The man is well known to our police here. I refuse to believe it, period."

"There've been other cases of distinguished men gone to pot in the South Seas, *monsieur le gouverneur*. This is quite a well-established tradition, you know."

"And what on earth do they mean by 'ensure personal security,' can you tell me?"

"The cable says we'll get more precise instructions later. The man is in immediate danger, I presume."

There was a silence. In a four-year tenure of office, this was the first time the Governor had received a message signed "Présidence de la République." It was as close as one could get to de Gaulle without first dropping dead.

"Who is threatening him here? And why? This is Tahiti, you know. Not Chicago."

Caillebasse felt the Governor was slightly out of touch. The reference to Chicago showed something like a forty-year information gap.

The Governor was a short, white-haired, and energetic man known for his rigid moral standards and the infidelities of his wife, one explaining the other.

"When is it that we last had a murder here? 'Ensure personal security'—this is positively insulting. I won't have anything to do with it. Pass it on to the S.D.E.C. That's the kind of thing they thrive on."

Caillebasse had now no way of sparing the man's susceptibility. There were moments when too much tact could ruin a man's career.

"The S.D.E.C.'s already been handling the case for more than a year."

The Governor's face reddened. "Behind my back?"

"I presume they weren't sure."

The Governor was a much-decorated hero of the Second World War. But time has a way with heroes. He was

63

...irement next year and all that was left in him ...as suspicion and pique.

And why is it that I'm informed only now?" he asked. "Don't answer, let me guess. The man is top security—I still don't believe it's he— and he's in danger. He may be killed, in which case the S.D.E.C. wants *me* to shoulder the responsibility. Correct?"

"Correct."

The Hong Kong plane was circling over Tahiti. The three men who were coming to kill Mathieu were looking down on the lush green island with the cold hostile eye of professionals who never know where they will be buried.

The man in white was leaning over his bike across the street from the restaurant, watching Cohn and his girl go in. It was a chance encounter, and it was lucky that he hadn't gone inside. After a year of close observation, he had acquired a considerable respect for "Monsieur Cohn's" sharp eye and truly remarkable nose for smelling out a rat. The game couldn't go on much longer. Paris was still hesitating, but the C.I.A. was getting nervous, and quite rightly so. It was highly unlikely that the Russians and the Chinese were still out of the picture. Chong Fat was the best informer the French had here, but his repeated assurance that the Maoists among the local population of six thousand Chinese were an insignificant minority was open to question. It was difficult to imagine that Peking was still unaware of the presence in Tahiti of the man who was a constant threat to their security and whose code name in the daily flow of top-secret messages flying between Paris and Papeete was "Elysêeus," a discreet allusion to the personal interest de Gaulle was taking in the case.

As soon as he saw the couple walk into the restaurant, Chong Fat began to gesticulate with all the proverbial frenzy of impassive Orientals. This grieved Cohn, who felt that a good Chinese restaurateur should stick to his menu and serve the traditional dishes of his native land. Seeing Chong Fat's face distorted with nervous fury was almost as if you were being served cannelloni alla Napolitana instead of glazed duck.

"What's wrong? Aren't we friends anymore?"

"Beat it, Mr. Cohn! The other day you broke open my cashbox and stole thirty thousand francs. You should be in jail. I forbid you to set foot in my distinguished establishment again!"

Cohn closed his eyes. The great cultural ⌐
reached Tahiti were undoubtedly praiseworthy, bu⌐
Chong Fat speak with that fine Corsican singsong ⌐
was truly too much, with that yellow background.

"Chong, you had it coming to you. Your ignoble ancestor of a father had grabbed well over thirty thousand
francs' worth of paintings from the man of genius who
brought fame to your establishment: Paul Gauguin Restaurant, Cantonese Cuisine!"

"Oh, Holy Mother!" groaned Chong Fat, in the best tradition of the Cannebière in Marseille. "My father fed Mr.
Gauguin free for months. You'll find it written everywhere."

"Your father was a Judas-Shylock who had Gauguin's
paintings and property seized to get his pound of flesh."

Chong Fat's face turned scarlet, in which the last re-
maining traces of yellow added orange touches. Holding
his head sideways, Cohn was admiring his artistic achievement.

"Leave him alone, Cohn," said Meeva. "He has children."

"I know," said Cohn. "I had to force myself."

Chong Fat turned on his heel and vanished inside his
office.

"He's going to kill you, Cohn," said Meeva. "You must
never insult their wives. With the Chinese, it's as if you
insulted General de Gaulle. Let's get out of here."

Chong Fat was coming back, brandishing Perruchot's
Life of Gauguin in Cohn's face.

"If you find a single word against my father here, I'll
feed you free for a month."

It was true, and that was why Bizien had a picture of
Chong Fat's restaurant in his folder, with a caption inviting the visitors to "try the genuine Chinese cuisine Paul
Gauguin enjoyed in his favorite restaurant." The menu
offered several of the Founder's favorite dishes, all typically Tahitian. There was Paul Gauguin barbecue, and
Paul Gauguin orange duck, and a Paul Gauguin fruit
salad. There was even a Chinese bouillabaisse, made from
a personal recipe the painter gave his good friend, the father of the present-day proprietor, Mr. Chong Fat, Jr.
Above the bouillabaisse appeared a reproduction of the
artist's self-portrait with the famous yellow halo around
his head. Cohn had always felt that Gauguin richly deserved that halo.

It was at that moment that Cohn heard in the dining
room behind the bamboo curtain the voices and the music

65

estra, "Jimmy Lin Pino and his Four Nitty-Hips," playing and singing "Alouette, gentille alouette" with much brio. For some reason, the idea of four Chinese in Tahiti singing "Alouette, gentille alouette" for Scandinavian and American tourists in the Paul Gauguin Restaurant, Genuine Cantonese Cuisine, threw him completely beside himself.

"You're screwing up French culture!" he thundered. "You want to turn everything yellow! There won't be a single white masterpiece left in our museums! Tomorrow, the *Mona Lisa* will have slant eyes! Vermeer's bourgeois, dressed like Buddhist monks, will be playing Mah-Jongg! De Gaulle will be turned into a mandarin eating rice with chopsticks! Nothing sacred, huh?"

Chong Fat's face looked like a yellow sheet wrinkled by a thousand nervous spasms. "I forbid you to insult me! I'm a true Gaullist!"

"That doesn't surprise me a bit."

"I'm an officer of the Tastevin!"

"Keep your hands off our French wines, you *risotto!*" shouted Cohn.

"I'm married to a Frenchwoman!"

"That's it! Now you're grabbing our women and our daughters!"

"Mr. Gauguin, I forbid you to come and make a scene here in my honorable establishment!" roared Chong Fat. "You've done this too often! I'll take you to court!"

Cohn held his breath. This was truly beautiful. He savored a delicious moment of perfection. Now he knew that, as an artist, he had reached maturity and was in full command of his talent. To hear himself called Gauguin by the distraught Chinese was a tribute that moved him intensely. He could almost hear the hearty laughter of his spiritual ancestor, defeated in Tahiti more than a half century earlier. He could hear it so clearly that it seemed to cover the voices of the Chinese group singing "Alouette, gentille alouette" for the tourists.

Cohn wiped away a tear or two. His victory was complete, and there was no more reason to stay in the damn place. He took Meeva's arm.

"Let's go," he said softly, his voice quivering with emotion. "We mustn't hate this Chinese Judas; he's just doing his job. But I'm warning you, Chong Fat, I'm going to hand out folders in front of your place telling the tourists I've never eaten here and that your father had my bed seized for a trifling matter of a fifty-franc debt. I'll put it into my autobiography. I have the papers to prove it, and

I'm going to show them to Bengt Danielsson, who's writing a book about me. Good-bye, bloodsucker."

Clenching a cigar between his teeth, his head held high under his filthy sailor's cap, Cohn withdrew. On the terrace of the Wimpy, where they stopped for a snack, they found Bizien bawling out Jesus Christ, who was having a beer at a nearby table. The Napoleon of Tourism was indignant. On Cohn's suggestion, he had hired Le Goff to play Jesus in the presentation of the Passion play, patterned after the famous Oberammergau staging, and that morning, a crown of thorns on his head, Le Goff had been dragging his cardboard cross everywhere, striking poses before the cameras. From nine to ten among the fishermen, from ten to eleven at the picturesque marketplace, then Jesus finished his morning in the slums, to show the foreigners that France was doing something for the workers. In the afternoon he was taken inland by jeep, and the tourists could see the tall silhouette appear here and there along the bus route, among the coconut palms. At Oberammergau, the performance of the Passion lasted only three days, less than Bayreuth's Wagner Festival, but Bizien had decided to give the Passion a permanent character.

Adam and Eve were already functioning on a hilltop of the peninsula, and "the death of Captain Cook" was performed twice a day at Point Venus. Cook had been killed and eaten in Hawaii, of course, but since Hawaii was putting on its own staging of Tahitian myths, there was no reason why they should not represent some of the best Hawaiian attractions in Tahiti.

All this had to be done with the utmost dignity and taste, so no wonder Bizien was furious to find Jesus sitting before a glass of beer at the Wimpy during working hours, the crown of thorns pushed back on his head like a worker's cap, and his cross thrown on the ground. That was not what he was paid for, he reminded him.

"I'll hire another guy if I catch you here again, Le Goff. What kind of a show is this? If the tourists see you guzzling beer, they'll think it's some kind of atheist propaganda. It's unprofessional. I told you I wanted dignity above all. At Disneyland they would've fired you on the spot. And for God's sake, get rid of that cigarette."

Le Goff threw his Gauloise away. It was obvious he didn't care much for his new job.

"So now I can't even have a drink anymore, is that it? Listen, I've been dragging that cross since nine A.M. I'm entitled to a break."

"All right, but next time, come in through the back door and have them serve you in the kitchen."

"Why? What's so disgusting about me? You mean to say that because it's Jesus, He has to be served in the kitchen?"

"It's a matter of realism, you idiot. You don't look convincing sitting here with a glass of beer in your hand and the crown of thorns on the back of your head. Dignity, man, we've got to have dignity."

"It's only a show. The tourists know that. I'm playing a role."

"That doesn't mean you have to drag your cross in bars. Why, it even shocks *me*. A little decorum, please. I should have hired a true believer, not the first imbecile to come along. Monsieur Cohn, that was your idea."

Cohn shrugged. "I thought Le Goff looked right for the part."

"That's not enough. It still takes a minimum of professionalism. Look at the Albert Schweitzer they show curing lepers, in Hawaii. It's got emotion. It's got authenticity. I wouldn't be a bit surprised if their man ended up by truly healing somebody."

"Sure thing," Le Goff grumbled. "The guy's getting twenty dollars a day. You pay me that and you'll get the real stuff."

"That's enough. Pick up that cross, Le Goff, and get the hell out of here."

"I'm meeting my *vahine* on this terrace."

"*What?* If I see my Christ here with a *vahine,* I'll sue you for damages and I'll have you deported for outrageous behavior. I have a cruise coming in, four hundred American Rotarians, landing here in half an hour. Do you want them to go back home saying that France has no respect for anything and that she's undermining the ancestral beliefs of the Tahitians?"

"All right, all right." He got up, swallowed his beer, straightened his crown of thorns, and walked gloomily away, dragging his cross.

Cohn, who was eating a six-egg omelette, shook his head. "An amateur," he said. "Nothing worse than working with amateurs."

"Do you want the job?"

"I don't have the right kind of face, the wrong kind, I mean. It doesn't look meek, gentle, and submissive enough. Look at all those Christs they're selling everywhere. They've taken the most virile, angry, and authentic man of all time, and with the help of the pederasts of the

Italian Renaissance, they turned Him into a sissy. The real Jesus looked probably the way they represented Him on the Byzantine archaic icons, the closest thing, anyway. But the Italian cheats who worked for the Authority of their times obliged with a yes-man Christ, a submissive lamb without a trace of indignation, of revolt. The idea was, of course, to induce submissiveness, to discourage protest and dissent. Propaganda. The painters were commissioned to promote the image of a Christ-mouse, a symbol of resignation and acceptance. The hell He was. I say the real Christ never bowed His head before anyone. He looked at them and reduced the bastards to steam with the fire in His eyes!"

Cohn brought his hairy fist down on the table.

"It's a disgrace!" he roared. "All this Gothic and Renaissance art, with their capitulating passive Christ, is blasphemy! Sabotage! I say, burn it all!"

Bizien's dark little eyes were studying Cohn's face curiously. "Don't take it so personally. Or maybe Christ was a friend of yours?"

Cohn was wiping out angrily, with a crust of bread, centuries of Gothic art from the bottom of his plate. Then he swallowed the bread. A few Renaissance masterpieces remained in his beard and Meeva wiped them out tenderly.

"Don't pay any attention to him, Monsieur Bizien," she said. "For him, Jesus is something sacred. He's not very tolerant."

Cohn belched.

On the quiet waters the Mooréa schooner was tracing a second horizon, more perceptible than the hazy line between the pale blue of the sky and the ocean. The now cemented islet of Mobu Uta mingled its last three meager clumps of coconut palms with the long metallic necks of cranes. Sixty-five years ago the oasis of Mobu Uta had been the favorite retreat of King Pomare V. Dressed in his uniform of a French admiral, the last Maori sovereign of Polynesia often paddled his pirogue toward that sanctuary. He always took along a quart of rum and a Bible. He was translating the Bible into Tahitian. Later, they would send out a boat and would bring him back, dead drunk, after removing the empty bottle from one hand, but leaving the Bible in the other.

From time to time Cohn would go out to the islet, settle under the last of the palms that had once thrown their shadow over the sovereign who died of cirrhosis of the liver, if not of the soul, and get royally drunk in memory

69

of the man in whom Gauguin had so fervently hoped to find a protector.

"Who are you *really*, Monsieur Cohn?"

Cohn was amazed. This was a crude, direct challenge, and, coming from a professional, it was surprising and almost insulting. Bizien was breaking the rules. A crook of his standing should know better than that.

"You must be kidding."

"Who *are* you, Monsieur Cohn?"

"All right, I'll tell you. But this is strictly confidential." He took a dirty notebook from his pocket and opened it. "I'm on the run. They're trying to kill me. Two assassination attempts so far."

"By whom?"

"The vultures. The big Powers, I mean. They're out to get me."

At the table behind them, the S.D.E.C. man who was listening almost dropped his glass. That took care of the amnesia theory. Cohn got a carefully folded piece of paper from his notebook.

"This is by the French philosopher, Michel Foucault. The new thinking force in Europe, and the most influential one. Listen. 'Man is but a recent invention, and the archaeology of our thoughts easily proves how recently he has appeared. And also his imminent end.' Yes, Bizien, 'his imminent end.' However, as I refused to conform to that request, Authority and Power have decided to hasten my demise. They're trying to kill the eternal rebel, Man, that perpetually subversive element in the power machine."

Bizien thought it over. "It won't work with the tourists," he said. "Too abstract. Too allegorical. Any other tricks you know? Something with your ears, perhaps?"

Meeva was staring at the two pros with respect and admiration. Sitting statuelike among the flowers of her cotton dress, she was listening to every word. Her beautiful face had that expression of deep intellectual satisfaction she felt whenever she heard things she was totally unable to understand. Bizien was looking pensively at the *provocateur*.

"You have a very beautiful nature, Monsieur Cohn."

"Sure thing. Ask Meeva. Are you talking performance or dimensions?"

"A cynic," Bizien said slowly, "often hides within him a bleating, bleeding, and idealistic lamb."

"And what if we talked about you?" Cohn suggested gently.

The Napoleon of Tourism sighed and wrinkled his forehead, lifting his eyebrows so high that they seemed to be reaching for the top of his bald head.

"Well," he said, "I, too, have an artistic nature and keep trying for perfection. I think I have tasted it once, at the foot of the Acropolis. I was accompanying a group of tourists who were visiting the Parthenon. I suddenly saw an elderly lady who was standing among the ruins of ancient Greece point to something in the distance. 'Oh, look, Marge,' she exclaimed. 'You can see the Hilton from here.' And she grabbed the camera. It was then that I made mine, once and for all, the famous saying 'If you can't lick 'em, join 'em.' That's all. I'm giving them a hand. I go all the way. Which makes me think—" He looked at his watch. "I hope you have not forgotten your painting, my dear Gauguin. The tourists will be there at five P.M. You'll be just in time."

Cohn got up. He took the check the waiter had handed him and put it on Bizien's table.

"What are we doing today?"

"The *Waterfall*."

Cohn's face brightened up. He took Meeva's arm. "O.K., let's go."

Chong's body filled the telephone booth in the back of the restaurant. He had built the booth twenty years ago, when still a slim and gracile young man, and now he barely managed to squeeze himself into it. He felt as if he were already in his coffin, and this was more than claustrophobia. The hail of bullets could be coming through the thin door any moment now. It had taken him more than five minutes to get Callum on the phone again and the three killers were bound to become suspicious. Professionals, Chong realized that the moment they had walked in. How this murderous trio got their weapons was a mystery to him. They couldn't have gotten that arsenal through customs. They had to have another contact in Tahiti.

"For Chrissake, Chong, get hold of yourself."

"Mr. Callum, it's the second time I am leaving them. They're no fools. They're going to kill me."

"They won't. They need you. Don't panic."

"Have you found the place?"

"I'm looking at it right now, on the map. I've been there before. But it'll take me at least an hour and a half to climb up there."

"Mr. Callum, I'm in mortal danger. Please hurry up."

71

"I have no orders. You understand? No orders. I'm on the wireless right now, but—"

"Mr. Callum, you don't need orders to save my life. I'm your best agent here. And you don't need orders to kill three Red rats."

"I'm not in charge of that bastard's security and—"

"Mr. Callum, I must go. Please. *We have one hour—*"

Chong heard an unmistakable creaking sound behind the door. He gulped. "I've told you I can't pay that much!" he yelled. "Fifty francs a kilo, that's robbery! *You understand?*"

There was a brief silence on the other end of the line.

"I understand," Callum's voice said. "All right. I'll be there. But give me one hour and a half, no less. And keep behind. Keep away from that boulder. Thirty yards. Grenades."

"Thank you," Chong yelled. "I'll pay that much. I'll do that. Thirty francs, yes. Thirty. Thank you." He put the receiver down with a shaking hand and opened the door.

10

The Vultures

Cohn was still hesitating, looking for the perfect angle.

Meeva waited patiently on all fours, her chin resting in her cupped hands, in that dreamy animal position of the *vahine* in *Otahi,* painted by Gauguin against a less exuberant background of white, yellow, and blue. But Cohn was no mere copyist. He had Meeva hold her head and torso a little lower, so that her rump would stand out royally against the blue background of heaven in such a way that the artist's eye could also enjoy at the same time the rump, the sky, the waterfall, the ocean beyond the rocks, and the gaudy profusion of plants on the slopes of Orofena. He also wished to include the distant sailboat that was gliding toward the peninsula, and waited for it to come closer so that it would look like a white butterfly sitting on that adorable ass. Now, if he could only manage to keep his eyes open right up to the end of the fire of action, he might well achieve a new masterpiece of joy. He put both hands firmly on her hips, grabbed her.

"Just a minute. Lean on your elbows—a little toward me, now—there."

Meeva assumed the pose obligingly. She knew, as did everyone else in Tahiti, that Gauguin was very exacting with his model when he was carried away by inspiration, and she had the greatest respect for Cohn's artistic needs, even though the latter never used paint, brush, or canvas. *Popaa*'s ways.

"That's perfect. Don't move."

He took off his pants and laid them on the sack, came down on his knees behind her, grabbed her hips, and attacked the subject boldly with broad confident strokes, but without undue haste, in full control of his medium, both his hands pressed gently but firmly against Meeva's buttocks. Around them, the exuberant vegetation was locked in a battle of color against color, each refusing to yield. The yellow and violet of the tall lordly *vestides* with their silver tops, the gray and purple cobralike *cormaraies* with thin red tongues, and the proletarian masses of every shade of green, broken only here and there by the ocher of a bare spot of the mountain's hide, with the peak of Orofena itself rising high above the flora battlefield. In the midst of his labor, Cohn, whose face had now assumed that extreme concentration and purposeful dedication that always adorned it at those moments of blissful self-expression, and whose movements and breathing were speeding up in the heat of action, tried to hold back his inspiration, for he knew, like all true artists, that nothing puts you back where you started faster than the final achievement. He dreaded completion; happiness brings within itself its own end. When climax threatened, he would raise his eyes and count the distant waterfalls booming in the confusion of giant ferns above the rocks of Ivahea. He was now beginning to feel as happy as a lowly cur when he raises himself triumphantly on all fours toward heaven. Yet something was missing from the approaching moment of accomplishment to be truly perfect: those two immortal horses, the pink and the blue, out there, among the *parapepe* trees, as in the Master's picture. He was clenching his teeth now, pressing forward faster and faster, and yet trying at the same time to postpone the movement of wretched fulfillment, but it was too late now for subterfuge, and the whole landscape was already beginning to capsize and to dissolve in a reddish glow and the only thing he could do now was to take Meeva along with him.

"Montjoie!"

This rallying cry of the Frank crusaders calling one another to join forces in the midst of a battle was addressed to Meeva, who knew it well and had no intention whatsoever to be left behind.

"Saint-Denis!" she yelled back, and she rushed to meet Cohn with such a determination that he had to bend over and lock her waist firmly in his arms. Far down below them, the ocean was throwing itself angrily against the black basalt rocks with a frustrated roar, as if for once the infinite felt envious, wishing it were a mere man.

Chong Fat had been sweating profusely ever since they had left the jeep. A tepid itchy mixture of grease and acid covered him from head to foot; it was as if his very substance was fleeting from him. A premonition of death, no doubt. For more than an hour now, they had been climbing up from the road along the steep western slopes of Orofena, but this physical exertion, though requiring all the energy he could muster, did nothing to help him to overcome his mortal fear.

The three Chinese were following him, and whenever Chong Fat began to falter, the tallest of the three, obviously the leader, shoved him forward with a hand that felt like steel against his ribs. The owner of the famous Restaurant Paul Gauguin, Genuine Cantonese Cuisine, hated the man deeply. He had the undernourished, skin-and-bones appearance of the true believer. His rimless glasses had the kind of fanatical gleam that always seems to carry the promise of prompt executions and mass graves. Chong grieved deeply to see such an expression on a Chinese face. Old China, *his* China had once been a civilized country.

The man who was carrying the rifle had a strangely American appearance for a Chinese Red. He was chewing gum and was dressed in tight stretch pants, Western boots and shirt, and a silver-nailed belt. There was a red tattoo on his forearm. He was also wearing a baseball cap, which somehow was particularly offensive. It was shocking and unnerving to see a Communist killer dressed up like an American one. The third man looked merely mean, suspicious, and abominably vulgar, which was as a Communist should look. At least there was some honesty there.

Chong blamed himself bitterly for his lack of acumen. He shouldn't have sent that report to Hong Kong. A tragic mistake. He hated the Reds with all his heart; they were destroying the China he loved, the land and customs of his ancestors. But he had no choice. Eleven members of his family were held hostages in Peking. He couldn't refuse to work for the Reds, but reported conscientiously everything to the Americans. This he did out of his full-hearted sympathy for the free world, his absolute devotion to Chiang Kai-shek, and his fervent hope for the overthrow of the hated Mao regime.

It had never occurred to him that Hong Kong would react so quickly and in such a murderous manner to his report. To all appearances, it was a harmless piece of information, the perfect item a double agent could pass on to one side without in any way endangering the vital interests of his other employer. It was therefore without the slightest hesitation that he had informed Peking that the C.I.A. was showing an extraordinary curiosity about a man whose name, real, or assumed, was Cohn, and who was a notorious scoundrel and good-for-nothing, an artist, in fact. He had added that in his opinion this was obviously a case of mistaken identity.

And now, this. Chong blamed himself bitterly for his biggest blunder, which was informing the Americans. But when he saw the three men walk into his restaurant and heard what was expected of him, he lost his head completely. He realized this thing was infinitely bigger than he could have ever imagined; he panicked and warned the C.I.A. man in Tahiti. A terrible mistake. Loyalty and devotion to a cause were always a mistake. You shouldn't try to be a superman.

He should have warned the French. They would've merely arrested and deported the murderous trio. But then Peking would have known that Chong had betrayed them, and his whole beloved family, his old father, and all his brothers would have paid for this dearly. Besides, the Americans had expressly forbidden him to say anything about this interest in Cohn to the French. Their secret services were indulging in a bitter feuding with each other. The three Reds had to be taken care of discreetly and immediately, and the last thing the C.I.A. apparently wanted was for the French to become aware that American agents were closing in on Cohn.

The restaurateur had never seen such an official interest in art and artists. It was so bewildering that at first, when he had been told what was expected of him, his Chinese curiosity had been almost as strong as his funk. "But why?" he had kept asking them. "Why do you want to kill him?" They were talking in English. None of them spoke Chong's southern Chinese.

The apelike squat Chinese, who looked a truly nasty piece of work even for a Maoist, had merely spat on the

75

beautifully polished floor of the restaurant, no doubt a deliberate display of Communist scorn for all private property.

"What do you care? What is he to you?"

"Nothing," Chong had answered firmly, relieved to be able to say something with total sincerity. He hated Cohn, as did almost everyone else in Tahiti. In some devious, cunning, almost fiendish manner, he made you lose face. An arrogant, aggressive *merde* like that deserved to be wiped out, if only for purely hygienic reasons. But then quite obviously hygiene was not why the Reds were after him.

And now he was panting and wheezing and climbing up and up in mortal fear. The American had promised to be very careful, nevertheless warning him to stay as far away from the killers as he could. Chong was making frantic efforts to do this, but running uphill on this rocky ground was beyond his strength and, anyway, the others had no trouble in keeping up with him. He was beginning to feel he was walking toward an almost certain death.

The man with the rifle was whistling a tune, and in the midst of his abject terror, Chong still found the energy to be surprised. It was a Beatles' tune. It was also a good excuse for a stop.

"That is a Western decadent tune you're whistling," he said.

The man grinned. "So what! I make my home in Hong Kong. I come from San Francisco. I don't care one way or another. I'm paid to do a job."

An American professional, Chong thought. He felt a little better. He preferred a straight, honest-to-God murderer to a Communist killer.

The tall Chinese pushed him forward once more. "Walk."

"You shouldn't have asked me to come with you," Chong told him. "I'm very well know here. If I am seen in your company, I'll be in trouble when they find the body. I won't be of any use to you here."

He was trying to avoid looking at the block of basalt barely a hundred feet away now. Beyond began the thickness of giant ferns and dove trees, with their white bird-shaped leaves. The ocher bareness of the mountain hung over the green, purple, and yellow wilderness, and the sky hit the eye with its savage merciless blue.

Meeva was still quivering when Cohn raised his head and saw a group of tourists making their way down the trail between the palm trees. They were taken everywhere by bus, but were left to walk a few hundred feet, which gave them a feeling of adventure and exploration. The men in Bermuda shorts and ankle socks were bad enough, but the worst were the gray-haired matrons in sunglasses wearing brightly colored pareus.

"There they come. Let's get to work."

The waterfall was fifty feet away. There was no need to hurry, but Meeva would insist on taking a bath first. No *vahine* could ever resist the sight of water. Cohn put on his jeans, his blue shirt, and his cap, after dragging them through the dirt so they would not look too clean.

"Hurry up."

She was standing in water up to her hips among the boulders. "Now, how is it again?"

"Damn it, Meeva, it's a classic. I've shown you the postcard a hundred times!"

"Do I put on the pareu?"

"Of course."

He threw her the red pareu with big white flowers. In Gauguin's picture, the pareu was white and the subject a boy. But Bizien did not want too close a resemblance, so that the show wouldn't appear staged. The tourists were supposed to run across this living tableau by chance. It was more satisfying. Authenticity. Meeva was paid fifty francs per session.

"Now get up on that rock and drink from the cascade."

"I'm going to break my neck."

"No, you won't. They've built some cement steps into the rock."

She climbed up the boulder and leaned over the waterfall. Cohn had to admit it was just about perfect. The giant fern tree to the left, the waterfall, the *vahine* drinking—

He sat on a rock and raised the wine bottle to his lips. He could hear the clicking of cameras behind his back, as Puccioni was giving them his usual crap. "Gauguin loved to paint women of abundant charms, which to him symbolized the fruits of the earth and the Garden of Eden before the original sin."

Cohn turned his profile to the tourists so they could take their pictures of the "outcast of the islands" with his *vahine*. He felt that with his conquering air, sitting on his rock, he probably looked like Prometheus. But the inspiration had left him. After the tourists had gone and Meeva came back to him, it took some time before he reached for the sacred fire again.

The basalt boulder was now almost directly over their heads. Jesus Christ, Chong thought, though he was a good Buddhist. Now. It will happen now. He will be blown up to pieces.

"Are you sure this is the place?" the tall Chinese asked.

"Of course I'm sure," Chong Fat assured him. "He's camping out there with his girl. By the stream, beyond the ferns. You saw his bike down there on the road. He's here all right. You don't need me anymore. I better go."

He felt the steely fingers against his back once more, hurting him.

"Walk."

"Please let me go now."

"We've got to come closer."

"Please—don't—"

Chong raised his eyes imploringly toward the top of the boulder. It was out of sight. Grenades. Callum was going to use grenades. He told him so.

"Please don't."

Then he thought he had heard a sound above his head, there on top of the boulder where Callum was, and he stiffened, closing his eyes, reduced to a state of almost total physical nonexistence, with only a shrill alarm sounding somewhere outside him, as if his immortal but prudent spirit had already jumped out of its unsafe premises.

Nothing happened. Maybe nothing would.

His mind remained completely blank for a while, then crazed shreds of thought began darting around once more. A wild hope was gushing from the darkest recesses of his fear.

Bill Callum wouldn't take the risk.

The American will let that bastard Gauguin be killed rather than blow up the wealthiest businessman in Tahiti, who was also the best friend and most trustworthy ally of the free world. Or maybe Callum wasn't even there yet.

They were now ahead of him. He started to back away and managed to put a few yards between them and himself; then, encouraged by this success, he quickly took a few more steps backward, tripped over a rock, and fell. The three Chinese glanced in his direction and the tall one with glasses came down and kicked him in the ribs. It hurt, and Chong felt almost grateful. The sharp physical pain made him feel less scared.

"Why did you do that?" he said, sobbing.

The other kicked him again. His glasses were frightening. Cold, glittering, deadly.

"You try that once more and I'll kill you," he said.

"You'll stay here till we're through. Just in case. Why're you so scared, you idiot?"

"I don't like this," Chong almost sobbed. "I don't like to have death around. It's bad luck."

The Hong Kong man whistled softly and pointed at something beyond the ferns. The tall Chinese raised his head, then left Chong and climbed quickly back to where the other two were standing.

They were now almost thirty yards ahead of him, but Chong still feared he was too close. He crawled backwards a few feet more and flattened himself as well as he could against the ground.

Then he heard the tall Chinese say angrily, "What're you waiting for?"

There was a laugh. Prudently, very prudently, Chong Fat raised his head a bit. The Hong Kong man was laughing. All three of them were looking at something Chong could not see. He was too far down the slope. The medium-sized Red seemed surprised, and even shaken. The leader of the murderous group was almost hiccuping with rage.

"Why don't you shoot?"

"I like the view, man," the killer said quietly. "I like it. He's good at it."

Curiosity was something Chong had never been able to resist. He raised himself a bit higher, got up on his knees, and as he still was unable to see what was happening beyond the ferns, he stood up and looked. His eyeballs almost jumped out of their sockets. Quickly he flattened himself against the ground once more.

That dog Cohn was surely the most shameless cur that had ever lived.

"He's great, man," the Hong Kong killer said with a trace of respect in his voice. "You've got to give him that. And he sure loves doing it."

"Shoot."

"Sure, sure. But let him finish first. Let him have his fun. You can't kill a guy before he's finished. That's un-American."

"I shall report you for this."

"He'll die better after he's finished."

"We'll never employ you again."

"I'll kill him all right. You don't have to worry. But I ain't gonna kill a guy just when he's about to hit the bull's-eye. I'll kill him good. But I go by my rules. You don't kill a guy who's just about to make it. You let him get there first."

He spat his gum on the ground, never taking his eyes off the couple. Then he said in a voice that seemed to the man who was holding his grenades ready on the top of the boulder, to be full of hatred and almost of despair, speaking as it were with the very voice of man's cynical nothingness, "Because, man, there's only one thing I respect, and it's screwing."

The four explosions coming in rapid succession shook Cohn out of his state of pleasant nonexistence. He yelled, jumped up, grabbing his pants, and looked down the slope of the mountain.

His first thought was that the extinct volcano of Orofena had miraculously become active again, in a fit of indignation long overdue. But he was suspicious of his mythological bent, and he got a firm grip over his imagination and over the ancient gods who were now nothing but art and had probably never been anything else.

"Nom de Dieu!" he yelled in a sudden flash of understanding. "The road! They're building their damn road through here! It's the end!"

Two hundred yards below, he saw a silhouette standing on a rock and he shook his fist and cursed the worker. The silhouette vanished almost instantly. Another man was running down the slope, falling, and getting up and running again, pursued by the avalanche of stone brought on by the explosion. Cohn kept yelling at the intruders for a while, until the wilderness spoke back to him in such a language of peace and silence that all sound and fury seemed to have been banned from the earth.

"Let's move on, Cohn," Meeva said, shuddering. "It feels *fiu* here."

Chong reached the dirt track and the car in a merciful state of half consciousness that left no room either for horror or for relief at his miraculous escape. His nephew was sitting at the wheel of the jeep. Chong jumped next to him and for half an hour remained inert in a semicoma. He had seen the first grenade flying through the air, and before it hit the ground, he had passed out and regained consciousness only when stones and dirt began to fall on him. Now emerging slowly from his gelatinous limbo, he felt his nephew's hand shaking him and he heard his voice, "It'll be all right now, *tonton*. It's all over."

Chong nodded, but it took him only a few seconds more to realize how mistaken both of them were.

"It's *not* over. I have to warn Hong Kong that the expedition has failed and that three of our good men were killed."

"They'll only send more men."

Chong shut his eyes. "I don't feel at all well," he said.

11

Tricolor

The grotto smelled of dampness and of granite. Somehow, the whining of mosquitoes and the buzz of trapped flies dashing blindly around were making the stifling atmosphere even more oppressive. A French naval n.c.o. in uniform, with earphones on his head, sat by the v.h.f. wireless, writing down the message. Two paratroopers in leopard-spotted fatigues were leaning against the roughly nailed together wooden door, their Thompson machine guns hanging, muzzles down, from their shoulders. A naked bulb was throwing its dirty, insect-soiled light over the black and ocher rocks, bottles of beer, and sleeping bags.

The man in white was smoking impatiently. The generator's heaving and panting filled the cave with its asthmatic breathing. It was catching, evocative of suffocation, and somehow managed to oppress your chest.

The n.c.o. on duty, whose name was Mozon, took the earphones off and began decoding the message. The man in white was reading the text over his shoulder. *"Ils y vont fort,"* he said angrily. "They lay it on rather thick. The guy's watched night and day, as closely as possible. The Chinese had perfectly valid visas. There was no reason to suspect them; Hong Kong had given no warning."

He threw his cigarette on the ground, picked up the message, and read it through once more.

"Why don't they put someone else in charge? I've had enough of Monsieur Cohn."

Mozon leaned back in his chair. "They've got a point, *mon capitaine.*"

"I know this point. It's the Americans that're really making them hopping mad in Paris. We have fifteen thousand troops in Polynesia. The Amerlocks have only one man here. Yet they pulled that one under our noses behaving as if their dear French allies did not exist. Grimaud."

One of the paratroopers leaning against the door removed the Gauloise butt from his lips. *"Mon capitaine?"*

"You're sure all of them are dead?"

"Positive, *mon capitaine.* Not that there was much of them left for identification. However, I've counted five slanted eyes."

"All right, but I do hope there isn't one of them still running around our Monsieur Cohn. Who's on duty today?"

"Deville and Roux."

"Get on the W.T. Tell them I'm taking over myself, for the next forty-eight hours, anyway."

"Bien, mon capitaine."

"Let's see our green friend now."

One of the paratroopers unlocked the door and pushed it open. The man in white walked out and inhaled deeply. The air was fresh and alive in that part of the cave. The entrance opened over the blue ocean and sky.

Chong Fat had collapsed in a chair, his face greenish, his roly-poly hands together as if for mutual support. The captain went toward the blue patch of sky and stood there, looking out, with his back to the Chinese.

"You're a stupid ass, Chong," he said.

"I had no choice."

"You should've warned us immediately. Why go to the Americans? What kind of Frenchman are you? Who comes first? The Americans or the French?"

"I am the staunchest Gaullist in Tahiti, you know that," Chong said in a nasal voice full of true emotion, entirely made of funk. "Please, I've told you, I'm helping our American allies. I've also told you repeatedly that I *had* to work for those Peking monsters. My family—"

"You should have warned *us.*"

"I couldn't. The Americans—"

"With whom are your loyalties? With America or with France?"

Chong's face quivered with anguish. "I assure you that the whole Chinese community here feels a hundred percent French. I myself—"

"Then why didn't you warn me?"

"The C.I.A. kills," Chong said in a mournful voice full of coffins, each of them carrying his body. "You know they do."

"We, too, kill sometimes," the captain said softly. "Remember that next time. You may go now."

Chong hesitated a moment. "Why's everybody so concerned about Monsieur Cohn?" he burst out almost imploringly.

The man in white smiled. There was still as much good old Chinese curiosity as funk in the restaurateur. "It's because Monsieur Cohn is that rarest of all things, a truly free spirit. That makes him dangerously subversive in our eyes."

Chong sighed. "You don't trust me, I see," he complained sadly. "Please don't make fun of me."

The man in white was no longer smiling. "You know, of course, that they'll be back." he said.

"Of course I know that," Chong Fat invented. "And they'll probably think that I've betrayed them."

"Probably."

"And they'll kill me too."

"Quite likely."

Chong took a bonbon out of his pocket and ate it for comfort. Then his face turned a kind of ashen gray-greenish yellow. A new fear had suddenly stirred in his heart. "The Russians," he mumbled. "How's it that the Russians haven't showed up yet?"

"They will," the man in white said quietly.

There was now something nerve-racking in the panic buzz of the flies.

12

Proud Ship,
Brave Captain

That night they slept on the ground by the half-empty lagoon, its waters carried out to sea by the mighty sweep of the tide. Some saw in that broad sweep the hand of the god Fatoua, who was looking for his seven sons, fallen from heaven. He was raising the seas in his endless search, for he little knew that his sworn enemy, the god of earth, Aheru, had long since transformed his sons into atolls.

Cohn lay on his back, his arms folded on his chest, smoking his night cigar, the one that made the last anguish of the day go up in smoke. Lolling on the clouds, the moon looked like Goya's *Reclining Maja*. It was that hour of darkness and silence propitious for the return of real names to the lips of village storytellers sitting around the fires before the skulls and bones of animals and of men who had died of untruth. The *popaas* had cut off the tongue of heaven, and thus the true gods could no longer talk to their people. It was also the hour that awakened in the heart of at least one *popaa* the craving for some prodigious and entirely reassuring lie, more beautiful than all the lies man had ever told himself in his terrifying loneliness.

Meeva was curled next to him under the stars, her face pressed against the sand in an attitude of submission and adoration that almost brought out of darkness the shape of some gigantic metaphysical foot.

Cohn fell asleep, but was awakened by a song. A reddish moon was floating in Meeva's hair spread over the phosphorescence of ocean and sky in that world of Polynesian nights without limits, perspective, or measure, and sometimes a falling star would drop from her hair as if carried away by the breeze. Knee-deep in the lagoon, the pagan goddess was raising her nakedness to the silver of the moon. Her body looked gigantic against the blue depths of the universe, with the head thrown back and the breasts held up in her cupped, caressing hands, blackening out millions of light-years in heaven. She was singing and at first Cohn could not believe what he was hearing; for a few desperate seconds he fought the reality of destruction and plunder that was so clearly perceptible behind those guttural words. For it was a German song Meeva was singing, a song a German *popaa* had taught her in her distant Tuamotus:

> *Ich weiss nicht, was soll es bedeuten,*
> *Dass ich so traurig bin;*
> *Ein Märchen aus alten Zeiten,*
> *Das kommt mir nicht aus dem Sinn. . . .*

"A story of times long past I can't forget—" Cohn recognized the famous Heine poem. It was all that was left of the first pirogue and of those who once were the Maori.

They spent the next two nights on the sands of Fiona, where three wide estuaries mingled the sweet waters of the mountains with the salt of the ocean. The old storm that had been gathering new strength for three days prowling around the island burst out at last far away from the shore with an angry snarl, having missed its earthly prey.

Lightning planted its yellow pulsating jungle over the horizon, its roots and branches shared between the ocean and the sky.

Then the motionless storm hung heavily in the dusk as if in helpless labor, unable to deliver itself and to give birth to the one who in times past was called Tahue, the god of limitless waters. The mountainside was stirring in an explosion of colors caught between lightning and sunset and gushing like fountains of purple, yellow, and bronze toward the sky, among the giant ferns so soothing and reassuring in their serene and petrified green. A tall white column of smoke rose from the village among the palms, at that windless moment of sunset when the daytime breeze was gone and the evening *maoae* had not yet begun.

Leaning against the faceless figurehead of a wrecked fishing boat that no one dared to remove or use for wood because wrecks are taboo, Meeva was combing the sunset out of her hair and the gesture was more beautiful, in Cohn's eyes, than all the celestial struggle above them.

The yellow flashes of the storm and the sudden copper glow of a black cloud that caught the last of the sinking sun was brightening her face with the earth's oldest lights. The caressing movements of her hand, holding an amber tortoiseshell comb, were soothing Cohn's heart with that feeling of eternity which a troubled soul always finds in passing moments of happiness.

Above the invisible village, where children and dogs could be heard playing, floated a green and orange kite, unless it was that never yet seen bird that would be sent to announce the coming of the "final night," the night without dawn, of which speaks the legend of Vairao.

Cohn was amazed to recognize in Meeva's song the *ute* of "the origin of all gods" of the Arii chiefs, which he had heard only once before, recited for him by Dr. Morteg, of the Smithsonian Institution:

> *Chief Tave of the Tautira Maroi*
> *Slept with the vahine Taurma*
> *Then with the woman Triterai*
> *It took two mothers to give*
> *birth to Chief Maraina*
> *Who slept with . . .*

There were over a hundred branches to the genealogical tree and Meeva recited them all, except for the last born, whose name must never be pronounced, so as not to expose him to the jealousy and wrath of the old but still reigning and powerful gods.

"They still chant that *ute* in the Tuamotus?"

"Of course not. It's my German *popaa* who taught it to me. They know all our *ute* in his country. They study them in the big schools where they keep all our past and all our *tikis*."

Cohn felt like crying. But it was too late for tears.

> *I am looking for the face I had*
> *Before the world was made.*

Before returning to Pouaavia, they made a detour to visit a friend. The sloop was raising its two motionless masts under the castles of clouds that the madrepores seemed to have built even in the sky, where all the grottoes, dungeons, walls, and labyrinths of the coral world were endlessly repeated. The reef barrier was thundering under the ocean's assaults, in a white chaos of water, sky, and stone, where a fleeting rainbow sometimes materialized only to be washed away by a new liquid cataract. Inland, the thickly massed vegetation was throwing its colorful infantry against the steep bare heights of Orofena.

Aboard the *Human Dignity,* "Professor Harkiss" welcomed them with open arms. This unfortunate employee of Bizien was bored to death. Except for some quick outings into Papeete at night, he had been stuck on the damn boat for over two months now. Matthews—that was the real name, inasmuch as a passport could mean anything —Matthews was complaining bitterly. Though he was pleased to be able to make a living, he felt that the promoter was beginning to exaggerate. Granted, it made sense to plant here and there a few "famous" characters whose edifying legends could be told to the tourists in a confidential whisper. But despite the occasional ironic smile on the face of Bengt Danielsson, the genuine *Kon-Tiki* relic in Tahiti, Matthews preferred to play the part of one of the crew of that immortal raft rather than that of Professor Harkiss. Oh, the story was convincing enough, and it was lapped up eagerly by the tourists; all Matthews meant was that, like anyone else, he was entitled to have his Saturdays and Sundays off. In Puccioni's presentation, Professor Harkiss was a scientist so profoundly shocked by the destructive use to which the big Powers were putting the fruit of human genius that he not only had given up his personal research in nuclear physics, as a protest, but also had decided to wake up the world's flabby conscience with a resounding gesture of self-sacrifice. He had set out for Polynesia on the ship he had christened the *Human Dignity,* and though—naturally enough, with a name like that—he had almost sunk twice during the crossing, he had finally managed to reach Tahiti. He was now waiting for the proper moment to slip into the area of fatal radiation, when the French nuclear explosion would take place in the atoll of Mururoa. Because of the very name he had chosen for his sloop, the authorities watched him closely, but he had every hope to be still able to make it, thanks to certain secret accomplices and wholehearted support of the people here. . . . It was a good, solid, contemporary cliché, and the tourists were delighted to be able to see with their own eyes "the spiritual son of Lord Russell and Gandhi," as Puccioni put it.

Matthews was paid five hundred francs a month by the France Oceane Tourist Bureau to play the part, and he did it conscientiously. But two months was more than he could take. Also, the scenery around him glowed with such beauty that he was beginning to feel like some kind of filth in its midst. And if that was not enough, Bizien forbade any drinking aboard. Matthews had vainly argued that it was normal that Professor Harkiss, a broken man, would take to drink to drown his sorrows. Bizien would have none of it; according to him, it was out of the question to get drunk aboard a ship called *Human Dignity.* Cohn felt that Matthews had a point and that on a ship flying such a banner the only thing left was to get drunk out of sheer despair. No *vahines* aboard, either: Matthews had to do everything himself. Bizien wanted something noble, truly tragic, inspiring, and deeply moving, so that the tourists would go home feeling they had had something for their money. Something Greek. That son of a bitch Bizien was obsessed by Greek ruins; he had run an agency in Athens once. Matthews hadn't the slightest intention of spending his life in the middle of a lagoon, surrounded by an almost unbearable sight of beauty, without going on the occasional bender that such a situation called for. The splendors of the landscape were giving him an inferiority complex and even some kind of obscure feeling of guilt. The other night, he went to Papeete, then had missed the early-morning bus back, and when the tourists got to the *Human Dignity,* they found no one aboard, which was only normal, ha! ha! ha! ha! Bizien flew into a rage and threatened to have Matthews deported from Tahiti for immoral conduct. He was pleased to see that Cohn apparently found this funny, since he was splitting his sides, but what about taking his, Matthews', place for a couple of months? Yes, he should try that: two months aboard the *Human Dignity* without a drop of liquor and no girls. Sometimes Matthews felt like tying a rock around his neck and jumping overboard. But besides that, what was the news?

Meeva was humming a tune, squatting on the deck, with her back to them. Her full brown shoulders were emerging from among the flowers of her green and mauve pareu, not unlike the ocher mountain that was rising out of the exuberant mass of vegetation over there.

"She looks *fiu*," Matthews noted.

"She's against the war in Vietnam," Cohn said. "I've awakened her social consciousness. By the way, did you know that the Maori located the soul in the bowels? You'll find this in the works of W. Ellis and Morenhaut. The Maori see a proof of it in the fact that the bowels are subject to painful cramps when the spirit is troubled."

Leaning against the ropes, Matthews was pulling thoughtfully on the legendary pipe of Professor Harkiss, while waiting for the tourist hour. "I know," he said. "That's why defecation was considered a sacred act among the Arii. It was the liberation of the body through elimination of the soul, which gods had placed in humans to make them weak and thus keep them in their power. The soul was a sort of fifth column, in the service of the gods. That's probably the origin of the mania Tahitians have, even today, of purging themselves constantly." He stiffened, his face became distorted with hate, and he pointed toward the shore. "Here they come," he said hoarsely.

A compact herd had appeared on the beach marching toward the pirogues. The shrill sound of transistor radios rose above the lagoon, and the latest popular tune, an arrangement of Bach in "haw haw" jazz, the latest trend in pop music, shattered the stillness of water and land. Dressed in pareus provided by the Tourist Office, each design on cotton reproducing faithfully a painting by Gauguin, the West was climbing into the pirogues, while on the invisible road the buses were maneuvering into position with a familiar noise reassuring for the visitors, who were at first delighted to find themselves surrounded by all this natural splendor, but soon became uneasy and frightened by it.

The first pirogues were already leaving the shore.

"Oh my God!" the Englishman groaned.

Cohn grabbed Meeva by the hand and stepped over the ropes. Before diving in, he looked at Matthews with pity. "Why don't you get the hell out of here?" he asked. "Take my advice. Chuck it all and go back to England!"

The poor "captain" sighed. "I can't go back to England. I have a wife and three kids there."

At Hitiau they stopped at Paava's school of painting and sculpture dedicated to a rebirth of Polynesian artistic tradition.

There were some thirty students there, mostly Chinese, and they were drawing their inspiration from Gauguin and Rousseau, or working out more typically Maori themes, based mostly on masks and fetishes figuring in Jean Guiart's book.

Every single piece of Polynesian art Gauguin had so desperately fought to save was now, sixty-five years later, in European and American museums and private collections; Tahiti was a culturally bare land. The head of the school, Paava, was supplying the world with forgeries.

He was a heavy-set Maori whose ancestors had come to Tahiti from Serbia and England. He received Cohn with open arms, though he was still trembling with indignation: he had discovered three copies of *Playboy* in the atelier; the students were passing them around behind his back.

"It's the end," he complained. "How can you expect them to recapture the secret of archaic Polynesian forms if they keep looking at these nudes? If these kids keep getting their ideas from *Playboy,* everything is lost. They don't seem to give a damn about their own cultural heritage."

Cohn left Meeva in the workshop, leaning against a window in a picturesque attitude of disconsolate longing, nibbling at the stem of a flower. She was clearly trying to stimulate the inspiration and taste for archaic forms in a good-looking and magnificently built half-Norwegian Chinese of Maori ancestry, who was wasting his evident energy on a piece of wood, knife in hand. There was a convenient palm grove on the beach just behind the school, and Cohn, always benevolently disposed toward nature, had no intention of interfering with what was taking shape under his eyes and would soon come to a head on the beach. Whatever Paava said, the Maori past was not completely lost.

A little later, he saw her on the beach, holding hands and comparing seashells with her *tane.* Cohn did not wish to interrupt anything so nice as this budding romance. So he sat down on the sand and waited patiently for Meeva to live her great love to the end. Then there would be heartrending good-byes and oaths of eternal love exchanged with total sincerity, but immediately forgotten, as befits these beautiful children of the moment. This thought filled Cohn's heart with a certain sadness. He enjoyed beautiful love stories, and he smoked his cigar moodily. The Bradfords' box of Monte Cristos was almost gone. There was nothing he liked more than smoking a good cigar while watching the ocean and listening to the sighs of true love.

The couple vanished in the palm grove and Cohn sat smoking peacefully on the shore. It was that twilight hour, when the sand was still warm from the sun, but the evening breeze was bringing in the coolness of the open sea and the scents carried all the way from the Marquesas while the copper sky, streaked with green, was already turning to purple; the dungeons of coral were beginning their evening watch after the departure of the tide.

The evening shadows were closing in on him.

Something stirred in the bushes out there, behind his back. There was the sharp, clearly perceptible click of a gun being cocked.

Cohn yelped, jumped up, and threw himself on his belly behind a palm. There he lay flattened against the warm sand. He could hear the waterfall thundering close to him. But there was no waterfall in Fiona. It was his funk. Fear was throwing his blood in panic gushes against his eardrums.

He began to crawl toward the *maa* bush.

Nothing there. Not a living soul.

It was his usual evening paranoia. Guilt has a way with shadows. . . .

He picked up what was left of his cigar from the sand. Then Meeva came back and found her *popaa* holding on desperately to the stump of aromatic Havana.

"What's the matter, Cohn? You look scared."

"This is my last good cigar." He stuck the butt in the sand. "How was he?"

"He's a pet, that little Tahea. Maybe I'll see him again, if I'm ever back in the neighborhood. But you know how these *tanes* are. They do it like rabbits. They don't like to work."

They slept that night under the monument to King Pomare, who had spent the last years of his life with the Bible in one hand, a bottle of rum in the other. On the roof of the royal tomb the local architect had built an urn, shaped exactly like a bottle of rum, a supreme Tahitian tribute to the memory of the departed sovereign. Gauguin had a letter of introduction to Pomare V, but a few days before his arrival His Majesty had passed away in a state of alcoholic stupor. The painter declined the offer to decorate the funeral chamber where the body of the king lay dressed in his uniform of a French admiral. Gauguin had given the reason that prompted him to decline the offer in a letter to his friend Monfreid: "They wouldn't let me paint the white man's Bible and bottle of rum above the coffin, one explaining the other and belying it at the same time. So I told them no, gentlemen, thank you very much. As you can see, I have remembered your advice and am on my best behavior here. I, too, know how to be polite."

13

Saint-Gauguin

It was the next morning, back home, that the miracle took place. Cohn had taken off his jeans and handed them over to Meeva to press. He was sitting bare-assed in the sand when he suddenly noticed that one of his legs was covered with a rash. There was also an open sore on his right calf.

"Meeva, come here, will you?"

She ran out naked, the way he liked to see her around the house.

"Look." He showed her his leg. The red open sore on his right calf was particularly ugly.

"Maybe it will go. Leave it alone."

He was examining the skin when it suddenly dawned on him. "Well, I'll be damned!" he yelled excitedly. "The stigmata!"

"The—what?"

Cohn leaped to his feet. "The stigmata! The stigmata of Gauguin! A thing like that is worth a fortune! Now I'm really *authentic!*"

"Cohn, what are you talking about?"

"Don't you understand? Gauguin had exactly the same sores on his legs and in the same places too. He had syphilis. Do you realize what that means?"

"Cohn! You've got syphilis? It's that slut Ounano! I knew it! I knew it!"

91

"No, you peasant! These are the stigmata of Gauguin. Now we are on solid ground! I've been authenticated! There's no arguing with a proof like that!"

Twenty minutes later, Cohn was taking off his pants triumphantly in Bizien's office. The promoter listened attentively, nodding approval. The canonization of Gauguin, if only the Church agreed to cooperate, could mean a new touristic gold mine, crowning the myth with immortality. He promised to talk up the matter with Bishop Tatin as soon as possible, but right now he had more urgent business to attend to. The Matson Line was bringing in six hundred passengers that afternoon, and they were to be taken around the island to see the *clou* of the new tourist season: thirty-two most famous biblical scenes as seen in the world's greatest paintings acted out by the Tahitians along the bus road.

Cohn was in such a state of creative excitement that he left the Tourist Office without his pants and had to walk back for them all the way from the Place Joffre. The next thing he did was to have a Wassermann test and was soon reassured. His blood was as pure as was humanly possible. The "stigmata" were merely a tropical skin infection.

On his way home from the hospital, Cohn blew a tire and tried hitchhiking to Pouaavia. But everybody in Tahiti knew him and as soon as they saw "that ruffian," they merely speeded by. After a half hour of waving and cursing, a motorbike drove up. It was Father Tamil, the Dominican.

Father Tamil was barely over thirty and had always been very nice to him, but Cohn avoided him like the plague: you simply could not trust a priest who had a Sorbonne degree in literature. Besides, the young missionary had a curious, ironic, knowing way of looking at him that made Cohn uneasy.

There was a trussed-up chicken on the back seat and Cohn took its place, holding the bird in his hands.

"How are we doing?"

But Cohn was not talking to local missionaries. He had not yet forgiven. Sixty-five years earlier, Gauguin had offered one of his nudes, *All the gold of their bodies,* to the Mission School. It was a clever stratagem. If he succeeded in having the painting accepted by these guardians of Polynesian virtue, his feud with the authorities over the prohibition of nudity could be considered as won. The painting had not been accepted. The prohibition of bare breasts and pareus in the "earthly paradise" had been implemented. The world's most splendid nudity had been hidden under the black garb of the French provincial *bigote*. Gauguin had described this in one of his letters to Monfreid as "The Third Coming of Civilization: the black veils of mourning, after alcohol and syphilis."

"I'm getting off here," he snarled.

The bike came to a stop.

"Mr. Cohn."

"What is it? I'm not talking to you bastards."

"You ought to give up. Your frantic gesticulation is useless. You know, it begins to look as if you were trying to force the Father to show himself. Why don't you try praying, like everybody else?"

Cohn let go with a string of obscenities, less from genuine feeling than as a matter of principle. At that very moment, a coconut fell from a palm at his feet, missing his head by inches.

"Jesus Christ!" he bellowed, jumping aside.

The young Dominican laughed. "Coconut harvesting by blasphemy! That should open new prospects to the lazy Tahitians."

Cohn felt like a loser. But he had a reputation to sustain. If there was one thing Cohn truly cared about, it was his honor as a liar. "You priests always turn guilt into a matter of original sin," he shouted. "With me it's much more recent than that. I ended up in Tahiti because I'm trying to forget. I am a murderer. My remorse crushes me. Two years ago, I dropped ten tons of bombs on a friendly Vietnamese village. Twenty women and children killed. The wrong ones. You may know the civilized man's noblest cry: 'Women and children first—' So long."

He walked away.

But it did not work.

Father Tamil described a perfect circle with his bike and caught up with him. "Give me back my chicken."

This time Cohn was truly licked. He gave back the chicken reluctantly, looking at the cunning young father with a certain amount of respect and with the feeling that he had a future pope before him.

The whole island was already talking about "the miracle," and Cohn, lolling in his hammock, began to receive little offerings of flowers, chicken, and fruit from the villagers. Meeva herself was now looking at him in a funny sort of way, displaying for the first time a certain shyness in their relationship. Cohn did not pay much attention to it until she flatly refused to give it to him.

"*E mea haama.* It makes me feel ashamed."

"What's the matter? Why do you feel ashamed all of a sudden?"

"We can't *foa-foa* anymore, Cohn. It's a sin now."

"What the hell are you talking about, you silly bitch? Since when has screwing become a sin, all of a sudden?"

"We better wait until it's over, Cohn. Maybe it will go. Father Tamil says that as long as you've got the stigmata, I must respect you as a holy person. He says as long as you're like that, your *fifi* is taboo."

"What?" roared Cohn. "My *fifi* is taboo?"

He yelled and threatened and begged, but Meeva was adamant. Taboo is taboo.

The following Sunday, Cohn cornered Tamil after Mass and told him what he thought of him.

"Of all the lousy tricks—"

The young Dominican merely smiled pleasantly.

"What d'you think you're doing?" thundered Cohn. "What right do you have to declare my *fifi* taboo? That's paganism!"

"Come now, come now, Mr. Cohn. It's you who's running around bragging you've got the stigmata."

"You know damn well that it's nothing of the sort! Tamil, if you keep declaring my *fifi* taboo, I'll sue you!"

The sore was beginning to heal and Cohn did what he could to make the best of it before it was over. He kept after Bizien anxiously. The canonization of Gauguin had long been one of the promoter's pet projects.

"Well, how is it going? Any luck?"

"I'm still trying. He's got to realize what this could mean for Tahiti. I'm having another meeting with Bishop Tatin today. But I don't think he'll cooperate. He's a conservative. They're still ages behind modern promotion methods."

Leaving an anxious Cohn in the street, the Napoleon of Tourism launched a final assault against that fortress of stubbornness that was the Bishop of Muano. His thick black beard and heavy brows began to bristle as soon as Bizien started to speak.

"Your Gauguin was a pig, and everybody knows it. He lived like a pig, fornicated like a pig, covered the walls of his house with obscene postcards, corrupted young girls, and died of syphilis."

"I know, but it was *deliberate*. Gauguin had deliberately assumed all the world's sins. There's definite proof of it. I'm referring to a letter he wrote to his friend Monfreid three days before his death, in which he states it quite clearly: 'This body, these sores, this agony, this wretchedness, all this slowly rotting carcass, what is it, if not Man since his very first step on earth?' "

"I wasn't acquainted with that letter," said Bishop Tatin rather suspiciously.

"It was sold for five million francs to a museum. Also, don't forget that in one of his first portraits, painted in Brittany, Gauguin represented himself with a halo around his head. The intention of deliberately sought martyrdom was already clear."

"My dear Bizien, the world will still see a lot more shame, fakery, and imposture, but there's at least one insult it will be spared, and it's the celebration of a Saint-Gauguin Day in Tahiti. I bow to the great painter, but the man was an absolute pig and that's all there is to it." The Bishop rose from his desk. "By the way, there's something I would like to mention while you're here. No one objects to your cultural activities. Neither do I have anything against your plan to bring out the 'earthly paradise' side of Tahiti, or the living tableaux drawn from the Bible and staged in a natural setting. But you should show a little more care in choosing your performers. Take that scandal with Adam and Eve last week. Really!"

"A most unfortunate incident. It will never happen again. I assure you."

"You began by putting them under an apple tree stark naked."

"It is difficult to present Adam and Eve dressed, you know. There's such a thing as realism."

"All right. As long as they sat under the apple tree, while the tourists took their picture— But you know how your Adam was making money on the side. Those who wanted to lay Eve under the apple tree were simply asked to pay two hundred francs. Most of the tourists are Americans, and you've done some bad damage to French prestige."

"I don't see what French prestige has to do with it. You know the Tahitians have no sense of sin."

"Your Adam was *not* a Tahitian. He's that notorious ruffian Sarrazin, who should have been deported long ago."

Bizien sighed. The staging of Adam and Eve in the Garden of Eden had brought him some of his worst headaches. First of all, there were no snakes in Tahiti, and it was of course essential to have one hanging attractively from the apple tree. Bizien had ordered a pair of harmless pythons from the Barranquilla Zoo, in Colombia. When the reptiles reached Papeete, Bizien had taken the crate directly to the spot he had chosen on the peninsula. A superb plastic apple tree had already been placed there, with truly beautiful red apples hanging from every branch. It was then that the catastrope occurred. When the crate was opened, they found inside two black mambas, whose bite brings on death within minutes. The Tahitian who opened the crate, and who had never seen a snake in his life, took one look at the heaving monsters, gave a yell of terror, and fled instantly, leaving the trap door open. The two reptiles were out with lightning speed and within seconds had disappeared in the wilderness. In an island that had never known any snakes, there were now two black mambas, probably reproducing like mad, just like everybody else in Tahiti. You could truly say that the "earthly paradise" had received the finishing touch needed to truly justify its name.

It was highly unlikely that the Barranquilla Zoo had made such a mistake. Bizien had his own theory about it. He was convinced that somewhere along the road his competitors in Hawaii had got hold of the crate and had replaced the harmless pythons with two deadly mambas.

He left Bishop Tatin and joined Cohn at the Noa Noa. Cohn gave him a somber look; he knew he was defeated. Bizien merely shrugged. They had at least one thing in common: they both had a craving for perfection. The canonization of Gauguin would have been a supreme accomplishment for the promoter and an indisputable artistic triumph for Cohn. But it was not to be.

"Well, we've got to keep trying," Bizien said.

They sat silently for a while.

"Have you ever been in jail?" Cohn asked.

The promoter's gloomy face brightened. "Never, Mr. Cohn. I was never found out. That's why governments keep employing me. Before taking over Tahiti, I spent many years in Africa and launched there three old civilizations completely unknown to anthropologists. It came off beautifully. Even UNESCO cooperated. But then, I couldn't miss. No white expert would dare tell a newly independent African republic, beaming with national pride, that they were created out of thin air and had no cultural roots of their own. This, of course, is not merely typical of Africa. It's generally held, Mr. Cohn, that the purpose of a national mystique as well as of a great national leader is to work toward the creation of the future. Well, that's not true. The purpose of a genuine nationalistic mystique is to work toward the greatness and glory of the past. Look at de Gaulle. He's done more for the French past than almost any other French national figure. That's what is known as leadership."

A few drops of warm rain were falling.

Cohn got on his bike and rode up to the House of Joy. There were moments when the irony of that name was almost more than he could bear.

An outrigger canoe appeared in the lagoon with four young men in bright pareus, with flowers behind their ears, their bodies glistening like bronze in the last glow of sunset. They were singing an old Maori *ute,* whose meaning was lost with the ancient gods. It spoke of the Milky Way, called "the long blue cloud-eating shark," and of the distant Venus draped in her cloak of night, *taurua o hiti ete a hiahe.* They were the four young German queers who ran the popular new joint, the Saint-Trop.

Cohn stretched out on the moist cool sand, pressed his face against it, and let the white foam flow over his hair and neck. Then, when the heartache and the guilt subsided, he walked back toward the House of Joy, his heart still full of that confused longing man carries in him like a promise or a premonition of some future birth upon another shore.

He pushed the door and walked in. Almost immediately he bumped into something in the darkness, something soft that scurried away. There was a sound of broken glass and Cohn heard a frightened breathing in the shadows.

"I have a gun in my hand and I intend to use it," he said. "You'll never get me alive, you bastards."

"Please, Mr. Cohn, don't shoot. It's only me."

"Who's me?"

"Fernand Bouton."

Because of that habit the local Chinese had of assuming French names, Cohn had some trouble remembering that his visitor was the tailor Wong Koo, who had a shop in the harbor arcade. He took the oil lamp and lit it. Fernand Bouton was at the far end of the room, holding a "painting" under each arm.

"So you're the thief who's been stealing my pictures, huh? Two were missing last week."

"I didn't steal them, Mr. Cohn. These pictures are ours."

"What? Maybe I promised them to your wife as a parting gift?"

"You know all about it, Mr. Cohn. My father gave Mr. Gauguin credit, but he never paid him. I have the bills to prove it, and you can look through our books; they've always been in perfect order. Mr. Gauguin kept promising

97

my father that he'd pay him, but he never did. His paintings are worth a fortune now, but my father never got anything. My father was fooled once, but it won't happen again. My father is an old man now, but he's never forgotten Mr. Gauguin. Everybody in Tahiti knows you've taken his business over from him, so my father feels you should pay off his debts. That's why he sent me over for these pictures. He feels they're his."

Cohn had a lump in his throat and almost tears in his eyes. He was overcome with gratitude. This Fernand Bouton was granting him one of the purest artistic joys of his life.

"Take them, young man. Take your pictures. Choose the most beautiful. Someday they'll be worth millions. In fact, my last showing in Paris was a triumph. Vollard writes me that— Forget it. Tell your distinguished father I've never forgotten what I owed him, I merely gave up thinking about it."

Fernand Bouton was radiant. "If you ever need a suit, Mr. Cohn, just drop by the store anytime you want."

"Tell your father he's real smart. How old is he?"

"Eighty-three."

"True wisdom, that's what it is, true wisdom. There are people who never learn from history and keep repeating the same mistakes. You know how much they got for a Gauguin painting in London last month? Six hundred thousand dollars. Your father's going to make a killing, I'm telling you that. Here, I'll sign them for you. You can't be too careful, you know, with all those forgeries around."

Cohn signed the pictures, Genghis Cohn. The signature was the part he always did himself. Fernand Bouton was beaming and bowing.

"Now be sure to keep them dry," advised Cohn. "Humidity, that's the enemy. Remember that."

"Don't worry, Mr. Cohn, we'll take good care. My father was a good friend of Mr. Gauguin's. Here, I'll show you something—"

He took a paper from his pocket and unfolded it carefully. Cohn raised the lamp and read:

June 2, 1898

One jar of gray ointment for lice.
One bottle of methylene syrup for the throat.
Dr. Joubart's balm for hemorrhoids.
Bottle of morphine, fifty centigrams.
Bottle of laudanum for internal pain.

Tell Wong Koo I shall pay him as soon as I receive the money, by the next ship, from my show in Paris, which has been a colossal success, all my paintings being sold at fabulous prices. If he wants, I can leave him as security the large painting I have just finished, entitled "Where do we come from? Where are we? Where are we going?" If that's not good enough, he can hold my guitar, which is in excellent condition and was made in Italy.

PAUL GAUGUIN*

Cohn studied the list for a long time, trying to engrave it in his mind—all of it, from the gray ointment for crabs to the balm for piles and from morphine, fifty centigrams, to laudanum for internal pain. Nothing was missing. Gauguin was the perfect tenant of the House of Joy.

He handed the paper back to Fernand Bouton. "You should offer it to the Musée de l'Homme in Paris," he said.

He walked out on the beach, lifted his eyes to the heavens, and looked for the constellation of the Dog among the stars.

14

The Vultures

It was a few days later that Cohn began to notice the danger signs. In the morning there were footmarks around the house that hadn't been there the evening before. There were sudden red cigarette glows in darkness, and no one there when he would walk up to investigate. Papers were missing, though he had been careful not to write anything on paper for quite a while now and had even given up his nightly séances of scribbling in the sand. But the two brutal, scary warnings came one afternoon as he was returning from Papeete and showed unmistakably that he had been found out. They were after his head again.

He had driven Meeva to Point Venus, where she had some important gossip to attend to, then went to see Bizien.

* Quoted in Perruchot's *Life of Gauguin.*

"You'd better remind that bedbug Verdouillet that he's supposed to deliver to me some of his old paintings. Puccioni's bringing a bunch of Gauguin fans over this afternoon and I've run out of pictures."

Bizien seemed surprised. "You mean to say you haven't heard the news?"

"What news?"

Apparently they had both underestimated Verdouillet's artistic integrity. Ordered to play Van Gogh for the tourists, though he had been painting in the Gauguin manner for more than thirty years, the poor man had bravely attempted to paint like the recluse of Arles. But then something quite unexpected happened. Struggling to get rid of Gauguin's style, Verdouillet hit, so to speak, upon himself. His recent work was beginning to show an originality that owed nothing either to Gauguin or to "poor Vincent," but had all the marks of an authentic and independent personality, that of Verdouillet himself, which was of not the slightest interest to anyone. The curse of authentic, original talent had stricken the wretch like a lightning bolt. No one was interested in "those smears." Puccioni did not even bother to take visitors to his studio any longer. Verdouillet was scared out of his wits. He put up a brave fight, trying to immerse himself in Van Gogh completely, sitting all day long in his garden, staring at sunflowers. Finally . . .

Bizien concluded his tale with a helpless shrug.

"He's in the hospital. He's always been a bit weak in the head. The fool ended up by cutting off his ear in a fit of authenticity."

Cohn was so impressed that he absentmindedly paid the check himself and rushed to the hospital.

He found Verdouillet in bed, a bandage around his head. The blanket was up to his sadly sticking out nose. The painter stricken with originality looked up guiltily at Cohn, then lowered his eyelids.

"I just don't have a Van Gogh in me, and that's all there's to it," he mumbled. "God knows I've tried, but whatever I did turned out to be only Verdouillet. I've lost my talent, that's all there is to it."

"Maybe it'll come back," said Cohn.

"You really think so?"

"All painters fall under some influence from time to time. You're passing through a period where you've fallen under your own influence, the influence of Verdouillet. It will go."

"Puccioni doesn't bring buyers anymore. I'm going to starve."

"I'll see what I can do for you," promised Cohn. "In the meanwhile, try to do some nice Tahitiain landscapes. Don't force yourself. Just try, gently, little by little. Copy some postcards. It'll come back."

"I can't. The stuff I do doesn't look like anything ever seen before. I can't help myself. It comes from *inside* me. Jesus! What am I to do? Who wants to paint like Verdouillet? *I* don't."

"You'll get over it," said Cohn. "Just take it easy for a while. But don't give in. Don't let that thing get you. The thing that's inside you, I mean."

In spite of the cheerful tone, he felt saddened as he left the hospital. If that wretched Verdouillet had been truly hit by authenticity, he was in for trouble and there was little one could do to help him.

He went to fetch Meeva and they were walking hand in hand along the Papeete waterfront when the first warning came. A black Citroën flying the French flag drove by, preceded by a motorcycle escort. It was the Government's official car and they had caught sight of the Governor himself, in his white and gold uniform and cap. The car rolled on a few more seconds, then slowed down.

Cohn gulped. His knees felt weak. The car was already continuing on its way, but there could be no mistake about what Cohn's eyes had seen.

The Governor of French Oceania had leaned out of the open window and waved to him, repeatedly, and with the greatest courtesy.

Cohn looked behind him, but there was no one. General de Gaulle's personally appointed representative in French Oceania had waved to him all right.

He had to sit down. He collapsed on a bench, his face ashen. "Christ!"

"Cohn! What's the matter?"

"The Governor—he greeted me!"

He raised a trembling hand to his forehead. The greeting could not have been intended for Cohn, a notorious, scandalous, debauched adventurer whose presence in Tahiti and deplorable way of life were resented as a personal insult by every man worthy of that name and who had been more than once saved from deportation only through the personal intervention of Bizien and by the shadow of his illustrious precedessor.

There was only one explanation possible.

The Governor of French Oceania knew who he was.

101

Meeva was laughing. "Gene, you're nuts. You're seeing things."

But her *popaa* looked so sick that she rushed into a pharmacy and came back with a bottle of castor oil, the universal Tahitian remedy.

"Drink that."

Cohn felt so awful that he did. But there's no purge strong enough. You need something more radical to get rid of yourself.

They knew who he was.

The Governor kept glancing back through the rear window, then laughed. "Incredible," he said. "They're still sticking to the amnesia theory. Can you imagine it? A man burns out his fingertips and has facial surgery— Why? To get rid of a past *he can't remember!* New French logic."

Caillebasse shifted his feet uneasily. "It's happened in psychiatry before—I mean, a man going into hiding and changing his face because of obscure, unformulated guilt feelings. You can keep your torturing feeling of guilt without remembering the cause. Amnesia wiping out all the past, all memories of it, except the obscure guilt—"

The Governor shrugged impatiently. "Philosophy. This is no longer psychology, it's metaphysics. Anyway, this man can't be French. He seems a typical American to me. They're a crazed nation. Gone mad. Their young people, the ones we see here, anyway, should be living in a zoo."

Caillebasse said nothing. It was hardly the moment to point out de Gaulle's personal interest in the case. But that, precisely, was on the Governor's mind.

"However, I'll play along," he said ironically. "For obvious reasons."

Obvious indeed. If the man was Mathieu, such a stubborn and such an outspoken refusal to believe this could cost dearly later. In fact, it proved that the Governor was an obstinate mule, which was exactly what Caillebasse thought of him.

"The General seems fascinated by the case," he remarked.

"He would be. French treasures, you know. The General's attitude to fifty million Frenchmen is exactly that of a farmer toward his herd of pigs. He loves all his pigs. He wants to keep them. He's resentful of America, because its President has one hundred and fifty million pigs more than he himself has. So, naturally, when it comes to an animal of Mathieu's talent and potential value, he hates the idea of losing the pig and seeing it fall in with another herd."

Caillebasse thought that the metaphor was highly interesting. He was going to remember it.

There was nothing but bright sunshine around, and so the impression of imminent doom that suddenly got hold of Cohn as they were approaching the *fare* could not be put to the usual sadness and foreboding brought on by the Tahitian shadows. He told Meeva to wait outside, walked twice around the house, then entered it with a beating heart, almost on tiptoe, as if the whole place had been mined during his absence. The house was empty. He sat down on the sofa and waited for something to blow up, for some hidden mine to go off. Then he realized once more that the mine was merely his hidden self and that there would be no explosion, no sudden death, nothing instant, in fact, that his anxiety was simply that of a man coming home to his fear.

Through the open door he could see a French cruiser, far in the distance. He got up from the sofa and started to walk back to Meeva, who was waiting for him on the bike, when he noticed the marks of footsteps on the floor. The sand of the footmarks was still wet.

Cohn took a cigarette from the bamboo table and stuck it in his mouth without lighting it.

The footsteps ran in on the floor and up the stairs, toward the entresol of the atelier, where he and Meeva had their bed.

Cohn stood still, staring. The footprints were going in. They didn't go back out. The man was still inside the house, up there.

They had come for him.

He was keeping his eyes on the floor. He did not want to see the gun that was probably pointed in his direction.

He waited. No sound, except for the panic humming in his ears.

He swallowed hard and glanced toward the cruiser imploringly. But no matter how scared you were, your funk sent no S.O.S. signals.

It was then that his terror managed at last to find a release in a mighty roar. "Get out of there, you bloody bastards!"

"There's only one of us here, Cohn," a voice said.

Cohn experienced a sudden untying of all his knotted sphincters, which threatened physiological disaster. Somehow, he managed to avoid the worst.

"Come up here, Cohn. Be my guest."

Callum. There was no mistaking that New England accent, which seemed to be the latest "in" thing back home since the Kennedys. Cohn always thought of America as "back home" and not only because of his mother or of the years he had spent there. He loved America because it was a country riddled with guilt, and that made it almost a civilization. He went upstairs.

Callum was spread all over the bed, smelling a rose and reading *Confrontation,* an American magazine published with strong financial C.I.A. backing for the purpose of attracting and identifying dissenters.

"I dropped in," Callum said amiably.

"So I see." Cohn nodded looking at the two hundred and twenty pounds of fat lolling on his bed. He added with total sincerity, "I am glad to see you, Bill. I saw your footprints downstairs and I said to myself, 'They're here and they're going to kill me.' "

Callum's face expressed a vague interest, that is, inasmuch as his features, sunk in fat, could manage to organize themselves into something like an expression.

"Who was trying to kill you?"

"The local bourgeoisie. The Authority, with a capital A. Law and Order. The 'decent' people. They hate my guts. The oldest conflict in the world, Bill. Artists versus the rest. They're right, too. We're naturals. For subversion, I mean. It's part of all art."

Callum farted. "Excuse me," he said, "but it saves a lot of words."

"You dirty fag," bellowed Cohn, rushing for the window.

Callum was so bearded, so fat, so filthy, and so much the very image of the typical un-American American intellectual that his head looked as if it had just been cut out from the cover of *Esquire*. On his forehead, there were the three marks—two red and one blue—of non-Zen, first class, second degree, which stood in underground metaphysics for "fuck you all" and gave the bearer the right to speak to Shiva even when he wasn't there; the marks were the spiritual equivalent of black belt in judo. He had gained this high distinction after his nonpilgrimages to Ramatou and after not spending six months in Binda's room of the ashram there, which made him one of the truly few "in the know." He was wearing a yellow kimono with a setting sun marked "U.S.A." in front and pictures of Vietnam atrocities on the back. His white silk pants and sleeves were covered in pop slogans, all of them from

Mao's little "Red Book." The sandals were made from sacred *behar* wood from Pondicherry and he wore earrings and a Coptic silver cross on his chest.

Cohn squatted on the floor and lit a cigarette. Callum's liquid eyes studied him for a while, then went back to the page of the magazine he was reading.

John William Callum had come to practice total dissent in Tahiti a year earlier, and during that time his reputation and stature had grown considerably back home, on the West Coast. He was now considered the leading figure of the latest American school of literature and painting, with deep social implications, which was known as "revolutionary abstentionism" or "creative negation." He was acknowledged as the most convincing spokesman of the *no* generation, a total dissenter who had successfully resisted the urge to write an immense masterpiece, so as to avoid making this contribution to a hated society and its "culture." His refusal of all creation was of tremendous revolutionary value, for it gave his nonwork a positive philosophical content of protest and rejection. Young abstentionist writers were coming to see him from all over the U.S.A. He was the unchallenged leader of the new artistic America that was triumphantly competing in the cultural field with the nonstatements and non-contribution of European nonpainting and nonliterature. The power of both the capitalistic oppression and human revolt could be heard clearly in the blanks of his nonwork. There was a Renaissance man in him as well, for he was also the guiding spirit of the school of painting that had succeeded *pop* and *op* and was known as *top*. Its adepts were at the very heart of the American cultural revolution and called themselves "blank guards." Callum's nonpaintings, vast empty frames suggesting the nothingness of being, showed nothing but the wall behind them, thus offering the sight of ruthless capitalistic and materialistic barriers against the artist's spiritual aspirations. He had also written a number of plays without text, called "nonhappenings" because they expressed the static aspect of our doomed social and moral order. In performing these plays, the motionless actors stared at the audience so as to communicate their total condemnation of the passive audience to the latter until the spectators began to go mad and shout insults at the actors; this was known as "awakening." Callum had also the reputation of being one of the best men in the Central Intelligence Agency. He had first come into contact with the C.I.A. in a matter-of-fact way as a potently influential literary personality, at the time when, under Allan Dulles,

105

the Agency secretly contributed to such distinguished intellectual ventures as *Monat* in Berlin, *Preuves* in Paris, and *Encounter* in England.

Callum's eyes were on the magazine.

"Listen to this," he said. "It's the editorial. 'The balance of terror is precarious by definition. It is always at the mercy of a new technological breakthrough, of a new discovery, and this explains why scientific genius represents such a potential danger to great powers. The facts are here. In the decade that had followed the "accidental drowning" of Professor Tchurek off the coast of Massachusetts, the United States had lost Rachmill, Lutchevsky, Gregory, Parks, Spetai, all from accidents or ill health. *Wallachs Bulletin,* published in Cambridge, estimated that in 1965 five Soviet scientists of the first order had disappeared from the scene. France lost Berner in 1963, Kovala in 1964, and Barlemont, Frank, and Gustavic. The figures for Japan were no less well known: Koshibashi, Soto, Okinada, and Kusaki in a single year. These deaths were always put down to natural causes. At the risk of being accused of cynicism, the editors of *Confrontation* feel that they have a very positive and practical suggestion to make. It would save the taxpayer a lot of money if the great Powers got together each year and agreed on the names and the number of scientists each of the Powers would undertake to rub off among their own nationals, so as to keep the balance of terror in perfect equilibrium. A kind of new-look Geneva Convention, in full accord with the spirit of the times and the paramount interest of peace.' How about that?"

Cohn was smoking, squatting on the floor, his arms around his knees, a smile on his mug, his eyes half closed against the smoke. They were taking him for somebody else.

"How did you find out?"

"Find out what?"

"That I am a scientist of genius."

Callum's almost liquid face congealed into an expression of icy disapproval. "Screw you."

"How did you find me out? Aside from going all through my papers and things, which is what you were up to again this time, knowing I was away?"

When Callum was angry, his voice rose from its usual hostile baritone to the pitch of a feminine, neurotic soprano. There were ripples of fat emotion on his face.

"I'm sure there're other people that have been searching your place, you bum. One of these days they'll find you

106

with a knife in your back. It's very amusing to be a kind of cosmic *provocateur,* which is your favorite little game, but sometimes you carry it a bit too far—"

Cohn grinned. He knew what Callum was referring to, and he was pleased to see that the incident still rankled. It happened a few months earlier, and Cohn considered the episode as one of his most vengeful artistic achievements. When he found himself unable to resist his creative compulsion, he would spend the night composing in the sand outside or on paper. Then he would tear his work to bits and throw them in the primitive latrines at the far end of the garden behind the house. One day, after a particularly self-indulgent night of creation, having carefully disposed in the usual way of the beauty he was pursuing for beauty's sake, he was awakened from his blissful sleep by Meeva.

"Cohn, Cohn—wake up."

He sat up in the bed, blinking. "What is it?"

"Listen."

A mournful cry for help rose from the far end of the garden. "*Au secours! À moi!*"

At first, he didn't recognize the voice. It was muffled and seemed to be rising from within the earth. Cohn jumped out of bed and ran into the garden.

"Help! I'm drowning! Cohn! Cohn!"

He galloped in the direction of the voice and saw what had happened. Somebody had been trying to get the scraps of paper from the latrines, the wooden planks had collapsed under the weight, and the man had fallen *inside.* The full implication of that *inside* dawned upon Cohn in all its horror. He walked slowly toward the place and crossed his arms on his chest.

"Hi there," he said.

Callum, holding his soiled face above all that materialism, was obviously in the last stage of exhaustion and horror. He was standing chin-deep in it and, decided Cohn, was on the verge of going under.

"You naughty boy," Cohn said. "This is private property you know. You're trespassing."

"Help me out, you—"

"Now, let's not be rude, Callum."

"Cohn, be human, for Christ's sake. I've been standing on tiptoes for hours—"

"I'm in a hurry, Bill. See you later. *Ciao.*" He turned to go.

"Cohn!"

"I didn't know you were so interested in my poetry, Bill."

"Get me out, you murderer!"

"Because there's nothing but celestial music there."

Callum gave a short, desperate, hysterical gasp and began to go under. Cohn waited till materialism reached to his ears, then grabbed him by the hair and yelled for Meeva. It took them a solid rope and half an hour of effort before they succeeded in dragging Callum back to shore.

Cohn was laughing, squatting by the bed, his back against the wall; Callum glared at him angrily. During the last three months, he had kept protesting, sending indignant cables, telling Washington that they were out of their minds, this was an obvious case of mistaken identity, Cohn was an adventurer, a con-man; and though he, Callum, had been unable up to now to discover his true identity, the idea that the man was Mathieu was ludicrous. Somebody was goofing. But to no avail. Though Washington was now avoiding any direct statement to Callum regarding Cohn's identity, the C.I.A. appeared to be sticking to their opinion, as well as the French. The facts that the French watched him constantly and that he himself had had to blow to pieces a Chinese murder commando were a sufficient proof of this.

"Well, anyway, I'm glad that you seem to have recovered completely from your encounter with my creations, the other day."

"You're going too far," Callum growled.

"Bill, I better tell you the truth. I'm the greatest scientific genius of modern times. I've made a fantastic discovery—"

"Sure, sure."

"I've discovered the greatest and the cheapest source of energy of all times."

"Let's hear that. What is it?"

"Shit, Bill. *La merde. Drek.* Soon all the big Powers will be cutting each other's throats to get hold of all the *merde* there is in the world. A true apotheosis of materialism."

Callum rose from the bed. "Anyway, I've got good news for you. I don't know why I'm doing this for you, but here it is. My American friends are very interested in your work. Your paintings, I mean. They're willing to buy all your output. But they're willing to do even more for you. They're offering you hospitality. Maybe you feel your Tahitian period's over—or almost so. You've made yourself a lot of enemies here, Cohn."

Cohn's heart jumped a beat or two. "So?"

"They'll be glad to welcome you in the States. You could work there undisturbed. Total economic security—security, Cohn. That's the thing for an artist."

Cohn flicked his cigarette with his finger. The ashes fell on the floor. "Is this from the C.I.A.? The offer, I mean."

Callum froze. "What the hell?"

"They say you work for the C.I.A."

"French paranoia. They say that of all the American intellectuals, since that unfortunate nonsense of Arthur Schlesinger's on T.V. This is *Ramparts* nonsense, Cohn. Besides, what they don't understand is that the intellectuals, those who did, I mean, never worked for the C.I.A. *The C.I.A. worked for the intellectuals.* Yes, Cohn, That's our America. They were taking orders from us. The miracle of true intellect, Cohn, is that it always comes out on top. It takes over. Well, let me know."

He got up with the curious unsteadiness of men with immense thighs and flowed downstairs, leaving his rose on the bed.

Cohn buried his head in his arms. He felt a soft hand on his shoulder and raised his eyes.

Meeva was watching him curiously. "Cohn, you look scared."

"I am."

"Why?"

He pressed his cheek against her hand. "And since when does a man need a reason to feel afraid?"

15

Tricolor

He spent a sleepless night, and next morning the terror and the anguish were still in him. The only man he could turn to was Bizien. He got hold of him at eight A.M. at his *vahine*'s shack.

"I have to get out of here."

Bizien asked no questions. Thieves' honor. "I can't get you out of the island secretly just like that. Security is much too tight right now, what with the nuclear test imminent."

"Well, I can't wait here."

"As bad as that?"

"Pretty goddamn awful."

"Give me time. Listen, why don't you go to the peninsula? It'll be easier for me to smuggle you out of there."

The Taiaropu Peninsula was the wildest part of Tahiti, a mountainous green chaos waging a constant battle against a dense and aggressive vegetation, with only the highest peaks emerging victoriously from the melee.

"It's the last place in Tahiti that still deserves the title of 'earthly paradise,'" Bizien said. "I'm opening it to Tourism. It's the ideal place for staging Adam and Eve in the Garden of Eden. You know the trouble I had with Sarrazin and his *vahine* in Pouaavia. Take the job. It's a perfect excuse to get out there."

Cohn felt a bit better. He walked back home, took his hammock, and slung it on the beach between two *purau* trees with their intricately tangled branches that seemed to bloom with a profusion of blue luminous flowers: the sky. Meeva came to lie beside him; her warm massive body protected him against the outside world. That's how the sunset found him, playing ostrich in the security of their silent embrace. Then the night came to hide Cohn, with its usual solicitude for fugitives.

The moon watched over its precious silver; the beach had the soothing whiteness of the first times and untarnished hope; the fireflies carried their sparks in the blue of the night, tiny Diogenes pursuing tirelessly their eternal quest.

They left the next morning, stopping for good luck at a much-revered Tahitian shrine.

It was a spring hidden deep in the thickness of the Vaiha Valley, where, according to the spoken tradition handed down by the Smithsonian Institution, the *ute* of the "god without end" had been born. The song itself was no longer heard in Polynesia, but snatches of the sacred text still survived on the mumbling lips of very old men.

They had to follow the bed of a rocky stream for more than an hour through a tunnel of vegetation, under weird trees that resembled slender mushrooms dotted with yellow and green; their tortured branches, covered with moss, were trying to join hands across the stream.

The growth was so dense here that it muffled the sound of the stream down to a murmur, and they had to watch for the lianas that stretched from one side to the other. It was on those *purau* lianas that the gods dried the skins of the human victims they had received as offerings, before putting them on, painted red and yellow, which, as everyone knows, have always been their favorite colors.

Cohn did not expect to find the "god without end" himself in his dwellings, since his only earthly image was kept under glass in the Heidelberg Museum. But the beauty of the place could be only that of its vanished master, who had prudently divested himself of it before being carried away, so that his magic still reigned over these untouched waters.

The spring gushed from the depths in a white froth where the mingled shadows of papaya trees, of jasmine, of dahlias, of ferns, danced briefly, then vanished with each new surge of waters and foam, only to be reborn again. Overhead, higher than the giant tufts of ferns with their silken plumes, rose the teaks, their bare dark bronze and gold hides showing through a satellite world of unknown plants with limp gray and black leaves that looked half cremated, as if bearing the mark of all the extinct volcanic fires that had convulsed the earth as if in angry search for some unholy seed. The stones, touched with moss, their basalt split by the slender, fragile stems of sulfur flowers, stood their black eternal guard over the misty galaxies of water droplets where rainbows quivered. Clouds of butterflies fluttered in a hothouse atmosphere above the crag where the god once stood and where—thus spoke Meeva —he had copulated with the first woman to rise from *moana,* "the great deep ocean." It was out of this union, of which speaks with deep awe the *ute* of the "god without end," that certain atolls were born, although it was impossible to tell which ones, for revealing their names would have brought on them immediate destruction by terrible tides.

Thus spoke Meeva.

Nothing remained of this past on the barren rock, except a thick layer of purple pollen fallen from the *baratanes.*

They were in water up to their hips, and in order to fulfill Cohn's artistic urge on the vanished god's throne, they had to climb through the thick bamboo grove that still surrounded the place with knightly white plumes of ancient chivalry.

As soon as he had reached the rock, Cohn's inspiration rose up to the challenge at this propitious abode. He spread out his pants on the basalt to protect Meeva's knees as well as his own, and when Meeva removed her pareu and offered herself to his creative genius, he gave way to

111

his creative urge, with that feeling of power out of which both gods and men are born.

On their way down, Cohn was surprised to see a familiar white form among the trees. Holding up his robe, a butterfly net in one hand and a small valise in the other, young Father Tamil was hurrying up the stream, knee deep in water, with a physical agility equal to his spiritual one. When he saw Cohn, he stopped and gave something like a sigh of relief.

"Well, I'll be damned," he said simply, and on the lips of a Dominican that expression could only mean a truly troubled soul. "So it's you."

"It's me," said Cohn, very pleased, for he got lost in his impostures so often that it was reassuring to hear his existence confirmed. "What's the matter?"

"I thought they were murdering you—I mean, someone, up there. I heard howlings as if an animal were having his throat cut. It almost sounded like a human sacrifice, although it's no longer practiced on these islands."

"It was me," Cohn admitted without false modesty.

"What happened? Somebody was killing you?"

"Meeva and I were swimming in bliss," said Cohn.

The Dominican seemed impressed. "And you always bellow like that in your better moments?"

Cohn lowered his eyes modestly, playing with his foot. Meeva was humming, holding a pin between her lips, arranging her hair.

"What the hell are you doing here with a valise and a butterfly net?" asked Cohn.

"I came to give the final rites to old Chief Wiriamu down there, in the village. I've always heard there're some rare butterflies here, so—Monsieur Cohn, you should not howl like that. You should leave something for the animals."

He watched them vanish in the dense green vegetation, standing in the middle of the stream, lifting his white robe and holding his butterfly net and his valise under his arm. Then he climbed all the way up to the summit, and knelt on the rock, on the very spot where the Maori used to make their offering to their beloved *tiki*, in exchange for a protection that failed to save Polynesia from the hands of better-equipped gods.

Tamil opened the valise, took out the shortwave set, and put it down on the sacred boulder, which was, he thought, his lips twisted in a thin, ironic smile, a very appropriate place. "God without end" was a perfect name for radio.

With the rocky chaos around, the radio waves needed

112

help. Tamil unscrewed the butterfly rod, took off the net, and pulled out the antenna. He connected it to the set and established contact.

"Mozon?"

"Mon capitaine? J'écoute, mon capitaine." Mozon's voice sounded both eager and worried.

"It's all right. You can recall the patrol. He certainly does not need any help. I thought they were murdering him, so I called for reinforcements. It was nothing like that."

Tamil pulled his white robe over his knees and sat down on the wet rock. He took out of his pocket a blue pack of Gauloises and lit one with his gold lighter, avoiding the spray.

"Still no answer from Hong Kong?"

"Complete blank. You know my views."

"You may well be right."

"They're going to use some local talent this time. Chong's list of 'possibles' had thirty-four names. Ages eighteen to twenty-six."

"Good Red Guard age," Tamil said. "We're playing a losing game. I wish Paris would listen to my suggestion. Tell him we know who he is. Tell him to stop running away from himself. He must've learned by now that he can't get away—neither from us, nor from himself."

He threw away his wet Gauloise, then lit another one. The radio set was silent, except for the usual sound of frying fish. The green, red, yellow, and white walls of nature around Tamil were oppressive, almost menacing. Flora against fauna, Tamil thought. Sooner or later, flora was bound to win, probably with fauna's help. He disliked the idea of de Gaulle's hydrogen bomb in the heart of Polynesia. It was a destruction, if not of the "earthly paradise," at least of one of the world's last myths.

"The other night he put in five hours writing on the sand, then he wiped out the whole thing with his feet, and even then waited for the ocean to cover the marks. He can't resist creation, then he goes and wipes his behind with it."

The wireless set laughed asthmatically. "You seem a bit upset, *mon capitaine.*"

Tamil looked at the flora around. It seemed to be closing in on him. Literature, he thought, myths. Gods without end. "You're damn right. First, it's lonely here. Ever been here, Mozon?"

"No."

"All this vegetation around seems a) to be waiting for

113

something; b) to have plenty of time, infinitely more than we have; c) to be waiting for us to go down and join the earth, so that it can at last feed itself on our phosphates, minerals, or whatever. In a place like this one, it's flora against fauna—"

"I didn't get that. Who against whom?"

"Never mind. I told Paris we should stop pussyfooting around with him. Tell him that a bloody nuisance like him, carrying such treasures in his head, simply cannot get away. He's just too dangerously unpredictable and you can never be sure on whose side he'll suddenly turn up."

"Just a moment, *mon capitaine.*"

Tamil waited, puffing at his Gauloise, his hands cupped around it to protect it from the liquid mist.

Then Mozon's voice said excitedly, "There's a KTSW signal from Paris, *mon capitaine. Decode it immediately. Will you wait?*"

"Hurry up. I'm getting soaked here."

Tamil threw his wet cigarette away. K was for K.G.B. The Russians were coming in, after the Americans and the Chinese. The Frenchman couldn't help smiling, almost affectionately. The family circle was now complete.

16

The Professional

The man whose name was not Victor Turkassi sat on the bed shivering in his pajamas, trying to put his foot in a sock. His hands were still shaking and his aim was poor. The sock kept missing the foot, and for a professional who would have to use his gun in an hour or two, that was hardly an ideal condition. He had spent the last thirty-eight hours wrapped in a blanket, with a temperature of a hundred and two, and he did not dare to call for a doctor or even for tea, out of fear of what he might say in his ravings. He had been suffering from malaria since North Vietnam, but had managed to keep this out of his K.G.B file. They didn't put agents who were subject to attacks of delirium in charge of Western Hemisphere operations, and the man whose name was not Victor Turkassi did not care to spend the rest of his days behind a Moscow desk.

He succeeded at last in getting into his socks and finished dressing: a suit of Philippine shantung, a pink flowered shirt, and a straw hat he had picked up in Waikiki, where he had just spent three difficult months cleaning up a network infiltrated by the Chinese. He specialized in straightening up "sick" networks. After the arrest of Colonel Abel in the U.S.A. he had salvaged an organization when the F.B.I. and the C.I.A. had already practically all the clues in hand. It was still operating. The man whose name was not Victor Turkassi was fully aware of his value, and he was dismayed by the mission he had been assigned in Tahiti. It was taking him back to his beginnings. He hadn't used a gun, except in routine training, for more than eight years, and he never carried one on him. He now left that sort of thing to his subordinates. Though he knew he had been given the order to proceed to Tahiti at once and to kill a "brain" there only because he happened to be in Honolulu, and the only operational agent on the spot, the irritation he had felt when he decoded the message had no doubt been at least partially responsible for the malaria attack that had delayed the execution of his instructions by almost two days. Now he was sitting on the bed fully dressed, assembling one by one the parts of the Luger he had scattered among his luggage and toiletries. His hands were still shaking so hard it took him ten minutes to put the gun together. Not too reassuring. He knew that at ten feet he was likely to miss his man. He'd have to fire point-blank.

He found it insulting that a man of his rank and value to the Service should be required to play a killer. He would lodge a formal protest at the proper time, but now he had to act. The order had reached him in Honolulu, preceded not only by a cipher indicating, as usual, an "absolute priority"—the inflation of "absolute priorities" was a constant source of irritation and conflict in the Service—but also by an "S" signal; it was only the second time in his whole career that he had received such "hot" instructions. The "S" message stood for "vital importance to the security of the U.S.S.R."

And yet, for all the obvious importance and urgency of the order, everything in the decoded message smacked of improvisation, confusion, and downright panic. He had felt it at first glance and it did nothing to soothe his temper. He prided himself on his professionalism and hated to receive instructions that seemed to have been spelled out by a bunch of amateurs. You'd have thought it was the British M.I.5 who were in charge, with their gentlemanly cricket players who had been taking orders for years from Kim Philby, the dedicated Soviet spy. The man whose name was not Victor Turkassi hated to see the K.G.B. giving every indication of bungling.

In the first place, it was obvious they were acting on information coming from Tahiti, which meant there was a reliable local source. He had reacted immediately, requesting contact. The information reached him two hours before his plane left, but the name was preceded by two question marks, which meant he was a double agent, and there was an additional cipher ordering him to avoid any contact with the man. Nevertheless, they did not hesitate to launch an operation of "vital importance" on the basis of information supplied by a questionable source. Neither did they hesitate to have it carried out by a man of his rank, which was K.G.B. colonel of top seniority, while the iron rule of any secret service in such a case is "If there is a trap, don't risk more than a mouse." But most infuriating was the part of the message under the cipher "For your personal security," something that had always made him laugh, but in the present case reeked of plain bureaucratic imbecility. The indication was "red red," which meant that if he were killed, all the necessary steps had to be taken to prevent his body from falling into the hands of local authorities. Such an order presupposed at least two agents, or a local organization. Yet he was being sent alone and told to avoid local contact. In other words, if he was killed, he was then required to dispose of his own body. The man whose name was not Victor Turkassi was proud of the Service to which he belonged, and he was thoroughly disgusted by this kind of nonsense. No "general orientation" data, either. He was to rush to Tahiti, kill a "brain" who was probably vacationing there, and bring back any document he might find.

The whole thing was probably connected with the French nuclear test at Mururoa, and there had also been rumors in the "scientific control" section of the K.G.B. that French scientists had been working on some kind of completely new device and were at the threshold of a breakthrough in the field of energy. It was inconceivable that an agent of his standing would be sent on an improvised mission without being given a more complete picture. It could mean only one thing: the Kremlin was hard on the K.G.B.'s back and, as it was always the case in such a situation, the K.G.B. panicked.

He loaded the revolver and put it in his pocket. He was so out of practice that he felt almost like an American

116

gangster. They were sending a colonel on a bayonet charge.

The man whose name was not Victor Turkassi was a Georgian with the shoulders and chest of a wrestler and thick wild eyebrows that looked even thicker and blacker under a bald head. A short hooked nose above a moustache and brown eyes like cockroaches. They had often told him he looked like Kaganovitch, Stalin's brother-in-law.

He left the hotel, got into the rented Volkswagen, and drove to Pouaavia, where he parked half a mile from the bungalow. He had explored the location a few hours after his arrival, but had found a Dominican priest and another man arguing by the door.

He walked leisurely around the house, among the banana trees. He had no idea of what the man he was going to kill looked like. Another of Moscow's thoughtful plannings. He would have to strike an acquaintance first, make sure of his identity, and proceed from there.

The lagoon was barely a hundred feet away. The whole thing looked too easy for comfort.

The door was wide open and he walked in, closing it gently behind him. He found himself in a painter's studio. There were a few canvases in a corner, a bed, and a staircase to the left. To the right, there was a curtain made of bamboo and seashells. He walked up to the curtain and raised his hand to draw it aside.

When he saw the muzzle of a gun pointed at him through the bamboo curtain, the man whose name was not Victor Turkassi had the instant reaction of the young agent he had been fifteen years ago. He jumped aside, pulling out his gun, and fired not more than a second later than the man behind the curtain.

The man whose name was not Victor Turkassi caught the bullet in his right side. He heard a groan behind the bamboo curtain, and he drew it apart.

The Chinese was fat, round, and he was sitting on the kitchen floor with his back against the wall, holding his belly in both arms as if he were nursing a baby. Tears were streaming down his well-fed cheeks, and so the man whose name was not Victor Turkassi knew that he was not a professional. He himself felt no great pain, though he knew that his liver and kidney had been hit and that he had no more than ten minutes left of his Georgian strength, reputed to be the toughest in the world. Between ten and fifteen minutes. Then he would be dead.

The Chinese amateur was still crying. On the floor,

117

there was his 8.6 Mauser gun, copybooks, and papers. The kitchen door was open, and from the outdoors came the peaceful sounds of an eternal summer.

The Georgian was still standing. It was no longer his strength that sustained him, but sheer willpower. He caught himself thinking of the wife and son he had left in Moscow; he had always known that in his profession a man should not have a wife and son. Natacha was thirty-three and Vassia was eight. Those were unnecessary, amateurish thoughts. *"Red red."* He had to get rid of his body at any cost before he died. That was all that mattered now. He took a step toward the door, with the intention of disposing of his body by throwing himself into the ocean. But his strength was ebbing fast now, and he dropped into a rattan chair by the Chinese. He looked down and pushed the copybooks on the floor with his foot.

"Anything—there?" he asked in English.

Chong Fat looked up at him with a sort of tender, dumb reproach. The tenderness was for himself and the reproach for the other. "A-american?" he stammered. "Then why? I—work for the Americans—for the free—world. Why—why have you—killed me? Who—who are you?"

"C.I.A."

"Then why? Why wasn't I told—that you were—coming? Why—this? The C.I.A. man here is—"

The man who was not Victor Turkassi was surprised by his own professionalism. A few minutes from death, he found himself watching the lips of the dying Chinese to learn the name of the C.I.A. agent in Tahiti. But Chong Fat was spitting blood now.

"My God," he mumbled at last. "I'm dying. Why—why have you killed me. I'm working for you—for the C.I.A. Why—"

"You fired—"

"I thought it was the Chinese!" stammered the Chinese. "They're here again. They had followed me—I saw the gun—I was scared—"

The man who was for a few more minutes Nikolai Vassilievitch Ordjonikidje sat stiffly in the rattan chair with his head thrown back, losing blood. He saw twenty fat Chinese whirling around him. But at least he was no longer seeing the faces of his wife and son. A needless sentimentalism. His eyes moved down toward the copybooks once more.

"Found anything?"

"Nothing!" whined Chong. "Nothing. Not a clue. Dear God!"

The man who was almost no longer Colonel Nikolai Vassilievitch Ordjonikidje, his eyes closed, clung with both hands to the arms of the rattan chair.

"For nothing!" yelled Chong. "You killed me for nothing!"

No. Not for nothing. The mountains, the children, and the vineyards of the Caucasia of his youth were passing under his closed eyelids. For them. He could see quite clearly the Terek and the *aouls,* and they still were exactly as in Pushkin's and Lermontov's days. For them. He heard steps and managed to open his eyes. He saw the bamboo curtain part slowly and the white figure of a man leaning over him. He made a desperate effort to die before it was too late. He had seen good men betray their country without knowing it, in their last breath.

He got up, hoping the effort would finish him off, and stayed on his feet, swaying, fighting his last enemy, which was what little life he had left in him.

The man whose name was not Tamil was looking at the stranger with the face and body of a Turkish wrestler who stood swaying before him. He grabbed him by the arms, made him sit down, and examined him rapidly. A bullet in the liver. A matter of minutes now.

Then he bent over the moribund Buddha who sat whining on the floor holding his belly in his arms.

"Chong Fat, you damn fool. I told you to keep out of this."

The Best Genuine Cantonese Cuisine in Tahiti was dying fast. Its owner looked up at the French agent with eyes so wide with pain and terror that they were no longer slanted. Outside, the ocean was beginning its evening roar against the reef.

*"Mon—capitaine—*I had orders—Peking— Eleven members of my family—hostages—had to. The Russians —too— No choice—I hate the Reds—but had to— Worked for the Americans—my convictions."

"And for France, out of patriotism?"

A tender smile fluttered briefly on Chong's lips. "Yes—I —am—French. Free French—Pacific battalion—Libya— Bir Hacheim—patriot—*croix de guerre*—*Vive la France! Bonne mère—"*

The man from the S.D.E.C. felt his throat tighten. The only Chinese in the world to speak with the authentic accent of a Corsican gendarme was on the point of joining his ancestors the Gauls.

"That doesn't explain why you were informing the Russians too," he said softly.

"Blackmail. The Chinese—told me—work for the Russians—then tell us—everything— Very difficult—situation for—respectable businessman."

The quadruple agent mumbled something that was more death rattle than words, and his eyes froze forever in an expression of boundless bewilderment, in which the man whose name was not Tamil recognized the very expression of this age. Then he heard the chair creak behind him and, looking back, saw that the Russian was up on his feet again, watching his own death on the other man's yellow face.

"You still have plans, I see?" the Frenchman asked coldly. "Catching a plane, perhaps?"

There were moments, like this one, when he was seized with savage hatred for his times and for all those who made the times what they were, starting with himself.

The man whose name was not Victor Turkassi felt a renewal of strength, the heart's last fight before bursting.

"I'm—an officer—K.G.B.—"

"How do you do, my dear colleague. Delighted." White with anger, the S.D.E.C. man pointed to the chair. "Sit down, *mon vieux*. Make yourself comfortable. A cigarette? How about a Scotch? Or vodka? Don't tell me you must go."

"The French and the Russians—"

"Yes?"

"Friends. You have—no interest—in having *ordinary* police—finding me here. Incident—bad for relations—between our two—countries . . .

"So."

". . . get rid—of my body—"

"All right, but only if you tell me your *real* name," the Frenchman said quickly. This was a golden opportunity. "Can you hear me? We'll find out anyway, but it would save us weeks of routine work. Hey, you, tell me your *real* name and I promise to dump you into the ocean as soon as you're dead. Or even before, if you insist. O.K.?"

The man whose name was not Victor Turkassi lowered his head like a bull about to fall on his knees. "O.K.," he said hoarsely. He straightened up. "My name is Victor Turkassi," he growled and fell dead in the arms of the man whose name was not Tamil.

17

Adam and Eve
in Their Garden of Eden

Cohn's two weeks on the peninsula were among the happiest and most peaceful of his life. Only the most determined tourists were willing to put up with a two-hour pirogue crossing to visit "Adam and Eve in Their Garden of Eden" and there were no signs of danger, no trace of the enemy, almost no fear.

The Napoleon of Tourism had done things with style. He had a hill cleared, not a very high or steep one, so as not to wear out the visitors. The hill dominated a lagoon where madrepores had agglomerated into a fantastically shaped coral. It had a magnificent view over the three Hutu Hutu reefs. Hutu Hutu was the master god who had created other, infinitely less powerful but useful gods; whenever he happened to feel displeased with his work, he would throw it in the sea, and out of such accidents were created some of the Tuamotus and a good third of the Marquesas. Thus spoke Meeva, slowly combing her hair, sitting at the edge of the night, while Cohn lay on the white sand that seemed even whiter in darkness. He watched her outlined against the Milky Way, combing stars out of the sky.

There were distant storms with brilliant marblings that thundered their way through heaven with all the violence of primeval times, when you could see the ruins of the sky fall into the sea. There were other, silent storms; their thunder did not reach the earth because it was stopped on its way down by the guards who watched over the peace of Arii chiefs, asleep in the clouds, which were royal dwellings where these masters of celestial archipelagoes rested after a busy day.

There was an abundance of falling stars, and they were unfaithful wives hurled down from celestial castles by the angry Arii. Actually, the sky did not exist. It was "another land inhabited in another manner."

The Milky Way was really a "long white shark that ate young clouds that had strayed from the herd." It was often crossed by shifting shadows, and it was among those shadows that you had to look for the spirits of the true kings, whom the Pomare usurpers had dethroned.

There were also those who saw in falling stars messengers that a god would send to his kin, carrying the announcement of some prodigious birth. But it was wrong to believe that the land of the sky was all inhabited, for the *ihoide,* or void, still held its own there, and this made all kinds of good things possible, for "nothing had happened there yet, and so anything could still happen." Thus sang Meeva, sitting among the stars, where her body covered billions of light-years; and then, when Cohn would finally pull his goddess under him, he had the impression of entering the Milky Way itself, and after giving her the full measure of his manly powers, his head still full of legends, he would raise his eyes proudly toward infinity and search the awed universe for the few billion new stars with which he had flooded the firmament in his glorious outburst.

In the morning, they went swimming in the lagoon, where the colors were already back at play—dark emerald giving in to the sulfur yellow of the sand, while the sun rose above shallow waters, with the muted grays of coral and the milky-white mother of pearl, broken to bits by the constant motion of surf, hanging its perfect half circle around the "neckless one," as the sun was still called by those who knew how the wicked earth had been decapitated in times past and thus lost its golden head.

Billions of madrepores had fossilized throughout the ages to form gray and violet masses of coral that looked, in their weird tortured shapes, like a petrified universe of grief. The still waters, where sulfur yellow was suddenly giving way to jade, and deep blue to emerald, ended along the reef in an almost perfect circle of orange and rusty brown of weeds and microorganisms, in an ephemeral and yet never-ending interplay of colors, with new shades appearing and vanishing in the wake of the sun.

Cohn was watching lovingly this strange labor of the ocean, where something always seemed on the verge of being born and yet remained absent, only the little flying fish appearing briefly over the surface. He took particular delight in the pearly whites and in the sudden, quickly passing mauves that the eyes would seize, lose, search for, and find and lose again with every change of light.

High above them, the abrupt mountain looked like an ocher fortress facing the battalion of swarming vegetation, with the red of flame trees, the yellow of mimosas, and the white plumes of the knightly bamboos rising above the unruly green peasantry of footsoldiers poised for some floral Austerlitz or Waterloo.

Meeva was swimming through the world of coral, with a flower behind her ear, trailing behind her the long black wake of her hair, which sometimes tangled with weeds or with clumsy little palpitating Sagittaria with lemon-yellow pods. Then, emerging from the blue, she would climb over a city of madrepores and closing her eyes, offer her face to the sun with a feline delight; she would begin to hum, then to sing a kind of inarticulate hymn in praise of life in which the happiness of the voice took the place of both tune and words, rising out of the ocean like that mythical island Cohn was yearning for, where man could find himself once more at his beginnings before the ruin of chance.

Their hut was hidden in a thick grove of coconut palms, fifty feet from one of the waterfalls that streaked the entire peninsula with their innumerable white threads.

The plastic apple trees had been placed on the cleared hilltop; two in bloom, and the third, under which Adam and Eve were entertaining the tourists, covered with tempting bright-red plastic fruit. The pretty nylon snake, painted orange, green, and black, hung limply from a branch. It was battery-operated, and Cohn turned it on when necessary with a hidden switch. Then the snake would lift itself up and amiably proffer to the tourists the apple it held between its teeth. Cohn and Meeva, entirely naked except for a modest loincloth, sat cross-legged under the tree. Meeva spun wool on a fifteenth-century French spinning wheel which, though slightly anachronistic, lent a greater pastoral authenticity to the scene. The tourists snapped their pictures and asked Adam a few questions. Cohn answered in a gentle voice, an expression of happy imbecility spread over his face.

What had prompted him to give up civilization and attempt this return to the source? Cohn replied that he had always dreamed of paradise and had finally decided to pass from idle dreaming to reality.

What had he done in civil life? Cohn's answers depended on his mood and whimsy. As a rule he played his most favorite contemporary cliché, the *ex. Ex*-guerrilla fighter at Castro's side, who had become disillusioned with the revolution and had ended up, brokenhearted, in Tahiti; an *ex*-doctor, who had been for years refusing to perform abortions and was now suffering from terrible remorse at the thought of all the children he had permitted to be born into the world. There was no limit to the *ex*'es he had in stock. Occasionally, he would simply introduce himself as

123

an "ex-'human being,'" leaving the full implications of this statement and of his feeling of happy relief to the imagination of the visitor.

Now and then, when his rage was getting the better of him, he would get up, draw the tourist aside, and whisper to him, "Say, if you're really interested in truth, I've got here some really filthy pictures of Adam and Eve in their earthly paradise. Twenty dollars a set, complete with a few Auschwitz pictures thrown in. Real filth, man, you'll like it —or I'll give you the money back. How about it?"

But the guide Puccioni was watching the outcast with a sharp eye, and Cohn had to be careful. He couldn't afford a falling out with Bizien, who was the only man who could help him now to leave Tahiti and reach that far-off, hidden, secret island that had to exist somewhere out there, in the Tuamotus. So he tried to behave, sitting under the apple tree applying himself to reproduce on his face the happy imbecility of the *maharishu* grin. Puccioni enlightened the tourists with the information that the cycle of biblical tableaux had been initiated in honor of the memory of King Pomare V, who had translated the Bible into Tahitian, skipping over the unnecessary detail of the sovereign's death in a state of complete alcoholic degeneration.

Cohn explored the peninsula and made friends with some of its "white savages," or "nature men." The guidebooks never failed to mention these cave dwellers; some were living there naked since the First World War. "In this century of relentless progress," writes Jean-Marie Loursin, "it is comforting to realize that the region of Pari is sure to remain for a long time yet the quiet hidden paradise of banana-eating blond Adams adoring the god Pan." The idea of "the god Pan" switched from ancient Greece to Tahiti had won Bizien over immediately. Some of the "blond Adams," however, were giving him trouble. Arne Björkman, a young Swedish giant with the features of a Polynesian Viking, who had lived naked in a grotto for the past five years, had become capricious and demanding. After he had been refused permission to fish with dynamite, he had started receiving the tourists dressed in a city flannel suit, tie, and suede shoes, lolling in a plastic chaise longue beside a transistor radio, a glass of Scotch in his hand, reading a novel by F. Scott Fitzgerald. It was pure vandalism. In the end, the authorities relented and looked the other way and he went massacring whole schools of fish with explosives. Another of the "cavemen" was caught posing for Grapps, an American soft drink, but too late: his pictures had already appeared in magazines.

There were a few nature men scattered in caves along the east coast of the peninsula, and Cohn sometimes went to visit a Frenchman by the name of Mahé, whose cave was located less than a mile from the hut. He was one of Bizien's favorites and, of course, he was an *ex*. Puccioni usually introduced him as an ex-captain of a Greek ship who thought he was the last to leave his sinking boat only to discover that he had left six hundred passengers aboard. For German tourists, he had a variant of the *ex* of which he was rather proud. He would point to Mahé, who stood half naked at the ocean's edge, as if turning his back on the world and his own past, and say, "No one really knows who he is, although there is reason to believe— You remember Martin Bormann, the Nazi criminal who vanished—" A pause, then Puccioni would whisper, "Well, one thing is certain. *He's not Bormann.*"

The effect was always most sinister. Mahé had confided to Cohn that he was really an ex-taxi driver from Paris who got fed up with traffic, to which Cohn replied that he himself was an ex-paratrooper in Algeria who was trying to live that one down. Mahé would nod approvingly and tell of his experiences as an ex-Communist Party member morally destroyed by the Soviet crushing of freedom in Prague, then Cohn would shoot back with a detailed account of his latest crimes just about everywhere, you name it, we've got it. Cohn knew perfectly well that Mahé was not a former taxi driver, just as Mahé knew Cohn was not Cohn, and that was enough to create between them a bond of mutual esteem based on that essential knowledge they had of each other.

The traces of man vanished from the earth with every sunset; there were rusty moons at the edge of violet storms. Cohn would leave the hut and walk naked into the twilight. The roar of waves over the rocks was reducing the waterfalls to silence. White flying chariots raised a purple and red dust in the sky and vanished in a fantastic leap over the mountain, while Cohn, faced with such an almost disdainful display of ease and magnificence, attempted to rise above his infinitesimal status and to defend his dignity by whistling back a few notes of Beethoven, as if to tell the universe, "See, we, too, have something to show you."

The nylon snake swayed gently on the plastic apple tree,

Meeva was spinning her wool, the tourists' cameras were busy; between two grins of blissful imbecility, Cohn would occasionally throw one or two of his *maharishu*-like pearls of wisdom to the visitors: "Simplicity is the answer." "Death is life, plus a loss of memory." "Ask me not, for only the unspoken word is true." Then he would burst into peals of a *maharishu*-like, hysterical laughter. Bizien had asked him to laugh a lot, to convey a feeling of the first couple's inner peace and happiness.

Father Tamil came to see them once or twice. He squatted with the couple under the tree smoking his pipe, while Cohn sang for him the praise of the absolute, in the shape of a woman's divine ass. Before leaving, the Dominican would offer the *pícaro* one of his boxes of chocolate candy, of which Cohn, who had a sweet tooth, was very fond.

Once, after hearing Adam sing at length his pagan *ute* of Eve's charms, he told him, "Did you know, Mr. Cohn, that, according to Bovis, the Maori you love so much considered materialism a curse? More precisely, materialism was the curse of *Te Tahu,* which means in language 'complete annihilation'?"

On his last visit, before leaving, he made a show of hiding something clumsily under his robe.

"What's that?"

"Oh, nothing. You won't be interested. Only a newspaper. Five days old. You don't want that *here,* do you?"

This Tamil was a real snake and Bizien should have placed him in the tree, instead of the plastic one.

"Come on, give me that—I knew damn well you had come into my little paradise only to poison it."

The Dominican displayed a mocking smile, as little Christian as possible, deposited the *Figaro* on Cohn's lap together with another box of chocolates, slipped out, and disappeared among the trees.

Adam passed a dreadful night.

The paper informed him that he had made another bombing error in Vietnam, reducing to ashes a friendly village, with twelve men, women, and children. They weren't the right ones.

In China he had shaved the head of a famous actress of the Peking Opera whom he had accused of "revisionism." The girl had leaped from the eleventh floor of a building. It underlined the positive aspect of Mao's China, however. It showed they had eleven-story buildings there.

126

In Brazil, he had caused disastrous floods, leaving more than a thousand dead or missing.

On the fourth page of the paper, Adam learned he was reproducing too fast. At the rate he was going, the earth would soon collapse under the weight of four billion people. That didn't surprise him. They had always told him he screwed too much.

On the other hand, in Germany, he had developed a new fertilizer that would make the most sterile soil blossom. The Jews were finally becoming obsolete.

Adam bled. His whole "I" was one great agony, from the South Pole to the North Pole, and from east to west. He stuffed himself with aspirin, and in the middle of the night, he sought refuge between Meeva's thighs.

She muttered, "Cohn, there're mosquitoes around," without waking up.

In the morning, he looked so ghastly that Meeva assumed a stern, knowing air and picked up her bottle of castor oil. This time Cohn put up a fight. He had at least one thing truly in common with Gauguin, hemorrhoids, and the doctor had told him that they were made worse by all this purging Meeva was forcing on him. And indeed, shortly before the arrival of a new bunch of tourists, he was seized with an excruciating pain in the rectum, a real dagger thrust. He adroitly explored the place with his fingers and felt a hard, unnatural obstacle there. He probed deeper and, with a yelp of pain, extracted a tiny metallic object.

Cohn glared stupidly at the object. It was no larger than a grain of rice, and he couldn't figure out how this perfectly shaped miniaturized ball of steel had gotten into him, or what it could be. One thing was certain. Despite all the frantic efforts he had been making during the past few years to purge himself, the object was none of the two things he had been trying to get rid of: it was neither the world nor his hidden self, even though Hamlet's immortal phrase rang in his memory:

> *I could be bounded in a nutshell, and*
> *count myself a king of infinite space. . . .*

Meeva felt the shiny piece of metal cautiously. "What is it, Cohn?"

"I don't know. The only way it could get there was if I had swallowed it and—" He turned ashen. He ran out, grabbed a rock, and crushed the pellet with a single blow. He kept staring at its electronic entrails, though one glance was enough. It was a microminiaturized shortwave transmitter, the sort of bait modern police make you swallow in order to know exactly where you are and in what direction you are moving. The ghastly bug could transmit over a couple of miles, sometimes considerably farther.

But who, how, and when had they made him swallow the filthy gadget?

He was already casting an accusing glance at Meeva, when the truth struck him.

"The candy, my God!" he bellowed. "The chocolates! It's the Dominican! He's a cop!"

He grabbed the candy box left by Tamil. There were still some twenty chocolates left. He crushed one with a mighty blow. The miniature transmitter spread out its electronic entrails on the rock. King-Kong Cohn started to beat his chest and tried to utter an awe-inspiring war-like cry, but the only sound that came out was a puppy's helpless yelp, and after a few titanic efforts to push some air down through his blocked throat, he gave up. And so it was that one more good fighter went down in defeat and fell K.O.'d to the ground.

18

Tricolor

The French Minister of Cultural Affairs, who was also one of the century's greatest writers, was looking at the photograph on his desk. Colonel Paul Dastier, in charge of the "scientific security" section of the S.D.E.C., while sinking deeper and deeper into the foam cushions of a very unmilitary black-leather chair, was trying to keep the upright stance of a professional soldier in uniform, feeling not unlike a captain going down with his ship. The dean of the Collège de France was standing at the eighteenth-century windows, staring at the Palais Royal gardens outside. The laughter of children was coming from the former playgrounds of long-vanished French kings.

"Yes, it's his eyes," Malraux said. "A kind of furious, angry gaiety. I remember well that—*light,* there is no other word for it. Quite well. As for the rest, there's a vague, familiar something, but the likeness is not as apparent as you say, *mon colonel."*

"Plastic surgery, *monsieur le ministre,"* the Colonel said. "We're almost sure of that."

"What about the voice?"

"Similar, but not quite. In fact, there's a marked difference. However, he may have had some of the vocal cords operated on. We don't know. It's difficult to look that far down a man's throat."

Mercier, his arms crossed on his chest, turned away from the window. "Plastic surgery, vocal cords operated on—I don't believe it. No man would try that hard to get away from himself. As for the eyes—"

He shrugged. Mercier was a tall, handsome man in his fifties, with a strong nose, a Lavallière tie, and a thick, perfectly groomed mane of white hair. Ten years at the head of the greatest French learning institution had left him with the permanent half-tolerant, half-sardonic expression of a man who has reached the limits of knowledge.

"As for the eyes, *monsieur le ministre*—Yes, I too remember what you call the 'light' in them. However, it also burns in the eyes of almost all great charlatans—a desperate gaiety. You can see it in Picasso's eyes—no disrespect intended for our national French-Spanish genius. I think Mathieu is dead."

The Colonel tried hard to give the impression of a rocklike impregnable position, while sinking rather hopelessly in all that decadent foam. "Dead, no, but buried. Buried deep within the man who calls himself Cohn. There are other clues— As you undoubtedly know, Mathieu had always had a strange fixation on Gauguin, even as a student. He had literally enshrined a reproduction of the painter's self-portrait above his desk at the Collège de France. Apparently, he saw in Gauguin the embodiment of some kind of basic innocence. Mathieu was obsessed by what he called 'our criminal destruction of environment, of the very air we breathe, of nature itself.' He had hundreds of scientists sign his nineteen-sixty-six manifesto against 'industrial and technological rape of life.' "

"Karkhoff," Malraux said.

The Colonel just stared.

"Yes," Mercier said, nodding. "The most famous of all the 'conscientious objectors,' I'd say."

In the ashram of Pondicherry, Karkhoff, whom Niels Bohr and Pahlen considered perhaps the greatest theoretical physicist of the age, had for twenty years been translating Vergil into Sanskrit, destroying even this humble contribution as he went along.*

Yet the world knew nothing about some of the world's most famous and gifted men whose refusal and dissent in face of the fantastic misuse of science and murderous technological and industrial rape of environment was taking the form of total withdrawal from scientific research.

"He saw in Gauguin a lover of life. And the whole tragedy of Mathieu was that he loved life too much. A crippling addiction—for a nuclear scientist."

"Thank you, *mon colonel*," Mercier said dryly, without a trace of irony, which was his favorite form of irony.

The Colonel's face reddened slightly. "What I mean, *monsieur le professeur,* is that a certain obsessive worshiping of life explains the no less obsessive preoccupation with genes, damage to environment, et cetera. All excess ends in morbidity. In Mathieu's case, it had become a neurosis, if not worse. He was bombarding the U.N., the Human Rights Commission, the governments, with vehement protest telegrams. Linus Pauling and Lord Russell are timid objectors compared to Mathieu. He was what we've come to call in France an *enragé.* A passionate, uncontrolled, antiscientific passion burning in a scientist's heart— Strange."

"A rage largely directed at himself," Malraux remarked. "If I remember correctly his last speech in New Delhi called for 'total abstention' in every scientific field even remotely connected with warfare. Yet he was unable to control his own creative urge. It was an almost artistic compulsion. Of course, his personal guilt feelings can easily be traced to the fact that it was his own brilliant work, his famous shortcut, that has made it possible for France to build the nuclear weapon that is to be tested soon in Mururoa. That is why, in my opinion, he's gone there—if it is him, of course. The murderer returning to the scene of his crime."

The Colonel nodded. "He has always been a very unbalanced person."

"Poets have always been laughed at as 'unbalanced' throughout the ages, or, in contemporary language, frowned at as security risks," Malraux said curtly. "I have known Mathieu. He's always considered himself as a *poet.* For him scientific research was pure, disinterested pursuit of poetry, of 'cosmic music,' in his own words. Now, when

Le Figaro, October 27, 1967.

other people grab your poetry or your music and turn it into a hundred-megaton bomb, it hurts."

"Two nervous breakdowns and one attempted suicide to get rid of his 'guilty head,'" Mercier said. "It is rather difficult to deny that right now the relationship between the governments and culture is rather like turning Shakespeare's work into a weapon of mass destruction."

He shrugged, looking sadly at the perfectly proportioned, carefully balanced gardens of the Palais Royal, with their geometrical design that bore the almost Cartesian mark of the Age of the Enlightenment, when man's newly acquired faith in his intellect and reason seemed to open unlimited vistas of happiness before him.

"It is only too easy to understand why he adopted Gauguin as his 'patron saint,' if I may put it so. A quite normal reaction against our misuse of our intellectual powers, of our brain. After all, the young people all over the world, all these flower kids and their love-ins, follow a similar pattern. It's Gauguin against Von Braun and Teller, lust for life against the scientific and technological 'overkill.' How far can you go against intellect without becoming a Nazi? In our kids' eyes, the answer is love—and sex. 'Guilt' for them is located in the head, not in sexual behavior, not in the rapport of the body with the fruits of joy. Quite obviously, in this mystique, Gauguin becomes a 'holy man,' the first dissenter, a kind of—no blasphemy intended—a kind of Christ of joy. Of course, Mathieu was an extreme case. During the London protest march in nineteen-sixty-three he was arrested for indecent exposure. He was at the head of the British students, three hundred of them, who had shown their bare ass to the police in Grosvenor Square. I did scold him a bit after that. A professor at the Collège de France— The answer was typical. 'There's nothing indecent about the ass. It's our head that needs looking into. I don't give a damn about what people do when they take their pants off. When it's havoc, beastliness, and murder, you'll always find them all dressed up.' That's Mathieu for you—"

"What are the *facts?*" Malraux asked.

The Colonel cleared his throat. "Well, for one thing, the character evidence is overwhelming. As everyone who had known him remembers, Mathieu's pattern of behavior was not at all one we usually associate with that of a scientist. The eccentricity, the exuberance, the revolt—*la bohème*, you know. The way of life of a nineteenty-century *poète damné*, Rimbaud, Verlaine—or of some of those incredible kids today. There was no end to scandals. The scientific genius had turned up in the wrong man, so to speak. Drinking, of course. As for sex—outrageous, really."

"An excessive love of life, you've called it that a while ago, *mon colonel*," Malraux observed, smiling. "It always leads to despair—if only because an excessive love of life calls for immortality."

"As a rule, scientists are self-centered, highly responsible, nonerratic individuals, *monsieur le ministre*."

Mercier laughed. "I could have your hair standing on end, *mon colonel*. But I won't quote any names. There's no such thing as a 'character pattern' that would be specific to scientists or artists. I admit Mathieu was an extreme case. Let's remember he was very young, the youngest physicist ever elected to the Collège de France. Twenty-eight years old then, if I remember correctly. It's true that he was a scientific prodigy whose behavior fitted our idea of an 'artist,' but this is merely changing one cliché to another. Also, do remember that he *was* a true artist, as true as Beethoven or Gauguin. It seems that you sorrily underestimate the inspired, poetical nature of theoretical research. Besides, it has always been my opinion that Mathieu deliberately overemphasized his antisocial behavior, sex, et cetera, as one of the aspects of his total dissent. By 'total' I mean not merely a refusal of society, but of the biological, moral, and intellectual 'historical' man. No wonder he was seeking release in sex. Besides, a 'genius' —I hate that word—in terms of understanding of the universe and of one's place and role in it, is often a tragic figure, because he constantly bangs his head against a wall, a wall that is the limit of our understanding. He knows that he will never know. No matter how far we search within the universe, the essential answer, or question, that of man's nature, place, and role within it, remains as much a question mark as in prehistory."

Malraux nodded. It was one of his lightning-quick, almost spasmlike nods. "And what happens when you reach the peak of knowledge and you find nothing but the same old mystery there?" he said. "You may find yourself seeking relief from longing and responsibility in *the fall*—Dostoevski, you know. *The fall* is a very respectable literary institution, but it's an illusion, of course. No matter how low you sink, you always find the whole world waiting for you there. *The fall*, yes—this indeed is, in my eyes, the strongest psychological argument for your theory of Mathieu-Cohn. But your man may still be a mere charlatan— or rather, a truly inspired charlatan, from what we've heard. Any other *proofs?*"

The Colonel waited a moment with a fine feeling of suspense. "We were able to get a specimen of his writing."

There was silence. The Army was modestly enjoying its brief moment of superiority, in the presence of two of the greatest minds in France.

"Not much, mind you. A few shreds of filthy paper. I'll spare you the details. Most of the time, this fanatic goes out on the beach in the middle of the night and writes in the sand, by moonlight. Then he shuffles his feet and destroys everything he has written or waits for the ocean to wash it away."

Malraux seemed delighted. There was something like true admiration in his grin.

"You mean he is still *working?*" Mercier asked. "But then, yes, of course he would. This is a compulsion. There is nothing he can do about it. Except to tie a stone around his head and— He has tried that once."

"Anyway, inasmuch as we can tell, the handwriting is that of Mathieu. Though in all frankness our experts would need more specimens."

"What is he working on?" Mercier asked.

"Not enough elements to tell. He even seems to be using some personal code."

"His last known work dealt with antigravitational research," Mercier said moodily. "My God, what a terrible waste!"

The Colonel sighed. Who could tell what magnificent new weapon France was losing? "That was when he had that nervous depression," he said. "His colleagues at the Collège de France are certain he was on to something truly big. Then the attempted suicide. I feel this was a tragedy. His refusal to work for his country, I mean. We've done everything we could to find out what he was up to, we succeeded in taking infrared pictures of his writing in the sand. Impossible to make any sense of it. New symbols, of his own device. We've gone through every shred of paper in his house—nothing. A truly fiendish determination."

"What was it that first attracted your attention to that man?" Malraux asked.

"We were conducting a thorough check on everybody in Tahiti, since it was the closest location to the nuclear-test site. Then we found out that burned-fingertips business. At first we thought it was some ordinary criminal. But then the other facts we've been talking about came up. For instance, the nights he spends 'composing,' as you would say. Writing his illegible formulas in the sand, and then

133

wiping them away— What fanaticism— what hate, yes, what hate! How can a civilized man—"

"All right. What steps have you taken?" Malraux cut him sharply.

"Every possible step. He's being watched night and day. There seems to have been at least one assassination attempt. There will undoubtedly be others. That's why I am asking your permission to tell Mathieu that we know who he is, even if there's a risk of another suicide attempt or defection. This hide-and-seek game is highly dangerous. It could end in disaster. France cannot afford to lose him or even to run the risk of letting him choose *the other side*. Let me put it this way: no great Power can afford to have Mathieu working against it. That goes for everyone, including us. His brain is of an invaluable industrial and military value, and the man himself is totally unpredictable. For all we know, he might suddenly decide to go along with Russia or China. This is a maximum-risk situation. Nothing is more dangerous than a brain of that caliber left free to do as he pleases, to go along with whom he chooses to go. We have to talk to him. We have to ask him to come back. It will be a tremendous loss for humanity if a man like Mathieu is killed, if he *has* to be killed, by the Russians, by the Americans, or by *us*—"

The Colonel felt instantly that he had gone too far. In fact, one quick glance in Malraux's direction told him that if eyes could burn, he would be on his way to the hospital.

"Needless to say, we have no such intention," he added lamely. "France—"

"Right, *France*," Malraux cut in in a dry, razor-sharp voice. "May I ask you to keep that word in mind?"

Monsieur le ministre,—"

Malraux was glaring at him furiously.

"You forget one little thing, *mon colonel*," Mercier said slowly. "You forget that Mathieu may not know any longer that he is Mathieu."

The Colonel kept staring at the illustrious "father of the laser." "You mean—"

"Yes, that's exactly what I mean. I'm not even talking about the electric shocks he received during his last breakdown. Neither am I talking about amnesia."

The Colonel gasped. "Lobotomy?" he asked in a curiously stricken voice.

"If a man goes as far as to have facial surgery, burn his fingertips, have his vocal cords operated on, break with himself as completely as possible, he can also have a frontal lobotomy performed, so as to dissociate himself totally

134

from his *misued*—misused by others—brain. But that's not what I am talking about. There's something else, and it is well known in psychopathology. There is a German word for it: *Selbstverdammung*. A deliberately self-triggered and yet absolutely authentic loss of identity. It is convenient to call this a 'psychotic situation.' Maybe so. But a conscience that cannot adjust to an unbearable fact often manages to suppress that fact from its consciousness. I told you a minute ago I did not believe your man *is* Mathieu. Allow me to make a correction. I believe your man is *no longer* Mathieu."

19

The Immortal

Cohn was paddling away with the force of a Viking racing against the pirogue of a Maori chief, and the craft was leaping forward over the waves with such a majestic display of power that Cohn knew that Justice, Dignity, and the Rights of Man were paddling by his side, though the outboard motor did not help a bit.

The thought that the enemy had treacherously invaded his bowels filled him with an indignation that the angry roar of his brother the ocean seemed to share. He had left Meeva wondering what *tupapau* had got hold of her Cohn, who now had but one thought: to get his hands on that fiend Tamil and send him to the hospital for six weeks, preferably with a few broken ribs.

In the village of Finae, a providential bus that Justice had placed there for him was waiting for its driver, and Cohn, to the great delight of the passengers, jumped in the seat and drove away, while Kuono the busman was galloping after his vehicle yelling, "Fire, fire!" the only word of alarm he was able to think of in his distress.

For the next five hours, the bus made a wild tour of the island, gradually losing its passengers, their chickens, bicycles, and baskets, while Cohn visited more churches, missions, and religious establishments than a good Christian in a lifetime. At the convent of Saint Joseph of the Little Apparition, he spread terror among the good sisters, whom he accused of hiding Tamil under their beds. He found no trace of the traitor, as if God himself were keeping the latter informed of Cohn's movements; then the bus gave up the ghost when it ran out of gas at Point Venus. Ten minutes later, a jeep pulled up; Cohn was grabbed by two gendarmes and driven to Papeete, where he was given a moderate beating and locked behind bars. He felt a bit better there. It was a pleasant feeling to find oneself on the right side of Law and Order once more.

Ryckmans wasn't there. It was "Saint Ryckmans Day," as the local cynics called it, the anniversary of the death of Modigo Tohe, who had been deported by the then Chief of Police of Batanga to Snake Island, eleven years ago, and who had died of fever in captivity. On September 18 each year, Ryckmans' photograph was displayed in every school of the African Republic of Batanga, and children were invited to spit on it. On that day also, Ryckmans had invariably his yearly psychosomatic attack, his face bled and he exuded a strong smell of roses like Saint Judas the martyr, for without him Modigo would have been nothing now, one more overthrown Nkrumah or a Keito threatened with Army revolt.

At seven A.M. the next morning, Cohn was served fried eggs, coffee, butter, toast, and a Havana cigar; then he was released with the sergeant-in-charge's apologies. Governor's orders, he was told by that completely stunned n.c.o. who kept staring at Cohn with cowed bewilderment.

Cohn shook his head. "I wonder how they found out?" he muttered. "You can't keep a secret nowadays. All I wanted was obscurity. How on earth did they manage to learn that I was de Gaulle's illegitimate son?"

The sergeant blinked, then his limbs crawled slowly to attention.

It took Cohn three hours by truck to get back to his pirogue at Port Phaeton. The fishermen there warned him that a storm was gathering and that he should not be provoking the great Papatoa, who was already blowing from the north and was known to consider all pirogues he found in his path as an intolerable insult. But Cohn attempted the crossing all the same, and he told the fishermen that if that old fart Papatoa should indeed rise in all his windy might, he, Cohn, would show him what the frail human breath could accomplish against all odds.

Cohn was fed up with Power in all its forms.

The sky threatened him with its black ink; the waves were lifting the motor higher than the collapsed sun, its purple skullcap vanishing behind each liquid wall; the reefs kept aiming at him in the greenish light of the day's rigor mortis; but Cohn reached the other side of the bay safely, which merely proved that his troubles were far from over and that life still had some new and even more fiendish blows in store for him. Ruling the waves, Cohn became so intoxicated with the fight that he began to sing a *ute* of confidence and hope, as a tribute to himself as well as to all the other human Vikings who had been forever challenging the universe with a paddle.

Meeva, who was watching her brave *popaa*'s crossing from a cliff, kissed him proudly as he reached, still singing, the top of the steps that had been carved in the rock for the convenience of visitors.

They stood huddled together watching the fireworks.

The storm was splitting the vault of the sky in a roaring, animal frenzy, and when the flashing cracks showed above their heads, there was a moment of total silence and stillness, and nature seemed poised at the edge of a liberating outburst that never materialized, as if some imperious taboo were holding it back. Then a new rambling promise came to deepen the frustration, the obscure labor of unseen forces, the heaving and the tension and the heaviness. Not a drop of rain from an atmosphere gorged with liquid, a vague third world, neither sky nor ocean. There were, captured in these mauve and gray celestial swells, weird, crazed birds that Cohn had never seen before and that the storm carried along from distant archipelagoes. The ghostly mountain floated above the mist, reverberating with the uproar of unearthly happenings. And then again the sudden yellow claws of the dark, violet- and purple-bellied dragons appeared heavenly, and Cohn sought in vain to recapture in their problematic existence a delicious feeling of primeval terror and awe that mere electricity was quite unable to offer. But at least Meeva's hand trembled in his, and he had to do with that.

"Let's go in, Cohn. I'm scared. They're mad at us up there—"

"They—" For a fleeting moment Cohn was thus able to savor "their" mythological presence and the long-lost naïveté of the earth. The hut was barely visible in the misty sweat of ocean and sky, and the coconut palms waved their glittering crowns graciously, with the blissful unconcern of royal families who mistake a revolutionary crowd for a cheering welcome. The great Matai held his breath and, the clouds herded against the mountain, waited for the kill in panting immobility, casting an occasional thunderbolt like a doomed bull's blind thrust of horns. The ocean had vanished under a vaporous mass,

137

only furtive white shudders of foam showing around the reefs in the wake of invisible waves.

Cohn devoured the chicken stuffed with bananas Meeva had heated up for him while gigantic shadows danced on the grass walls and vanished each time a moth burned in the oil lamp. Outside, the storm still labored in its heaving pregnancy; there was nothing but a shattering stillness and the incipient coolness of liquid masses suspended in the sky. He collapsed on the bed, and Meeva snuggled against him and fell instantly asleep in his arms. He felt her thigh against his belly and all the flashing apparitions of a yellow world outside the window faded away in the warm thickness of the black, glowing hair flowing over his face.

Once, when the heavens hurled a particularly majestic thunderbolt against the mountain, Meeva stirred and woke up for a few seconds to murmur, in tender reproach, "You eat too many bananas, Cohn."

He didn't know how long he had been asleep when he felt a sudden apprehension that became anxiety as soon as he became aware of the beating of his heart. He lay still, trying in vain to control the growing terror born out of the extreme frustration of the storm that surrounded him with its raging impotence and its ephemeral fires. But the fear was now becoming a panic, and Cohn slipped out of bed and walked naked into the night. He was instantly caught in a thickness of damp wool, and for the first time since he had known the Tahitian night, not a single firefly came to brighten the darkness with its earthbound star.

Shuddering, he went back into the cabin, then rushed out again and started to run until he found himself at the top of the hill surrounded by a white pulsating brightness of the electrical storm.

He was gripped by an animal terror, a premonition of immediate danger so vivid that he turned around suddenly; it was then that he caught sight of the two silhouettes outlined against the flickering white night. Relieved by this apparition, which was merely human, Cohn raised his hand in a friendly wave and greeted them with a welcoming "Ahoy!"

What happened next was so totally unexpected, and was followed in such a rapid succession by other and no less stunning events, that Cohn simply stopped thinking and feeling and stood frozen in the constant silent fluttering of lightning that kept him in its throbbing spider's web.

The two men were facing him and he clearly saw the machine gun pointed in his direction. At the same instant, a long, insistent burst of fire erupted from somewhere to his right, and he saw the two men falter, drop their weapons, and fall to the ground in a friendly heap, while another volley of shots followed, as if to make sure of their immortality.

Cohn did not move. He no longer had legs. He wanted to yell, but all he managed was a kind of puppylike yap.

The entire hill was held in the mortal brilliance of continuous silent electrical discharges. Then the *huano no* pulled in its yellow claws and the night covered again the immodest nudity of the earth.

A hand touched his shoulder.

"Help!" bellowed Cohn, who did not want to die without uttering one of those inspired words that sometimes sum up in a flash man's entire history since the beginning of time.

"Come now, Mr. Cohn. Calm down. It's all over."

Tamil. Cohn looked at the Dominican and at the machine gun in his hands without surprise, for his total stupor left no room for further astonishment. The beam of a flashlight stabbed the darkness. The two bodies lay one on top of the other, in reassuring immobility.

Tamil was wearing the black raincoat and cape of a Breton fisherman over his white robe and kept his hand on Cohn's shoulder. "You're out of danger. They're nice and dead. Come over. See for yourself."

The two Chinese had their eyes wide open, staring emptily at emptiness.

Cohn had never seen them before. "Why on earth—"

"They only wanted to kill you, Professor Mathieu. Quite a lot of people have been trying that. You've been quite a worry to us."

Cohn swallowed hard. "This is an obvious case of mistaken identity," he said grandly, though being stark naked did little to help this display of haughtiness.

"Of course, of course. Come on. I think it'll be wiser to let your girl sleep in blissful ignorance. Some people never get used to the sight of stiffs. In my profession—I mean, as a churchman, of course—"

"Spare me your cynicism."

"I'll have my two yellow colleagues out of here in no time. We'll find them an idyllic little cove with welcoming water—as the tourist brochures say. In the meantime"—he put his arm around Cohn's shaking shoulders—"I think a jug of hot wine will take care of your gooseflesh, Professor —I mean, Mr. Cohn. Your friend Mahé will be happy to extend to you the French Navy's famous hospitality."

Cohn groaned. "Mahé? Tell me, is there anybody at all in Tahiti who is not a cop?"

"Undoubtedly," said Tamil in a tone that aroused Cohn's suspicion because of its excessive emphasis. "However, we do have fifteen thousand soldiers here. With the Mururoa nuclear tests coming up, all the big Powers have sent some discreet observers. And then, of course, last but not least, there was you, Mr. Cohn. I presume you'd rather keep that amusing name for the time being. For France, and for other naughty, naughty Powers, your brain is much more important than fifteen thousand soldiers, or even than the Mururoa tests themselves. God only knows what new and brilliant flowers of genius may be blooming right now in that wholly unpredictable and compulsively creative mind of yours. We treasure you. Believe me."

Cohn by now was ready to believe anything. Tamil led him away, cowed, naked, and trembling, and even though there were still some admirable flashes of lightning and roars of thunder in the sky, the fugitive had now so little fight left in him that he didn't even have the dignity to answer these majestic affectations with a few resounding farts. He was out of breath.

"We had to set up a whole organization to protect you, Mr. Cohn. No doubt you'll be pleased to know that you're costing the French taxpayer half a million francs a year, not counting the sleepless nights of the man responsible for your safety—your humble servant."

Ten minutes later Mahé, or rather Chief Warrant Officer Mozon, was welcoming them heartily to his cave. The "nature man" was wearing his Navy uniform and with him there were two heavily armed marines in paratroopers' battle fatigues. Mahé-Mozon saluted Tamil smartly and Cohn, caught naked in the net of implacable reality, released a torrent of insults on the head of the false *ex,* or *ex-ex.* Mahé listened to this string of pearls with the quiet interest all French military always show for literature. Then he invited them to what he termed the "Navy mess." Behind the heavy plank door Cohn knew so well, there was a wireless set and two frogmen, whom Tamil instructed to take care of the dead Chinese in such a way that they would not rise to the surface again.

Cohn collapsed into a chair and closed his eyes. He opened them again only after two jugs of hot wine, which Mahé served him with sugar and cinnamon. The two S.D.E.C. men were looking at him with that solicitous attention butchers always show to prime meat.

140

"Feeling better?"

Cohn mumbled a few insults, but they lacked true inspiration and sounded rather like an admission of defeat. Mahé got out a uniform for him, but Cohn refused indignantly to put it on. Bare-assed he was and bare-assed he would always remain, despite all those garments of light in which the greatest charlatans of history were attempting to dress the eternal cur. He gulped some more of Mahé's stuff, and the wine was now bringing back some of that sacred indignation without which a man's heart withers away.

"Why did they want to kill me? I mean, apart from the general consideration that man is something that cannot be tolerated?"

Tamil looked hurt. "Mr. Cohn, you are much too informed a person to ask such naïve questions."

Cohn's eyes narrowed. His hand tightened around his glass. His powers were returning, and with them that aggressive irony which was the only weapon the infinitely small could use in battle against the infinitely great. The weapon could not achieve victory, but it helped the helpless to survive.

"Even with Gauguin, they didn't attempt a downright killing," he said. "He was a thorn in their side, a living challenge to Law and Order, and yet they did not use a gun on him. Why me?"

Tamil nodded approvingly. "It was a very interesting idea," he said. "The choice of Gauguin's character, I mean. What could be farther removed from technology and science than this embodiment of lust, love for life and nature? Yes, a perfect disguise. The two poles of man's psyche and history. Oppenheimer and Gauguin. You've tried very hard, *monsieur le professeur,* and you did brilliantly."

"Funny," Cohn grumbled. "We don't have, in French, an equivalent to 'kiss my ass.' There's always been a cultural gap between America and France."

"Continue, by all means. You're very convincing. It's almost as if your beloved nature had blundered somewhere along the road. A mix-up in genes. Scientific genius found its way into a man who had the psychological makeup of an artist, and the artistic gifts intended for him went elsewhere. Yes, you did that very well. But you never had a chance. We've always known. And not only us. A distinguished Russian colleague and a good Chinese agent killed each other a few days ago. Two dead. Then three more, plus two tonight."

141

Cohn added up. "That's not nearly enough, seven dead," he stated soberly. "They underestimate me. I deserve a lot more than that. Remember that with my Mururoa effort alone, you'll be able to destroy an entire capital. Am I or am I not the father of the French bomb? Seven dead! That's what I call ingratitude."

He was beginning to enjoy himself. It was rather fun for old Adam to be changing identity once more. He had been Attila the Hun, Genghis Khan, Saint Louis, Napoleon, Pasteur, de Gaulle, not to mention Eichmann—why not the father of the French hydrogen bomb? A man is a man is a man, as Gertrude Stein once didn't say, and that meant there was no backing away from anything.

"That terrible Foucault," he mumbled. "The latest in philosophy, you know. Not only does he announce the 'imminent end of man,' that hangover from the humanistic age, but as the bastard refuses to die, he decides to hasten his demise. He tries to have me killed. I call that cheating."

"Very funny," Tamil said. "No end to laughs. They won't miss you the next time."

Cohn thought it over, then shook his head. "Nothing doing," he said firmly. "I am immortal."

"Then have another drink."

Cohn did. What else could a man do when faced with his real self and a no-exit sign written all over his skin? He had a drink and another and another.

A yellow web of lightning hung over the grotto's entrance, then darkness again and a distant roll of celestial drums—

Tamil was looking at him with curiosity. "You suffer from a case of moral elephantiasis, Mr. Cohn," he said. "A gigantic swelling of moral conscience, that is. The megaloguilt of people like Bertrand Russell, Jean-Paul Sartre, and yourself is a case of monstrously inflated ego, inflated to the point that your skin ends up covering the whole globe. They—and you—resent mankind's misbehavior as a personal offense. You don't seem to realize how incredibly aristocratic such an attitude really is. You should stop torturing yourself the way you've been doing for the last three years."

Cohn glared at him. "I've been torturing myself for the last two thousand years, and that's a minimum!" he roared.

"Yes, yes, we all know you have it in you. But even without you, without your shortcut, France would have found a way to build a nuclear weapon and it would have been tested here. So all this drama of coming secretly to Tahiti, the scene of your 'crime,' all this mimicry and acting out of your total dissent, your ironic 'aggression' against our present moral and intellectual ways— An overinflated conscience can be treated and cured. Your doctor in Paris, Dr. Birdek, who took care of you during your two last breakdowns, could certainly, had you given him the chance, restored you to that peace of mind and absence of remorse that a great scientist needs to pursue his work today, whatever the consequences. Scientists should shrug off 'consequences' for which they cannot be held responsible, and this is exactly what is known as 'disinterested research.' "

Cohn was no longer listening. The terrors of the night, the exhaustion, and the three jugs of wine were now leaving him in a semicomatose state where all that remained of his consciousness was a longing, confused and yet shattering in its intensity.

"I am looking for the face I had before the world was made—" he muttered and brought his fist down on the table with such force that a roll of thunder echoed through heaven.

Tamil laughed. "Congratulations," he said, but the irony was lost on Cohn, who vomited, slid from the chair, and fell to the ground in merciful oblivion.

Tamil took a cigarette and lit it.

Mozon shook his head. "I still can't believe it. I can't imagine a man capable of willfully suppressing his true self so completely. If he is Mathieu, then he no longer knows that himself."

Tamil shrugged. "That's what they think in Paris too. They're convinced that he's suffering from a total loss of identity. Deliberately self-triggered. In psychiatric terms, Machner's *Selbstverdammung*. They're wrong, of course."

Mozon helped himself to the wine. "And what if he were deliberately, cunningly trying to make us believe he *is* Mathieu?"

"Risking his life? To what purpose?"

"Sheer hate."

Tamil threw his cigarette away. "The Army does not pay you to have that much imagination, my friend. It would take a hatred of heroic proportions. Besides, you seem to forget that our most helpful, if amateurish agent has supplied us day by day with small but conclusive facts about our friend here, and the total of these tidbits amounts to an overwhelming evidence."

Mozon sighed. "I don't know. What I *do* know is that

143

no one can keep away from his true self with such an unfailing determination."

The captain nodded. "Nothing new there," he said.
"The Jesuits knew all about that. For them a man who
keeps away from his true nature with an unfailing determination, as you put it, is the very definition of moral and
spiritual progress."

His ironic eyes remained for a while on the naked
human form lying in its vomit on the floor of the cave. "A
puritan," he said slowly. "Difficult to believe, but true. An
extreme case of human yearning for dignity. And the ulti-
mate release from this torturing thirst is *the fall*. You see,
it isn't so much his personal contribution that crushes him.
More likely, it's the millennia of universal guilt, including
that of the quiet and unknown Power that gave birth to
man in the first place. Very difficult. No wonder he's been
so desperately trying to become a cur. There's got to be
peace and innocence in being a cur. Or is there?"

Mozon emptied his glass and looked at the prehistoric
creature lying on the floor of the cave in all its nakedness.
"Well, I guess it isn't easy, *mon capitaine,* to be a great
man and *only* a man, all in one."

"It isn't easy to be a man, period," the Captain said. "So
he's trying to get rid of the scepter and the crown. All
right, give me a hand. Let's carry our Adam back to his
Eve. Who knows, maybe they'll start something different
this time."

20

The Balance of Terror

Meeva's bare breasts sailed among the stars as she sat paddling at the head of the pirogue, while Cohn, one hand on
the tiller, the other clutching a bottle, watched the paddle
plunge now into the Milky Way, now into the phosphorescent cosmos of microorganisms, each of them carrying
perhaps within it the germ of a new universe. He felt like
the great Te Tumu, or "the First One," descending from
heaven for the nuptials with his bride, Atea Nui, or "the
Infinite Brightness," in the great pirogue given him as a
wedding gift by the "god without end," sole master of the

144

"Key of the World." All that was missing were Ferdinand the bull, the Last of the Mohicans, Snow White and the seven dwarfs, and Mickey Mouse.

As for the "god without end," he was probably a French undercover agent. But one still had a right to optical illusions, and as he watched Meeva's paddle move among the light-years, sometimes shaking off a falling star, Cohn raised his face toward the infinite and looked at it as an equal. He, too, was a power to be reckoned with, the great Cohn, the King of Cohns, and he was not to be impressed with aimless shots of rocketing worlds and galaxies on the celestial billiard table.

He was as drunk as the last of the Pomare kings.

An unexpected inspection tour by Bizien had put an end to their idyllic retreat in the Garden of Eden. Since the discovery of a shortwave transmitter in his ass, the new assassination attempt, and the now continuous buzzing of S.D.E.C. agents around him, Cohn had given in to a despair that ended up in an almost uninterrupted bout of drinking. Things came to a head when an Adam reeking of booze began bawling Eve out in front of a group of Dutch, English, and Scandinavian tourists.

Pointing an accusing finger at the little herd of visitors, he yelled, "See them, you bitch? None of it would've happened if you'd taken your pill regularly!"

The tourists were deeply shocked, and Bizien, despite his fondness for Cohn, had to be firm. Adam and Eve were once more driven out of the Garden of Eden.

Now the motor was panting, Cohn was steering, and Meeva was paddling, sitting in a picturesque pose at the head of the craft. From time to time she registered a vehement protest.

"Cohn, it's *fiu*. Why do I have to paddle when the motor's working?"

"It's strictly for artistic and mythological reasons," snapped Cohn.

The *vahine* figurehead, outlined in black among the stars, was a delight to the eye.

He added as an afterthought, "They tried to kill me, you know."

"What? Who tried to kill you?"

"The watchdogs."

"You're drunk, Gene."

"Don't you dare to call me Gene, you vulgar cow! Show some respect, god damn it! I'm that mythological creature, Man!"

And at the proclamation of such unparalleled greatness,

145

Cohn saw distinctly that the stars had turned white and the constellation of the Dog took to flight, its tail between its legs.

Cohn felt better.

But Meeva kept grumbling. "Listen, Cohn, I'm not saying that you're a lousy lover, no, but don't think you're god all the same. Why've they tried to kill you?"

"Those idiots took me for somebody else. Some scientist by the name of Mathieu. Father of the French bomb, Mururoa. That sort of thing. Crazy."

"Well, and aren't you Mathieu?"

Cohn almost swallowed his tonsils. "What?" he roared. "Who, I? You're nuts."

"I don't know, Cohn. Why couldn't you be that man? You're almost anyone I've ever met."

Cohn was pleased. For a *pícaro*, this was a great compliment.

The most urgent thing now was to ensure his security. On the third day after their return from the peninsula, Cohn went looking for Tamil and found him, as he expected, at the H.Q., French Strategic Command, Oceania, in Marshal De Lattre Street. There he handed him a letter.

"Please see that it gets mailed. Since you bastards open all my mail anyway—you may read it."

Cohn was informing Richard Helms, the C.I.A. director, that the offer he had repeatedly made to "Professor Mathieu to continue his work in the U.S.A. was gratefully accepted. Professor Mathieu could be contacted in Tahiti, where he had made himself quite known in certain artistic circles under the name of Genghis Cohn."

"This is a copy," Cohn warned the Captain. "The original's already on its way, as well as similar offers of my services made to China, Russia, England, and even to Albania, just in case it starts to get big too. In case you're interested, it's Matthews, who flew to Ecuador last week, who's taken the letters with him."

Tamil threw the envelope in the paper basket. "You can't be serious. You're a member of the Collège de France."

"Yeah, well, I'm a born defector. I'm willing to defect to anybody, at any time, anywhere. I'm not discriminating. It's all the same shit to me. Besides, my mom was a nice American lady from Sacramento," he added and felt surprised; it was the first time he heard himself tell the truth. "But that's not the point."

"What's the point?"

"I intend to go on enjoying my sex life. The Chinese

146

and the Russians have already tried to bump me off. That still leaves the Americans. Now that they've been informed of my intention to throw all my talents on their side, they'll leave me alone. Why, the C.I.A. will go to any lengths to protect me. You know, I'm sure that Bill Callum is their man here."

Tamil went "tss, tss," shaking his head. "You don't say?" He wasn't even bothering to fake genuine surprise.

"Mathieu they want, Mathieu they'll have. Just ask, we've got it. By the way, you seem not to have paid enough attention to Matthews, the former captain of the *Human Dignity*. He is safely out of your reach now. Continuing his disinterested theoretical research somewhere in South America. *Matthews—Mathieu*—you haven't given it much thought, it seems."

The dark, fierce eyes were laughing, and the Captain experienced a slight passing moment of unease. But for the last year he had been receiving a day-by-day report on Cohn from his most reliable agent and the truth was plain: he was Mathieu.

"Stop trying so hard, *mon cher professeur*. Since your last nervous breakdown—"

Cohn appeared genuinely baffled. "I didn't know it was a nervous breakdown. I thought it was a bad attack of conscience, if you prefer. Can you imagine Leonardo lovingly painting a madonna, for the sheer beauty of it, only to see it turned into a weapon of destruction? And can you imagine what they'd have done with my work on antigravity, if I didn't give that up? Every bit of paper in my house—"

The Captain indulged in one of his thin, steellike smiles. "I know. I also know that for all this exquisite moral conscience, there's been a mistake somewhere along the line. Scientific genius blundered into you, while the artistic gifts that were intended for you fell somewhere else —In other words, you've been miscast. Mixed-up genes. Fate played one of its sardonic tricks on you."

Cohn decided that without the Dominican's white robe, which lay on a chair, Tamil had a thoroughly unpleasant personality.

That afternoon he went to Mother Nouna's for lunch, in Taorea. She always treated him to her famous "pig *poi meia*, as the gods liked it," cooked in banana and pineapple juice.

"What's wrong, Cohn? You look *fiu*. Is it true you'll be leaving us soon? They say you're somebody else. Sit down.

Have some pig. Pig's great for morale. It'll make a man of you. Eat. It's on the house."

Cohn was in a bad mood. He felt so nasty, in fact, that he was almost eager to become Mathieu again. He would go to the Collège de France and invent them something really filthy. Something truly worthy of the destructive breed of these biological and spiritual misfits. Suddenly sickened, he pushed the pig away.

"You don't like it?"

"I've had enough."

Cohn was thinking that God had forbidden the Jews to eat pork because he didn't want them to become a race of cannibals.

Stuffed with *poi meia,* he stretched out for a little siesta in the shade of some *tamanus.* The light was so dazzling that the palms looked like charcoal-black silhouettes against the sky, and in their motionless pirogues suspended in brilliance, fishermen floated in a mirage that was neither water nor air, but a kind of radiant void.

His sailor's cap over his face, Cohn was beginning to doze off when he was suddenly crushed by an avalanche. He yelled, attempted to fight back, kicked someone successfully in the groin, then felt his head burst and felt no more.

When he came to, he saw a good old familiar sight: he was back in jail once more. Through the bars he saw the prison courtyard, and facing it, the entrance to the Kit Kat, where sailors from all over the world rushed to look for the *vahine* of their dreams and left with a dose of clap.

It was the first time the police had resorted to real violence with him. It cheered him up considerably. There was still hope. They'd probably found out that he was not Mathieu after all.

He was sitting peacefully in a corner, not thinking at all —a fantastic intellectual achievement—when he heard a discreet "psst, psst" from the courtyard. He leaped to the window, his vocabulary at the ready. But it was Meeva. She was squatting under the window in her best red and white dress, with three other *vahines* she had brought along to support her in her grief.

"Why do you do terrible things like that, Cohn?"

"What have I done now? Anyway, it's a lie."

"They say you've beaten up Our Lord and Saviour Jesus Christ."

"What?"

"The police are mad. You can get a year, Cohn, for beating up a cop while he was performing his duties."

"Now what—"

Then it came back to him. He had completely forgotten that bit of trouble with Jesus.

It had happened the day before. Cohn had gone fishing, which meant sitting peacefully in his pirogue, leaving the fish alone. He was returning to the *fare,* his head still pleasantly filled with the surf's uproar and freed from any trace of thought, the purpose of all truly fruitful meditation. He ran across Jesus in a papaya grove. He had laid his cardboard cross in the grass and was eating a garlic sausage. There was a bottle of red wine beside him. Cohn had never seen the guy before. It was a new Jesus. The last recruit to play the part, after Le Goff's resignation, was a Belgian who had originally come to Tahiti with the Club Méditerranée.

"Hi."

"Hi."

Cohn looked at the cross. He didn't like to see it like that, lying idly on the ground. It wasn't right. It was made to be on a man's back.

"How's it going?"

"It's no picnic. I've been at it for about a week. Had no choice."

He spoke with a strong Corsican accent, and there were whiffs of garlic every time he opened his mouth. He was picking his teeth with his dirty nails now. Cohn watched him critically. The man didn't look right for the job at all. Heavy set, vulgar, and his crown of thorns seemed completely out of place on his thick skull. His eyes were mean and stupid. At the most, he might have been cast as Barabbas.

"You don't care much for the job, huh?"

"Would you?"

Cohn was beginning to get mad. Somehow, he felt personally insulted. Choosing a lout like this for the role struck him as a provocation. There was a limit to what even the tourists would buy. Bizien was losing his touch.

"The chief of police called me in and barked, 'Pozzo, you're to report for duty to Mr. Bizien at the Tourist Office.' I've been under a two-week confinement for getting drunk on duty, so it was that or the jug. They even threatened to send me back to France, God forbid."

Cohn was beginning to perceive the horrible truth, but he struggled against the evidence. "So you were—assigned the part?"

"Sure," Pozzo said. "I'm a cop."

Cohn roared like a wounded animal and went for

149

Pozzo, his fists flying. The gendarme was no weakling and he tried to put up a fight, but he was up against the mightiest indignation that ever roused a man's heart. The idea that a cop had been chosen to play Jesus was more than even Cohn could bear. Pozzo ended up in a hospital with two broken ribs.

Meeva was staring at her *popaa* reproachfully through the window bars. "Why you beat up Pozzo, Gene?"

"He insulted me."

"They say you'll be in jail for at least three months—"

She began to cry. Cohn's heart filled with warmth. Say what you want, love was a wonderful thing. It had to exist somewhere.

"I'll wait for you all my life, Cohn, even if it takes three months."

Cohn had tears in his eyes. Three months for a *vahine* was much more than what Petrarch called eternity.

"You're a good kid. I love you too. With all my heart. Don't screw too much. You know how they are, the *popaas*. They don't understand it. They'll think you're cheating on me."

"If you wish, Cohn, I won't screw at all."

"I'm not telling you to perish. Just don't do it with too many guys. Stick to half a dozen."

Cohn heard the door open and saw the gendarme Christophe come in. He was the palest and the most shaken cop he'd ever seen.

"Please, we're terribly sorry, Monsieur—Monsieur Cohn. We've made a dreadful mistake."

As soon as he walked into Ryckmans' office Mathieu knew it was all over and that Cohn's days were coming to an end. To his surprise, he didn't mind that. On the contrary. It would be interesting to see what he could do as Mathieu. There certainly were possibilities there.

There was such an expression of fear and respect on Ryckmans' face that Cohn felt almost sorry for him.

"I must explain—I cannot tell you how deeply sorry we all are, Monsieur—Monsieur Cohn."

Mathieu wondered if that brief hesitation was merely the effect of Ryckmans' throat knotted with respect or if he had barely avoided calling him by his real name.

"I'd taken the afternoon off, Monsieur—Cohn. Well, of course, they weren't aware of the Governor's instructions concerning you—"

"What are the instructions, exactly?"

"Utmost discretion—help on every occasion. Corporal Pozzo will be severely punished."

"I'll take care of him myself."

"As you wish. Of course, an artist of your stature—I understand the Governor's been looking at some of your paintings. I was even told he's bought some. Now, the Governor's placed a car at your disposal. Allow me—"

He accompanied him to the car under the completely stunned eyes of the *gendarmerie*. Cohn had the extremely satisfying impression that Authority would never be the same in Tahiti. He helped Meeva into the official black Citroën, as the military chauffeur, cap in hand, held the door open. Meeva looked at her *popaa* in terror.

"My God, Cohn, what have you done now?"

He didn't want to frighten her. Besides, he didn't have his new act completely ready. You can't become Hitler, Napoleon, Joan of Arc, or Mathieu at the drop of a hat. It takes some focusing, some genuine inspiration. You have to get a good feel of your new identity before you can truly give your best. You can't switch from crusader to penicillin, from cathedrals to destruction, and back without a minimum of preparation. Man was the greatest impersonator and the greatest improviser of himself that the galaxy had ever been blessed—or cursed—with, but it still took some time before you could develop and master a new routine of destruction, and the time it took was known as "stagnation" in the history of civilization.

"Cohn, please! What've you done? Why are they all after you? Who are you? Really, I mean. They're saying all sorts of good things about you now. The Tahitians here always knew that you were a bastard, but now they think you're something even bigger than that. Please tell me."

"I'm one of those revered shits who've made it all possible. My personal contribution is the French bomb. The one they're going to explode here, in your 'earthly paradise.' In Mururoa. *E mea haama*. It makes me feel ashamed."

She thought it over. "Well, it's not your fault."

"Not my fault?"

"You couldn't have known they'd drop it here, your bomb. Maybe you thought they'd drop it on someone else."

Cohn was impressed. There was good French logic there.

151

21

Onward, Christian Soldiers

Air France informed him there was a first-class ticket to Paris waiting at their office and would he please notify them forty-eight hours ahead of the day he chose to leave. A motorcycle cop brought him an official envelope, "with the compliments of the Governor of French Oceania." Inside there was an invitation to dinner and a clipping from the *Figaro*.

The French scientist Marc Mathieu, who had disappeared two years ago after leaving a suicide note, is rumored to be alive. The young physicist, who had been deeply disturbed by the decisive role played by his theoretical research in the development of the French thermonuclear weapon, is reported to be recuperating after a long illness in an unspecified location kept secret by the authorities, in French Polynesia.

Two guys he had never seen before were now following him discreetly everywhere. They even prowled around the *fare* at night with flashlights. In the morning, looking for a sandal under the bed, he noticed a small round object stuck on the wall. A mike. He searched the place thoroughly and found two more, one by the sofa on the ground floor, one by the bed upstairs.

Returning home one morning, after a night at sea with the fishermen of Port Puah, he found Meeva squatting on the floor, staring at a mail bag forwarded to him from Paris. There were invitations to symposiums, lectures, meetings; requests for articles, for interviews; letters of congratulation; degrees *honoris causa;* and the Institute of Advanced Studies at Princeton wanted to know if he would accept the position left vacant by the death of Oppenheimer. There was also a personal note signed Chávez, assuring him that "everybody is so happy to know you're getting well. Madeleine and the kids await anxiously to hear from you. Madeleine still loves you."

"Who's Madeleine, Cohn?"

"Obviously that guy Mathieu's wife. The shit's trying to peddle his wife and kids on me."

One morning he ran into Bizien on the terrace of the Vairia. The great promoter greeted him with his usual polite indifference. He asked no questions, but then Cohn couldn't resist showing off in front of such a connoisseur.

"I suppose you've heard the news."

"What news?" Bizien asked, simulating curiosity.

"They've discovered my true identity."

Bizien sympathized. "Terrible."

"An absolutely unique coincidence. Interpol was after me for various swindles, so I had plastic surgery done in Venezuela. And what happens? By one of those freaks of chance, the surgeon gives me almost exactly the features of a great French scientist who disappeared two years ago and who has probably committed suicide. They'd been looking for him everywhere, so naturally they recognized me— Now they're all begging me to go back and to do some more work for them. A better and bigger bomb. How about that?"

"Very nice," Bizien said and went on sucking an olive dreamily.

"Naturally, you don't believe me."

"Oh, but I do," Bizien said politely.

"And you know what? I'm thinking of accepting the offer. Why shouldn't I? They're practically begging for it. I'm going to invent them something so goddamn awful that the whole earth'll be cleaned up for good."

Bizien nodded. "Great. Let me know so that I can go some other place in time."

"After all, I'm capable of almost anything. I'm a man, am I not?"

"It can happen to the best of us," Bizien said.

"I'm capable of almost anything. Hitler, you remember? And Albert Schweitzer? And the Crusades? That's all me."

Bizien's cold little eyes rose slowly from the glass he was holding in his hand and met Cohn's inspired stare.

"The crusades were very poorly organized," Bizien said sternly.

Cohn didn't know if the great promoter was tactfully changing the subject or if he was expressing his regret for not having been there to take charge of things.

Cohn took the bus back to Pouaavia, but continued past it and got off at a stretch of sand and coral past Bengt Danielsson's house. It had been Gauguin's favorite retreat in Tahiti, and Cohn visited it regularly. A light *faarua* was blowing; just strong enough to draw the palms out of their torpor, and their crinoline of shadows undulated gently on the sands, soothing to the eye. The fishermen sat still in their immobile pirogues and looked as if they were themselves caught in a net of light thrown over ocean and sky by some translucid power. The surf lay prostrate on the coral reef. The huge gray crabs darted away and dived into their holes; in thousands of dugouts a miniscule heart was beating in a gigantic terror.

As he walked past a broken pirogue, Cohn came upon a couple making love. The man was a British Labour M.P. who was visiting Tahiti for the World Health Organization. The *vahine* was one of the daughters of the biggest grocer in Papeete.

Cohn stopped, bit a cigar, and watched the fireworks with a critical eye. "How is it?"

The Labourite raised his head slightly. "Get the bloody hell out of here."

But Cohn, in spite of all, was still interested in world affairs. "Tell me, do you think Britain'll make it? I mean, will it succeed in entering the Common Market?"

"Listen, Cohn," the girl yelled. "You have no right to insult me."

Cohn was genuinely surprised. "I'm not insulting you. I'm asking a polite question."

"Just because I'm doing this with one *popaa* doesn't mean that I do it with everybody! Common Market yourself, you bum!"

"All I want to know is—"

"Sit down, old boy," the Englishman said, still striving hard, like a good Socialist, toward the construction of paradise on earth. "Make yourself comfortable. I'll be with you in a minute."

"Do you have a match?"

"You'll find a lighter in the right hand pocket of my trousers."

Cohn leaned over to look in the pocket. He was never to know it, but the gesture saved his life.

The man who was holding the rifle with telescopic sight had already begun to press the trigger. He was standing in a coconut grove on a dune some five hundred feet from Bill Callum's bungalow, and he had taken a good, careful aim when Cohn's head suddenly disappeared out of sight behind the pirogue. He swore and lowered his rifle. The man was a Negro, dressed in a blue-silk suit; he had removed his sunglasses and had put them down on the sand.

154

His companion, who was crouching in front, a pair of binoculars in his hands, relaxed.

"It's all right. Plenty of time. Anyway, it's better to wait till he's alone. No witnesses."

"Well, I could handle the three of them. No problem."

"Sure you can, but we aren't here just to have fun, you know. So don't show off."

Cohn was impressed by this typically English phlegm. You'd think that guy had a third eye someplace. He put the lighter back.

"Anything else I can do for you, friend?" the Englishman asked.

Cohn walked away, a bit hurt. His tactful allusion to the Common Market having been received glacially, he was not going to press his candidacy. A man has his dignity.

He continued on his way. Bill Callum's bungalow was visible now to the left, in its thick garden of *uru* and banana trees on a hill above the beach.

The Negro, whose name was O'Hara and who was one of the C.I.A.'s best sharpshooters, raised his rifle again. At that distance, using a telescopic sight was a waste of talent. He removed it, aimed at Cohn behind the ear, then his head jerked back; he still managed to press the trigger, stood there a moment with a vaguely surprised air, and fell dead to the ground. His companion was following Cohn through the binoculars when he heard the two shots.

"What the—"

He glanced back. O'Hara was lying in the sand with a streak of blood trickling out of the corner of his gaping mouth.

Vessely's stunned freeze lasted just the two seconds it took for the conditioned reflex of a thoroughly trained agent to take over. He flattened himself against the sand and looked around. He saw nothing but scattered palms, too thin to hide a sniper, and Cohn, who was dashing like a hare toward Callum's bungalow.

Only then did Vessely think of looking for the killer in that direction, and what he saw was so completely beyond the grasp of logic that for a few seconds his mind went completely blank.

Bill Callum was standing on the veranda, rifle in hand. It was obvious that he had fired the shot.

Vessely opened his mouth, but his voice was gone. All he managed were a few gasps.

Callum had killed O'Hara.

The agent now had the impression that he had suddenly changed planets, that he was in a different, weird universe totally devoid of meaning. Callum was the C.I.A. "resident" in Tahiti. He was in charge of the whole operation, and yet it was he, Callum—and there couldn't be the slightest doubt about that—who had just deliberately killed one of the two men sent, at his own request, by Operations to do the job. He had killed O'Hara.

Callum had gone raving mad. There was no other explanation.

He had now put his rifle down and was gesticulating madly, obviously trying to attract Vessely's attention. He probably wanted him to get up, and then, with a burst of fiendish laughter, he would kill him too.

The agent crawled to the blue Air France bag by O'Hara's head and opened it. He grabbed the W.T. set and switched it on so high that he could hear the signal coming from inside the house. He saw Callum leave the veranda and run inside. He toned the signal down. For the first few seconds all Vessely could do was to yell profanities, while Callum was panting into the mike, trying to catch his breath.

"You killed him, you fat bastard! Don't try to tell me it wasn't you, because—"

"I'm not trying anything," Callum was yelling. "I know damn well I did it—I had to. There's nothing else I could have done to stop him! I have *orders,* you understand? *Orders!*"

"Orders? What orders?"

"Counterorders, if you prefer!"

"What are you trying to tell me? That Operations gave you the order to kill O'Hara, you— Who gave you the order? Peking?"

"For Chrissake, Vessely, shut up. I'm telling you, I received new orders from Washington. They came in two hours ago. I've been all over the damn place, trying to get hold of you. You were supposed to make contact every three hours."

"We were tailing the guy. There was no time and no place for contact. He took a bus and—" He heard a nasty familiar sound, glanced toward the body, and saw the black face, his glassy eyes open to the flies. He began yelling again. "Holy shit, you'll pay for this Callum. And don't try to tell me Operations gave you orders to kill O'Hara, because I swear to God I'm going to cut your throat, you queer!"

"Have you finished your little bit of hysteria?" Callum

156

was obviously on the verge of hysteria himself. "I didn't receive an order to kill O'Hara, of course not. But there was no other way. You understand? *No other way!*"

He was almost sobbing now, and Vessely calmed down.

"O.K., I'm listening. But you better make sense."

"I received new orders two hours ago——"

Vessely almost blew up again, but he succeeded in checking himself. He couldn't stand the sight of O'Hara's dead eyes. It was the first time a stiff affected him like that. The climate maybe.

"You already said that."

"A double-two order."

Vessely swallowed hard. So Callum had not gone crazy after all. It was much worse than that. Someone much higher up had gone completely nuts in Washington.

"I suppose you know what that means? *Double two——*"

"*The subject's personal security must be assured at any cost,*" Vessely translated automatically.

"Good. I'm happy you're still capable of thinking. Because I myself— Jesus!"

Vessely glanced at the body more calmly now. It was beginning to look all right. An occupational hazard. "Don't get excited, Bill. Look at O'Hara. He's much worse off than you, and he's not a bit excited."

"Very funny— I didn't mean to kill him, of course. I was aiming below the knees. But I'm not a killer. So I missed. Too bad, but that's *his* luck. I had to stop him from shooting somehow. And it was the only thing I could still do. I've been looking for you to tell you that I had new orders, then I came back here and the first thing I see is O'Hara taking aim. Why didn't he shoot the first time?"

"The guy went out of sight. Behind the pirogue, out there."

"I ran into the house, grabbed my rifle—just in time, too. Holy Mother, I was aiming real low."

"You'd better go on a refresher course, Bill. Practice shooting now and then. Preferably on a bottle."

Callum wasn't listening. "The rest of the message says I'm to make sure Mathieu reaches the U.S.A. safely. This, forty-eight hours after your arrival and the confirmed order to kill the 'brain' as a potential defector to the enemy and a threat to the security of the U.S.A. I suppose he's agreed to work for us after all. You know something? This thing's getting out of hand. I mean, that little desperate game the big boys are playing against each other. The brain-power game. Eleven top scientists rubbed off in the last few years, so that this damn balance of terror doesn't tip suddenly to the other side's advantage. The people are bound to wake up sooner or later. It makes less and less sense."

"Well, there's someone here for whom it makes no sense at all, and it's O'Hara. What about the body? We can't risk the French finding it."

"Dump it into the ocean. The sharks'll take care of security. But make sure to get him beyond the reef. Take my pirogue and—"

There was a silence.

"He's coming over here," Callum said. "Stand by."

Cohn was galloping toward the bungalow with the mighty speed of a man who had just heard a bullet whiz past his head. He was convinced that the shot had been intended for him, or rather for Mathieu, and though he wasn't particularly devoted to the latter, he felt it his duty to save a head that harbored such wealth of genius. As for himself, it wasn't that he loved life so much, it was rather that he was afraid of dying.

He made it safely to the door, which was open, and jumped inside.

Callum was standing in the middle of the room, huge stains of sweat all over his flowery shirt, panting heavily. "Wha-wha-what?" he stammered, fighting for breath.

"They—they—sh—sh—" Cohn wheezed away and collapsed in a chair while Callum dragged himself toward the sofa and sank deep into the cushions, his head and neck emerging from his two hundred and twenty pounds like a pale, depraved lily. In Cohn's opinion, the worst thing about the head was the earrings. It didn't help at all to know that they were genuine holy Tahotaki, which meant that they had been blessed by Shiva's left hand, the right-hand blessing being given only to the *tahotaki suma,* after castration to remove the source of all filth on earth. Against these fat cheeks, they looked like an insult to homosexuality.

Callum knew he was repulsive and he hated himself, which was probably the reason for his remarkable career as an undercover agent. The only way he could live with himself was to know that everything about his personality was but a disguise, that his real self was that of a much-praised C.I.A. man. He thought of his loathsome appearance as a camouflage. He'd gotten enormously fat and repulsive the way other good men get killed in the line of duty. He hated Buddhism, Zen, avant-garde intellectuals, and everything that looked like Bill Callum so deeply that he could put up with himself only because he knew that his true identity was elsewhere. More precisely, it was in the files of the Personnel Division, C.I.A., Washington, D.C.

For several weeks now, Callum had been so completely obsessed by Cohn that he was beginning to see him even when the latter wasn't around, just as others see rocks and snakes. His happiest day in Tahiti was the day he had received his orders for "preventive action," but now he had had to shoot one of his own men to save Mathieu. O'Hara's death was a particularly sad loss, because he had been the only Negro killer the C.I.A. could boast about. At a time when the American Negro was demanding equal rights, the presence of a black killer in its ranks had kept the C.I.A.'s reputation clean as far as racial discrimination was concerned.

Cohn's face was haggard, and he was out of breath. So, for different reasons, was Callum. The two men were looking at each other with utmost mistrust.

"What's the matter, Cohn? You look terrible."

"Van Gogh," Cohn said simply, as if it explained everything.

Callum felt a twitch in his left buttock, which was always a sign of a disastrous nervous condition. "What?"

"Van Gogh. He's tried to kill me again. Took a shot at me. Sheer murderous envy, that's what it is. Just because he can't sell a damn painting. Back in Brittany, he tried to cut my throat with a razor, now he's trying to shoot me. I'm telling you, Bill, our Vincent's gone completely off his rocker. They should take him back to that clinic in Arles. Can you imagine that? Coming all the way to Tahiti just to get me, simply because my last exhibition in Paris was such a triumph. Did you know that? There's even talk about giving me the Legion of Honor! No wonder that failure Van Gogh's hopping mad—envious bastard."

Callum's sphincters were all knotted with sheer hate. "Screw you. Keep your crap for the tourists."

Cohn was now feeling an irresistible urge to tell the truth. Exhaustion, no doubt. "All right, Bill. I better tell you everything. You might as well know. Give me a drink."

Callum got up and filled the biggest glass he could find. Then he collapsed on the sofa and closed his eyes. He felt he was going to have a heart attack.

"Bill, I'm sure you know half the story. My real name is Marc Mathieu. I'm some kind of a scientist."

"Oh?"

"Yes. I've made a fantastic discovery—"

Callum closed his eyes again. "Please, don't give me that bull shit, Cohn. You can do better than that."

Cohn nodded. He certainly could. He could hear the ocean shivering in his sleep. The air was filled with a sweet fragrance, always heavier after the day had died, and it suggested the presence of a willing and voluptuous femininity. The Tahitian night again. The sweetest of all the whores in the world. Cohn filled his lungs with its immaterial presence.

"No wonder, Bill, that Law and Order, Power and Authority in all their forms are after me. Trying to get rid of me before happiness hits the world. In their eyes I am the number-one enemy. You see, I've developed a product, soluble in water and air and so infinitely catching that it could completely revolutionize screwing such as we know it. Instead of a few miserable minutes, the orgasm would last six hours and you could go again at will. Paradise on earth. The end of idle screwing. That's what socialism's been always aiming at. Imagine de Gaulle or Mao—"

Callum leaped from the sofa and began to dance a kind of maniacal cha-cha-cha, clutching his fists. Cohn was pleased. To make a mountain of lard dance like that was no mean artistic achievement.

"Get the hell out of here, you pimp!" yelled Callum, stamping his feet. "Out, out!"

Cohn experienced the tragic feeling of having lost a dear friend. "Now, Bill, you mustn't—"

"OUT!" Callum was pointing his fingers toward the door in a gesture of such melodramatic impact that Cohn felt like an unwed mother thrown out in the cold with the fruit of her sin.

"All right, Bill, I'll go. I guess I'm not wanted here. Call me, if you wish to hear the *real* truth—"

Bill Callum let go with a string of obscenities that conveyed for the first time in a tangible manner the scope of his literary talents.

"Thanks, Bill. I'm glad you feel that way."

Cohn emptied the box of cigars, looked for matches, and withdrew calmly from the scene. The night greeted him with her soft caresses. He lit a Havana. In the darkness, the little glow could help a sniper, but he had regained all his cocky self-assurance. He had already handled the Chinese, the Russians, the French, and the Americans, and he was prepared to give the enemy a breathing

160

spell. Besides, by now they were probably beginning to think that he was immortal. As long as man's survival depended on screwing, Cohn felt that he had nothing to worry about.

22

The House of Joy

He reached the House of Joy in a pleasant state of euphoria. The *fare* was half shadows, half shiver, and from the coral laid bare by the tide was rising the heady intimate smell of marine nudity.

Cohn pushed the door.

The *tane* jumped from the sofa, grabbed his pants, and leaped through the window.

"Oh, excuse me," said Cohn.

Meeva remained peacefully on her back, naked and splendidly open. Her contented, completely relaxed air reassured Cohn. His abrupt arrival hadn't spoiled anything. She smiled at him; Cohn winked back and went to the washbasin. His personal towel was still wet and it smacked of man. Cohn was shocked.

"God damn it!" he shouted. "As soon as my back is turned, somebody creeps in and uses my towel!"

"I'll get you a clean one. Why is it you've always got to make a fuss?"

"And what kind of manners is this, jumping out of the window without even saying hello?"

"He's shy."

"Shy? Look, he's even used my toothbrush. This is really too much!"

"Cohn, honestly. When the guy came in, he didn't know he'd be needing a toothbrush."

"Who is he, anyway?"

"How am I to know? I ran into him a couple of hours ago. We didn't have time to talk."

"Anything to eat?"

"I fixed a dinner for you, but he ate it all."

"I don't like that guy," Cohn decided. He walked over to the sofa. "I'm not going to moralize. But when a woman lets a fellow use her man's towel and toothbrush,

161

and then lets him eat her *popaa*'s dinner, then something is wrong. I have to tell you that."

Meeva was about to burst into tears. Nothing hurts a *vahine* more than to be told that she didn't take good care of her *popaa*.

"I thought you were dining out. Cohn, you know I love you with all my heart."

Cohn softened. He took her hand and caressed it. She was a true *vahine*, Meeva was. She knew what was important. Love. Nothing else mattered much, really.

He kissed her. She put her arms around his waist, pressed her head against him.

"Was it good?" he asked gently.

"Very sweet. The good Lord does things all right."

"Yes. You've got to give him that. He sure invented a few good things. But he still left us with a lot of work to do."

She thought it over. "Well, we don't have to do it. Nobody can force us."

Cohn was impressed. Wisdom.

The oil lamp gave just enough light to respect the night's peaceful shadows. The surf lay still. Somewhere in the distance a rooster, confused by the brightness of the sky, kept announcing dawn with all the conviction of a false prophet. A lizard fell on the mosquito net, his belly throbbing in a terrified immobility, then dashed away. Meeva held her *popaa* tight in her arms. She knew that he, too, was scared, that he soon would be gone. She didn't know why he was so disturbed. Neither did Cohn, for that matter. That's what he found most disturbing about anxiety.

"Cohn."

He looked down on that beautiful face with its feline nose and high cheekbones lying in the splendor of her flowing hair. She was trying to tell him something. Cohn wondered what strange, different thoughts lay hidden behind the dark eyes of that royal creature that long-vanished gods had left behind in their flight at the beginning of reality, when their kingdom on earth had come to an end.

"Cohn, scratch my back."

A *vahine*'s erotic imagination knew no limits. He began to scratch.

She purred. "Oh, Cohn, you're so good. You are the best, Cohn. Here, under the left shoulder—"

Cohn reigned. He had always known he was a superb

lover. He could scratch a back for hours without weakening.

"The Governor's cook told me you're going back to Paris. They need you there. She says you're important. Please tell me before going. Don't just run away. I've got to know, now that we're going to have a baby."

Cohn froze. "We're going to have a baby? Since when?"

"The *toubib* at the hospital told me. I'm going to have a baby."

Cohn broke out in cold sweat. "Jesus. I hope it isn't mine. Poor little bastard."

"I don't know if it's yours, but you're welcome to it. I sure want you to be his father. Everything I have is yours, Cohn."

He knew the Tahitians well enough to take this for what it was, a token of true love. Cohn was deeply moved. He even felt an unexpected surge of pride at the thought of becoming a father. That old, old male vanity.

"Do you have any idea who did it?"

"Of course not. How could I?"

"Don't get mad. I was just asking. I'll take care of it. Gee, it sure does something to one."

She smiled sweetly and caressed his hair. "You mean it?"

"Of course I do. Who wouldn't? I'm not different from anybody else. Though I must say I didn't know I had it in me. That paternal thing, I mean. Gee, I sure get a kick."

"I knew you would."

"I hope it's a boy. Isn't that funny, I never thought it'd do that to me, being a father, I mean."

"He's going to be very handsome, you'll see. I never went to bed with anyone who wasn't good-looking. You'll be proud of him."

Cohn's heart was filled with warmth. He had the sudden impression that he had achieved something in life, after all. It was the first lucky break he'd had in a long, long time. He wiped away a tear.

Meeva kissed his hand. "Don't cry, Gene. I'm so glad I've made you happy. I always wanted to give you something."

"This is simply wonderful!" yelled Cohn. He was getting truly emotional now.

She pressed her cheek against his hand. "I'll give you more kids, Cohn. As many as you want. I love you."

Cohn was crying. This was a blessing. A son he hadn't fathered had a good chance to start with. He could grow up to become someone, truly different. Perhaps even a man.

"Don't cry, my Cohn, love."

Cohn was sobbing now. It was wonderful to be able to give your son a real chance, which was that he had nothing in common with you. He wouldn't be of your blood, so you could truly love him. Cohn had never felt better since he had lost his parents.

"Come on, let's celebrate. Let's go dancing." He began to worry. "You can dance, can't you? It won't drop out or something?"

"Of course not. It doesn't drop out just like that. It holds on real tough."

"Which reminds me. I've caught crabs again. Got to get some ointment. I don't know at all where I keep catching them. Not a clean place left anywhere."

"It's that bitch Ounano. She's not French, if you ask me. A savage."

They left the *fare* and walked into the night, holding hands. Blue, white, and silver stirred gently at their feet.

"When are you going back to France, Cohn?"

"What makes you think I'm going back?"

"For the last few days, you've been looking like a whipped dog. Will you take us with you?"

"No. I wouldn't do a thing like that to my son. Besides, France is not a place for a *vahine*. They don't know about innocence back there. They'll think you're just another whore. But we'll make it, somehow. All three of us. Some other place. We'll escape. There're other, still new, undiscovered islands, lost, unknown atolls where no one's ever been. We'll go there. We'll find a way. You'll have our son there. A new, completely different start. We'll give him a break."

He almost believed that, too.

> *I am looking for the face I had*
> *Before the world was made.*

The man and the woman were walking slowly along the shore. Cohn was singing.

23

Free Spirit,
Where He Danced

Mathieu didn't want to leave Tahiti without paying a final and loving tribute to the identity and character of Genghis Cohn, with whom he would be soon parting company forever. A public demonstration of humility, an act of contrition, would clearly indicate his intention to put an end to his feud with Authority and to bow his guilty head before Law and Order. Besides, he wanted to add a finishing touch to the artistic legacy he was leaving behind in Polynesia.

At eleven o'clock that morning, Bizien was returning from the harbor with a busload of tourists he had gone to welcome in person when the *President Roosevelt* docked in Papeete. At the corner of the rue Paul Gauguin, a dense and unruly crowd of Tahitians was blocking the way. There was a considerable amount of excitement and even of tension in the air. The bus had come to a stop. Straining his neck, Bizien saw a *tableau vivant* that he himself might have mistaken as part of his *Passion of Paul Gauguin*.

In the arcade in front of Fong's barbershop, the gendarme Pozzo, in uniform but with his pants rolled up and his feet bare, sat on a chair before a basin of water. He was holding his feet in midair, as if he were afraid of losing them. His face had an expression of bewilderment, almost pathetic in its mixture of suspicion and stupidity.

Dressed in a white robe, Cohn was on his knees before him, trying to convince Pozzo to entrust his extremities to him. The gendarme demurred, raising his feet as high as he could.

Bizien felt his heart fill with gratitude. He knew he was in the presence of true greatness. An elderly lady who was studying the brochure of the tour asked him what the excitement was about.

"It's a famous episode from the life of Gauguin," Bizien explained. "It's called 'the washing of the feet.' It's now part of Tahitian folklore and staged every year on the anniversary of the painter's death. One of the most moving moments in the life of that great rebel who had repented toward the end, something that is all too often overlooked. You'll find it tomorrow in the new brochure we're printing."

Bizien hurried out of the bus. The first person he saw was Ryckmans. The crowd of Tahitians was getting out of hand. There was a threatening murmur and quite a few shouts. Ryckmans gave the promoter a worried look.

"What's going on?" Bizien asked.

"Subversion," Ryckmans said darkly. "Yesterday when he came to tell me that he wanted to wash Corporal Pozzo's feet in public, before leaving Tahiti, as an act of humility and repentance because of all the trouble he's given us here, I knew he was up to his usual tricks again. I said no, politely, but firmly. You can't do that to a gendarme in uniform. But he started a row, so I telephoned Government House. Well, I was given hell, believe it or not. Told we mustn't antagonize him, lest he refuse to go back to France. Paris orders. Apparently, he could defect to the Americans or even to the Russians. Had to be treated with kid gloves. So I called Pozzo in and told him he was going to have his feet washed in public by Monsieur Cohn, it was in the national interest. He wanted no part of it. He has his dignity. I had to promise him a promotion. That's what we've come to here, Monsieur Bizien. I'm asking for a transfer."

Bizien pushed his way through the crowd. Cohn had finally succeeded in getting hold of Pozzo's feet. Never had the face of a Corsican gendarme expressed such indignation since Waterloo. Cohn was carefully soaping his feet, scraping the nails, inspecting each toe closely. It was a thing of beauty, but Bizien didn't fully realize the Machiavellian aim of the operation until a chorus of hostile shouts began to rise from the crowd.

"This is an outrage!"

"Look, they're forcing us to wash their feet now!"

"Down with the cops!"

"Down with dictatorship!"

"Nazis!"

"Fascism shall not pass!"

"Don't let them do that to you, Cohn! Fight! They have no right! This is fascism!"

"Down with the police state!"

"Spit on him, Cohn! Be a man!"

Cohn hung his head in humiliation. On his knees, covering Pozzo's hairy feet with soap, he was the very image of slavery and degradation.

"Don't, Cohn, don't! Slug him! We'll help you!"

"Look what they're doing to a man!"

"There's no law that says you've got to wash a cop's feet!"

"Down with the oppressors! Down with colonialism!"

Cohn was getting nervous. Where the hell was Taroa? He'd given him precise instructions and a good tip. The situation was ripe. Now was the moment. What was that skunk Taroa waiting for? It was then that Taroa's powerful voice rose above the crowd, and the words of "La Marseillaise" echoed with all their heady might:

> *Alons, enfants de la patrie,*
> *Le jour de gloire est arrive.*
> *Contre nous de la tyrannie*
> *L'étendard sanglant est levé!*
> *Aux armes, citoyens!*

There was a roar, and the Tahitians rushed forward as a single man in response to the immortal call to arms of their ancestors the Gauls. Corporal Pozzo was lifted from his chair by a hundred hands and hurled through the barbershop window. Ryckmans was seized as he was trying to start his car, his pants were pulled off, and he was dumped into the ocean. When his head popped up again, the choicest insults were hurled at him.

"Torturer! Fascist!"

"You've got blood on your hands!"

"Judas! Imperialist!"

"S.S.! Hitler! Colonialist!"

The sound of glass breaking was now coming from all sides, as "La Marseillaise" still rang proudly in the air Cohn was raised on the Tahitians' shoulders and carried in triumph through the streets, while the Chinese hurried to close the shutters of their stores. They were already under attack. With that infallible instinct of crowds, every good Tahitian knew the yellow bastards had something to do with the outrage. His open arms raised in a V sign above the people, Cohn, wildly cheered, was making a deeply moving farewell speech that no one could hear but everyone applauded. On the coral reef, his brother the ocean was adding his thunderous approval to the cheering of the populace. Then Cohn had himself carried to the street corner, grabbed a lei of orchids from the neck of one of the *vahines* who had been welcoming the tourists, and hung the flowers around the name "rue Paul Gauguin," his eyes filled with tears at the idea that his trampling dance in Tahiti was over.

24

The Finishing Touch

He was booked on an Air France flight to Paris the next day. He spent the afternoon in Meeva's arms. Her eyes were full of that resigned sadness of the Tahitian *vahine* whose fate has always been to be left behind by her *popaa*. Yet he couldn't believe he was going to lose her forever. He kept pressing her hand, the last link with his lost true self, with innocence, with the man he was before the world began. She was going to give him a son by an unknown father, a son who, with a bit of luck, wouldn't have a drop of his blood in his veins and whom therefore he could truly love. Then she put on her prettiest dress, the red one with white flowers.

"Where are you going?"

"Dancing."

He knew she would dance for hours, then make love on the beach with a *tane*. She was truly miserable, in the Tahitian way. Cohn was feeling loved for the first time in his life.

The final blow came toward six in the afternoon, just as the swollen yolk of the sun was collapsing over Mooréa.

As always when he was about to assume a new identity, Cohn felt nervous and apprehensive. It was a kind of stage-fright that usually disappeared as soon as he knew there was no turning back. He had always managed to get by, somehow, even though he had died a billion deaths, his only tribute to conformity. The seventeenth century in Spain had been his favorite; he had had a ripping good time with Church, King, and Authority there, to the point that they had to hang him a couple of times, and once, in Sevilla, the Inquisition had filled his stomach with water until he burst. His favorite identity had been that of Lope de Vega, not only because he had written a thousand plays under that name, but also because he had fornicated happily to a ripe old age, defying all the conventions of his time and never praying for his sins. Now he was bracing himself to become Marc Mathieu once more, the eccentric genius, and he was determined not to let down his public. After that—there was no telling what new adventures were awaiting him. The only thing that mattered was to keep inventing new identities for himself along the *pícaro*'s difficult road, and this was known as creativity. Yet in spite of all his past triumphs, the fear that he might fail and that sooner or later he would be found out was always present in him. All he could do was to put his unshakable faith in himself into his act, and then it was quite possible that one day Man the impostor would attain authenticity at last. His stagefright was only natural, considering the immensity of the stage and the magnitude of the task ahead of him. Yet to feel reassured he had only to remember all the past identities he had successfully assumed along the way. It wasn't much of an achievement perhaps, considering the talent, the agony, and the millennia of effort he had put into the act, but it was better than nothing, and it was still known as a civilization.

Cohn was sitting in the sand in front of the House of Joy, smoking his last cigar, watching the sun go down, when he saw an elderly man walking toward him. It was the distinguished-looking tourist he had noticed that morning on the terrace of the Vairia. They had exchanged a few words about the weather. A German, Cohn recalled. He resented this intrusion. The bastard was going to spoil the sunset.

The gentleman approached him. He was really a very civilized-looking guy. He wore a gray-flannel suit and he held a panama hat in his hand. His face was pleasant, with a full elegant nose.

"Excuse me."

Cohn didn't move. No one in Tahiti has the right to disturb a man peacefully smoking his cigar, facing the ocean, and enjoying the sunset.

"Mr. Cohn, I believe?"

Cohn had a kind of built-in alarm when it came to sensing trouble. It was located somewhere around his buttocks, and when danger threatened, the buttocks contracted and emitted little cold shudders up his spine. This radar was now operating furiously.

"Forgive me for intruding, but I'm looking for my daughter."

"This is not that kind of house," Cohn said severely.

"I know she doesn't want to see me. But her mother is very ill. She's dying. It's really a matter of weeks, perhaps of days. I want Liebchen to come back to Frankfurt, if only for a few days."

"There's no Liebchen here," said Cohn firmly. "God forbid." Liebchen! That's all he needed.

"Allow me to introduce myself. My name is Kremnitz. I'm a professor of international law in Tübingen. As a very young man, I went through the usual romantic crises of youth. The old dream of escape from civilization, from the Western world—you know how it is. Youth. I came to the Tuamotus and married a Polynesian girl there. In the end, of course, I went back to Germany with my wife and daughter. She studied anthropology at the University of Tübingen. A very bright girl."

Cohn relaxed. A false alarm. His radar was out of order. He'd have to have it fixed.

"Liebchen is one of those rebels always in conflict with everything. Family, the consumer society, the materialistic rat race—she was disillusioned with everything, even with Cuba, where she had spent a few months. The typical crisis of young people today, who have everything but who feel that something essential is missing. Some kind of lost innocence, I suppose. The illusion that you can retrace your steps, go back to the source, so to speak. The feeling that civilization has chosen a completely wrong direction."

Cohn took the cigar from his lips. "Listen, why don't you go and look for her at the Club Méditerranée? That's what it is for. People like your daughter, I mean. You're sure to find her there."

"Please forgive me. I didn't come here to bother you with my family problems. But it's been more than a year since we've last heard from her— We've made some inquiries. We've learned that Liebchen had been to the Tuamotus and that then she came over here. She's been living here for some time under her Polynesian grandmother's name, Meeva."

All of Cohn's sphincters went out of control. The cigar fell from his lips. "WHAT?" He jumped to his feet. "What name did you say?"

"Meeva. I believe you know her."

Cohn slapped his thighs and doubled up with laughter. "Liebchen, huh?" he roared. "Liebchen! Holy shit!" He was convulsed with laughter and tears were streaming down his cheeks in an excess of mirth. He couldn't stop.

The professor was looking at him in hurt surprise. "Excuse me, but I really don't see what—"

"Liebchen!" Cohn managed to gulp some air just as he was going to choke. He clenched his fists, raised his face toward heaven; the Son was getting ready to unburden himself to the Father, when he remembered that he was born an orphan and that there was no one up there. He spinned and ran toward the ocean.

The cove was a hundred yards from the *fare*, where the spring empties into the lagoon among the mangroves. The pirogue was tied to a palm, and Cohn checked the rope. It was long and strong enough, just what he needed. Now all he had to do was to find a heavy enough stone, since the "heavy heart" was an invention of literature and had never helped anyone to sink to the bottom. He finally found a rock that he could barely lift, and managed to drag it into the pirogue.

Night had fallen. It even seemed to Cohn that it had hurried down, so as not to miss the rebel's end. The night loves exemplary endings. Cohn raised his eyes again. The celestial spheres pressed around him like a festive crowd. He looked for the constellation of the Dog, but he couldn't find it. It was very busy and couldn't look after all its children.

He began to paddle. He didn't have to go far. You had to be a self-deluding dreamer to believe, as Gauguin had written in his diary, that it was possible to "keep your bow pointed obstinately toward a hospitable shore, the house of liberty and beauty."

The lagoon was quivering with billions of phosphorescent lives and it seemed to Cohn that the light-years above shone with an almost triumphant brilliance. The galaxies were on the Father's side, on the side of an implacable Authority that accepted no defiance of its Law and Order. The ocean carried in its fold the small silver change of the infinite.

When the pirogue reached the middle of the lagoon, Cohn laid down his paddle. He tied the end of the rope around the rock, made a noose of the other end, and fixed it around his neck. Then, mistrusting that old cheat, the self-preservation instinct, he tied his wrists together. As the cur stood in the pirogue, his hands tied and the noose around his neck, he raised his eyes once more toward what for want of a stronger word men called heaven, and he saw that the stands were packed, the circus full. He could almost hear the peanut and soft-drink vendors. A million yellow eyes were watching.

The stone was much heavier than he thought. His tied

171

wrists hampered him. The narrow pirogue was rocking dangerously, and he was afraid of hurting himself.

He finally managed to lift the rock, holding it against his belly. He filled his lungs, then realized that he was only giving in to nature's trick that would only prolong his agony. He exhaled, closed his eyes, and jumped overboard.

He didn't sink.

He opened his eyes and found he was floating at the end of the rope. He had dropped the rock too soon and it had fallen inside the pirogue.

Cohn's breast filled with such an indignant rage that the ocean foamed and waves rose around his head. With all the fury and total absence of faith of a genuine atheist, he let go with a flood of blasphemies against the Father. He was so mad he forgot the nonexistent Father liked these outbursts of impotence and marks of recognition in his faithless Son and that the nature of the feelings He inspired meant little to Him, as long as He remained a source of inspiration.

Cohn tried to climb back into the pirogue and start all over again. He soon realized he'd never make it. His tied hands hampered him. Cursing, he pulled on the rope to make the rock fall out, but succeeded only in pulling the pirogue toward him.

He tried to sink to the bottom through sheer willpower and with no outside help, but after each dive, as he was beginning to suffocate, he struggled, gasping for air, back to the surface.

He floated in the water, torn between humiliation and relief for having once more escaped death by a hair's breadth. Then he began to swim back with mighty knee jerks toward the shore. But he had to drag the pirogue with him, and with his tied hands, he would never make it. He was swallowing water and began to panic. He was in danger of drowning, God forbid.

He floated on his back. The pirogue stood still in a patch of moonlight. There had to be some lovers on the beach. He began to yell. "Help! Help!"

It was rather humiliating for a notorious cynic to be found in such a romantic situation as trying to commit suicide, but he could always accuse the police, the missionaries, and the local bourgeoisie, who had put a noose around his neck, had tied him to a rock, and had tried to get rid of another subversive artist. Everybody knew they had persecuted Gauguin to the very end.

"Help! Help! Murder!"

An hour went by and Cohn was beginning to be scared

172

out of his wits. Then he saw a pirogue leave the shore and start slowly toward him in the moonlight.

"Help! They're murdering a good man! Help!"

It was Meeva.

She was standing in the pirogue, paddling. Her hair was undone and she hadn't had the time to put on her dress. She was stark naked in the moonlight. Cohn's nose was sending scornful snorts above the water. This German nymphomaniac had been screwing on the beach like an innocent *vahine*. Only a German whore could behave like that. Coming to Tahiti to soil the last innocence of the world, the only place where guilt and sin didn't exist.

"Whore! Sex maniac!"

The pirogue drew near him. Meeva was crying. But Cohn had had enough of salt water.

"That's right, shed a tear, you bloody hypocrite!"

"Cohn, my mother was a true Maori from the Tuamotus, I swear she was!"

"Your mother, I don't even want to think what she was!"

"You know that everybody here has a few drops of European blood—"

"A few drops! Ha!" He almost managed to laugh. "Liebchen!" he shouted with laughing irony. "Liebchen!"

"I lived in the Tuamotus till I was twelve years old. My mental and psychological makeup is entirely that of the Maori people—"

Cohn closed his eyes. If there was one horror he'd never believed possible, it was to hear the words "mental and psychological makeup" on Meeva's lips.

"It is true that my father is German, but I have to say for him that he'd always been against the Nazis—"

"Sure, and now, with a daughter like you, he's made up for it!"

She was kneeling in the pirogue, trying to help him out of the water.

"Don't touch me!"

"We'll go back to the *fare* and you can beat me. Then we'll make love."

"German pervert. Go away! I don't want to live with people like you and me!"

But he had no fight left in him. He ended up in the pirogue with enough stone in his heart to build yet another cathedral.

"Cohn, please listen to me. I wanted to go back to my origins, become a Maori again. Can't you understand that?

I had to find some kind of simplicity again, the lost innocence—"

"Yeah. That's why you had to study anthropology for five years at the University of Tübingen. To recapture your lost innocence. *Merde! Merde!*"

"I went to Cuba, but Marxism is a profoundly materialistic doctrine. It's gone all wrong, somehow. Have you read Marcuse's *One-Dimensional Man?*"

Cohn was getting goose pimples. Here they were, two bare-assed Westerners, sitting in a pirogue in the middle of a Tahitian lagoon, talking about *The One-Dimensional Man*. His *vahine* was a hippie. He leaned over the water and vomited. Then he lay on his back in the pirogue and stared at the light-years glistening with all the beauty of nonexistent worlds. He didn't even push her away when she took his hand.

"How much did they pay you for spying on me, Liebchen?"

She was sobbing now. "I had no choice. They threatened to deport me. I had no money, no resident's permit. I love you, Cohn. I love you with all my heart."

"If you mention the heart to me once more, you one-dimensional whore—"

"I had to take them every scrap of paper you left lying around— But they knew you were Mathieu anyway."

"What did they tell you about me?"

"That you had had some kind of shock and you had deliberately suppressed your true identity, because you were unable to face it."

Cohn laughed. There is simply no end to the help a crook could get from up-to-date psychiatry. "Sure, Machner's *Selbstverdammung*," he said. "A classic case. Right. Then?"

"They photographed your work, you know, the writing you did at night on the sand. They became truly worried."

"Who took the picture? You?"

"Yes." She began to sob again.

"Don't cry, Liebchen," he heard himself saying in a voice so full of kindness that it scared him. Authenticity. He was a goner.

She kissed his hand. "We have been happy together, Cohn, haven't we?"

"Yes, but it was because we didn't know each other. You see, Liebchen, when a man and a woman know very little about each other, they can be truly in love. That's where the beauty lies. But when they get to know each

174

other, it's no longer possible. No illusions, you see. Nothing but bare-assed truth."

He sat up. The pirogue lay still in the moonlight. He began to paddle toward the shore.

"Cohn, listen to me. I know you don't want to go back. I know you don't want to work for them. I can help you. I know an island in the Atura atoll. No one's ever been there, except me, when I was a little girl, with my maternal grandfather, old Ouana, the Chief of Atura, who is still alive. He could take us there. No one will ever know. We could start all over again—"

The face I had before the world began—

Cohn was paddling. The shore was much closer than he thought.

"I could have my baby there. Wouldn't that be something? A completely new, clean start—"

Now, after all those lies, Cohn feared the worst. "Whose is it? The baby, I mean."

"I told you. I don't know."

"You're sure it's not mine?" He didn't want to do that to his kid. He was already being a good father.

"I don't know. With all those *tanes*—"

Cohn was paddling. A vague, hesitant hope was stirring in him. He didn't want to look too closely into it, lest it vanish, disintegrating under his knowing, ironic eyes. He was his old laughing self once more, yearning for some new, completely different birth upon another shore.

They were almost there now.

"How far is it from here, your island?"

"Very far. We'll have to start from the Tuamotus. You can't imagine how lovely it is. When you've lived a lot, you no longer can imagine it. But I've been there. I've never forgotten."

"You were a child then. You were looking at it with different eyes."

"We've got to try."

They were reaching the shore. Cohn stepped into the water and pushed the pirogue.

"Do you have a map?"

"It's not on the map. But old Ouana will take us there. We can still make it, Cohn. We've got to try. There's nowhere else we can go, is there?"

Cohn raised his eyes. On the mountainside, where Bizien had set up his Moses, the neon lights were glowing yellow, orange, and red; they were still testing the Burning Bush. Headlights were sweeping the new road above Pouaavia. The STAI bus was taking its first load of tourists along the Stations of the Cross to the Crucifixion, which was opening that night in the official presence of the Governor. At the nuclear test site of Mururoa, France was working day and night to catch up with it.

The man and the woman stood naked on the shore, waiting to be born.